THE FINAL WHISTLE

THE FINAL WHISTLE

K. T. PRESTIDGE

Copyright © 2022 K. T. Prestidge

The moral right of the author has been asserted.

Apart from any fair dealing for the purposes of research or private study, or criticism or review, as permitted under the Copyright, Designs and Patents Act 1988, this publication may only be reproduced, stored or transmitted, in any form or by any means, with the prior permission in writing of the publishers, or in the case of reprographic reproduction in accordance with the terms of licences issued by the Copyright Licensing Agency. Enquiries concerning reproduction outside those terms should be sent to the publishers.

This is a work of fiction. Names, characters, businesses, places, eventsand incidents are either the products of the author's imagination or used in a fictitious manner.

Matador
Unit E2 Airfield Business Park,
Harrison Road, Market Harborough,
Leicestershire. LE16 7UL
Tel: 0116 2792299
Email: books@troubador.co.uk
Web: www.troubador.co.uk/matador
Twitter: @matadorbooks

ISBN 978 1 80313 490 1

British Library Cataloguing in Publication Data.
A catalogue record for this book is available from the British Library.

Printed and bound in the UK by TJ Books Limited, Padstow, Cornwall
Typeset in 11pt Adobe Garamond Pro by Troubador Publishing Ltd, Leicester, UK

Matador is an imprint of Troubador Publishing Ltd

PROLOGUE

He couldn't take his eyes of the elegant woman as she walked into the club with poise. Slowly, she walked up to the bar in her five-inch heels, red with little black bows on the front. He examined her body, noting the soft curves of her hips, and her flat stomach, wrapped up in a skin-tight red dress that stopped just below her knees. Next, her soft neck, slender and pale against the lights of the club. Finally, her hair and eyes were mesmerising. Her hair was jet black but her eyes were light, close to the colour of the whites of her eyes and, from a distance, he couldn't place the colour but they seemed hauntingly beautiful.

Her solitary status surprised him the most. He watched her for close to five minutes, standing by the bar. Not a soul walked up to her. There were no female friends, and no man close by. She didn't look at her phone, an indication she may have been stood up. He hoped it was his lucky day and she was alone. If so, he would be keen to meet her.

Her beauty was so hypnotic he failed to notice his friends come back into the club, smelling of sweet e-vape smoke. It was a habit he abhorred, and as such choose to stay inside while those around him partook in the social activity. They called him a spoilsport, however, he was happy to leave them to their habit. He didn't want to be the judgemental one crying about second hand smoke.

"Hey, Mikey, did you miss us?" the most senior of the group, Alex, asked him. He didn't hear to begin with, still staring at the woman across the room. It didn't take Alex long to click where his attentions lay. Michael felt the heat rise to his cheeks as Alex glanced at the young woman to take her in.

"Well, Mikey, we are heading off if you want to come with us. I'm sure I'm not the only one who's getting bored of the place. Right lads?" The younger man knew Alex's game. He was goading him into making a decision. Stay and speak to the woman at the bar, or continue their evening drinking session? Although not a fan of mind games, he knew they would work. If Michael left, he would regret not trying to strike up a conversation, even if it led nowhere. But if he remained and she did deny his advances, his evening was over. Alex would withhold where they were going, he knew he wouldn't catch up with them again.

The intrigued part of his mind won over, he decided to strike up the courage to start a conversation. He knew that regrets would play on his mind more than an early night. His friends said their goodbyes and departed. Before Alex turned, Michael noticed a hint of a smug and knowing look on his face. He'd find a way to get him back tomorrow.

•

As I walked into the Lone Wolf, the premier singles club in Salford, I believed it wouldn't be my night. Billed as a sophisticated place to relax and meet like-minded singles who were looking for a good time with no commitments, its reputation for good alcohol and a safe environment meant that more people were just coming for the atmosphere rather than to connect with others. Tonight was no exception, very few of the men in attendance were eligible or single. Many were either with groups of friends or in a quiet corner getting to know an attractive young woman. The short walk to the bar only made me more self-conscious, as I felt overdressed and older than most patrons. Although in the past it was a twenty-one-and-over club, the financial difficulties made the owners lower the age to eighteen, and, with the large student population in Manchester, the younger clientele started to grow.

Sighing, I walked up to the bar, briefly staring out at the room with my elbows resting behind on the slightly sticky dark wood. It didn't take me long to accept that nobody was interested in me, so I turned and decided to purchase my own drink. Going back to an empty house so early was pointless, it wouldn't hurt to have a couple of drinks to get over my tough day.

A young barman was eager to come to serve me. For a brief moment I thought the night was looking up, until the band on his ring finger glittered in the club lighting. It was at that moment I realised it wasn't my lucky day. Although I was not fussy about male attention, married men were an avenue I vowed never to cross. It became too complicated when an angry spouse found out. I also didn't want to be the cause of a marital breakdown. Instead of reciprocating his flirting, I paid for my overpriced gin and tonic and moved elsewhere. A plan that was thwarted when I ended up with my drink down me.

"My dress…" The words were spoken so softly I wasn't sure if I had uttered them. Around me I could hear the sniggers of a couple of young women who found the scene delightful, so I fired them an angry warning shot and they skulked off into the crowd. After getting over the shock of my £13 drink going down my new dress, I looked up to the man who had bumped into me. The night was definitely on the up.

He was significantly taller than me, even in heels I was only chest height on him. It allowed me to stare at his stunning pectoral muscles just that little bit longer. Slowly, I started to look higher up, making a note of his strong arms rippling against his leather jacket. When I finally took him in fully though it was hard not to notice how stunning he was. His skin was as dark as his hazel eyes, and his short, curly hair looked like something I would want to put my hands through. My night was starting to get more interesting.

"I'm so sorry, miss, I didn't mean to ruin your lovely dress," he replied, with an exhilarating South American drawl. If I wasn't mistaken, I placed his accent from New Orleans. A fascinating area of American I had visited multiple times. I could see the guilt in his eyes as I looked into them, wanting to start fresh I made light of the situation.

"Could I borrow your shirt?" I asked playfully with a grin. He looked quizzical, but it didn't take him long to peel it off and hand it over to me. "I'll be right back," I replied, handing over my handbag as he was putting his leather jacket back on in a bid to show that I wasn't just going to run off. As I made my way into the ladies toilets I noticed him go to an intimate little corner, clutching my bag to ensure that it wouldn't get stolen. It made me smile that he was so concerned about it.

After a little while I walked back out in my new outfit. The shirt that the young man had handed to me was too big, but I was able to clip it together with the belt from my dress; the sleeves were rolled up and the top two buttons of the shirt were undone. It was at this moment I noticed everybody's eyes on me in the room. I had clearly peaked the interest of a lot of men. But tonight, I only had eyes for the young South American stud. Nobody else mattered.

"My name is Sammi. How about you?" Extending my hand to him as I sat down on the opposite side of the table. He took it in a firm grip, the touch made my skin feel like it was on fire.

"Michael, pleasure to meet you, Sammi," he responded. "I am sorry about that dress." His syntax was quite adorable and it just made me smile even more. Not wanting to start off on the wrong foot, I just laughed it off and gave a warm and bright smile.

"You shouldn't worry, Michael. Everybody makes mistakes. How about you go get us a couple of drinks and we can get to know each other a bit better," I said, as I sidled my chair up closer to him. He nodded his head and got up to walk over to the bar, not before kissing me full on the lips.

"Sorry, I had to do that," Michael whispered, as we pulled away from each other. "I'll go get those drinks now." He left me sitting a little stunned, I had never been kissed so passionately by any man, let alone one I had just met. It seemed like the night was going to continue on the up.

•

For the first time in what seemed like months, Joseph finally had a night to himself. Normally by this time he would be servicing his first client of the evening. Sometimes in a hotel room, others at the clients home if they didn't mind people being aware of their use of escorts. He would spend a couple of hours pleasuring them before potentially going to meet another client, the cycle would continue all evening. It was exhausting, and an issue with being one of Marcos' favoured escorts for both men and women.

Normally, a gay club would be his number-one destination, however, he wanted to unwind and felt bumping into some of his potential clients wouldn't be a relaxing experience. Even when not on the job his boss expected him to be professional at all times, and he didn't want to feel like he was on the job tonight.

"Hey Joey, You gonna come in tonight?" the bouncer who spotted him shouted out. Joseph turned around and smiled at the man who he had been with on more than one occasion, his most favoured client. He was tall and lightly built. There was a large tattoo of a snake that ran down his neck and onto his back. Something that Joseph used to play with when they would lie in bed together.

"Unfortunately not, darling, I'm looking for a new adventure," Joseph replied, the bouncer blushed a little and looked to the ground. Joey couldn't help but stare at the man ahead of him, a man who he had shared a bed with on many occasions. He wanted nothing more than to walk up to the bouncer and give him a long kiss on the lips. He couldn't though, the man's wife was co-owner of the club. That's why the bouncer paid, he couldn't admit the truth to the woman he'd married as a teenager that he was still finding his sexuality.

As he turned around, still thinking about the bouncer in his bed, he literally bumped into a group of men. One of whom he recognised instantly.

"Evening, my little gay freak. What are you doing out here?" one of the men goaded, as he put his hand on Joseph, he was clearly the mouth of the gang. There was a slight accent when he spoke, possibly from Eastern Europe. Joseph was convinced he looked familiar, however, he wasn't sure where he could place the face.

"I… I'm sorry." He was scared of what was going on. He was only talking to the bouncer, a little flirtatiously but he was really only being friendly, and it seemed like he was going to pay for it. He twisted his arm away from the large Eastern European man, but before he could run away from the situation to safety he stumbled as he was almost pushed onto the floor.

"Look out will you," he said, smirking from ear to ear. His friends were smiling as well, enjoying their little game of terror. There was only one man who didn't smile though, somebody he was well acquainted with. He knew it was a stupid thing to do, he should have walked away, but fear makes you do reckless things. As Joseph was about to find out.

"Help me please," he whispered softly to one of the group. Five of the men instantly turned round with puzzles looks on their faces.

"Oi, Smith, you know this faggot then do you?" the mouthpiece said, the words stung Joseph, taking him back to his childhood when he was frequently mocked by his family for his sexuality. His scum family who forced him out when he was younger.

"Never seen this batty boy in my life." The words hurt, but not as much as the actions. The man pushed him hard to the floor, discarding him like a toy he no longer wanted to play with. As Joseph fell, he hit his cheek on a kerb. The pain was intense, he was convinced he had broken a bone and that a couple of teeth had been knocked out. For a moment he just lay there in stunned silence as some of the group laughed at his misfortune. Suddenly he picked himself up and ran before his attackers realised he was crying.

ONE

At first I wasn't sure if I was hearing correctly. It sounded as if my mobile was ringing for the past two or three minutes, which was strange as it would normally click to voicemail within just thirty seconds. It was only once the fog lifted from my mind did I realise that it was the fourth time my phone had rung that morning. All the calls came within just seconds of each other. Before answering I knew it was my boss trying to get in touch with me, the constant ringing meant it was of the utmost importance. Slowly, I wriggled away from the man next to me, picked up my phone and went into the living room so I didn't wake him. When I answered I tried to make myself sound like I hadn't just crawled out of bed.

"Oh glad to hear you're alive, Samantha." The passive aggressive greeting from DCI Jackson, my boss and occasional tormentor, was not lost on me even when suffering from extreme exhaustion.

"Sorry, sir. I didn't have a good night last night, I was feeling very unwell," I responded, while ignoring the comment, knowing it wouldn't pull the wool over Jackson's eyes. Sadly my reputation preceded me, with many of my colleagues being aware of my nightly escapades and my lacklustre attendance record. Jackson was aware, but hadn't used it as an excuse to relieve me of my post... yet.

"Yeah, sure. Just get here. I have a suspicious death on my hands, and at the moment you are the only competent detective I currently have. We are on The Quays. You'll see where when you get here." Short, sweet and to the point as always. The phone slamming made me jolt a little, however, I shouldn't have been too surprised, it was the way he normally conducted all of his business.

After spotting the time I ended up groaning in frustration, not even 5am yet. If I was lucky I had up to two hours sleep last night, mostly due to the young man I had left in my bed while taking the phone call. Silently I walked back in to see him still in his peaceful slumber, snoring softly. I grabbed a few clothes off the floor, not wanting to rifle through my drawers, all the time praying he didn't wake up. Dealing with the night before wasn't high on my priority list and I was anxious to leave before any awkward conversations.

I locked the bathroom door and turned on the shower, letting the water run to heat a little before jumping in. As I turned my face towards the shower head I closed my eyes and felt the water falling down my head and neck. The heat rejuvenating my tender muscles and washing the sweat off my body from the previous evening. I grabbed my shower gel and lathered the sponge, enjoying the coconut scent as I ran it down my body. I shampooed my hair, enjoying the feeling of my fingers as I massaged my sore head. After stepping out and wrapping myself in a towel I felt refreshed and renewed.

I stared at myself in a mirror for the moment… noting my dark circles and bloodshot eyes. It was evident I was in a poor state. I went to pick up the hair dryer but decided against it. Knowing the noise would awaken the gorgeous man in my bed. Just the memories of how he touched me and breathed my name made me shudder in anticipation.

After drying myself and brushing my hair I put my clothes on, noting I could have done with a fresher set and mentally reminding myself to wash them more frequently. I then walked out, closing the door softly so my companion could enjoy his slumber. Even after our one-night stand I believed I could trust him in my own home. It was just a gut feeling that I had after the way he guarded my bag when we first met. I just hoped he wasn't still there when I returned.

•

It was only when the door finally shut that Michael realised the warmth beside him had disappeared. He awoke instantly and started to look around for the raven-haired beauty that had made his night. The soft touch of her lips; the way she looked up at him with her haunting grey eyes and her soft moans as they made passionate love would stay with him forever. He hoped it wouldn't be a one-time deal but he was under no illusions. This was a one-night stand and it was unlikely he would ever see her again.

Sighing, he got out of the comfortable bed, but stopped briefly on the edge of it with his head in his hands. He was still woozy from the booze that they had drunk together. What was it... five...no... six tequila shots they downed? Licking the salt off her shoulder, and sharing the lime from her gorgeous mouth. It was an experience he had never tried before, but knew he would want to try again, especially with her.

Now his own mobile rang. He sighed and answered, but not before spotting the time... 5.15am? He was curious about what kind of career she had, if she needed to be called in for critical work so early? A cheerful, and still slightly drunk Alex, pulled him out of his thoughts and back to the real world. Michael couldn't help but wonder if he had been to sleep yet.

"Hi Mikey, I hope you had a really good night. But enough about that. Got a phone call from Fernandes this morning, like really early. He heard about us being out drinking last night so wants us down the training-ground gym from 7am doing a lot of workouts as punishments. Thought I'd let you know. I'll see you down there." Before Michael could respond Alex was already gone. The phone call with the hyped, and highly caffeinated Alex, had lasted all of fifteen seconds, possibly twenty at a push. If he didn't know his friend any better he would have assumed he had taken cocaine the evening before, but Alex wasn't the type of man to do drugs. Michael then called a taxi and made his way home for a shower and a change of clothes, not wanting his friends to know he had been out all night.

TWO

The soft morning sun rose above the thick dark clouds which threatened rain. With one hand off the wheel I looped the sunglasses over my sensitive eyes. Hoping that they would provide some comfort to the morning glare. As I pulled over to the side of the kerb by the nearest coffee shop, I had to wonder if I was in a fit state to continue driving. By my calculations we left the club at around 11.30pm and ended up drinking at my flat afterwards, the result was that the last alcoholic beverage consumed was around 12.30 this morning. Resulting in just under five of the possible twelve units of alcohol being fully removed from my system. If I was stopped by a colleague, it wouldn't just be a drink driving charge but also the end of my career.

Unsurprisingly the coffee shop was full at 6am, meaning I had to join the back of a long queue with one weary looking teenager serving behind the counter. In the early 2020s the world was hit with a double crippling recession. The first in 2020, caused by an outbreak of Covid-19, which resulted in hospitality and travel industries being shut down for extended periods of time with around 25% of the working population furloughed. The consequence was a devastating economic collapse with rampant unemployment. When deaths started to decline the government managed the removal of lockdowns poorly. Instead of being honest about death figures, these were overinflated. Decisions were made on incorrect data and subsequently the lockdown was extended.

By the time things improved, more controls, such as face masks, were brought in to give people confidence to go outside. Something I personally refused to police. It caused arguments with my colleagues but I stood firm, I didn't believe we should be policing such a trivial issue when we needed to be supporting communities with real crimes such as burglaries and assaults. I was ostracised and held back in my career for having such a view, as my superiors put me down as a Covid denier, but I didn't care. I had my principles and refused to change them because of Covid.

The situation was a mess, and could have been fixed with honesty, but with a government that refused to face up to their mistakes, they just doubled down on their lies. It wasn't until a hastily called election did the matter start to improve. Terrance Marshall, the husband of a good friend of mine, became the first fully Liberal PM since David Lloyd George. Not only did he win some of the traditional Conservative vote, but also the votes of millions of people who were happy with the decision to leave the EU. It was only then did the rampant fraud and dishonesty that was being peddled by some of the biggest offenders become public knowledge. Furious at what he learned, Terrance gave them an ultimatum, be prosecuted for their crimes or resign in disgrace. Many took the latter option.

He wasn't done there though. A measure was passed in Parliament by his party that all parliamentarians who voted for the Coronavirus Act 2020 and lockdowns were blacklisted and political parties were informed they would need to ask them to resign. At first there was pushback, but only when Terrance threatened to blacklist the parties themselves did they comply. Over three hundred by-elections were called and an entirely new Parliament was formed. Many were unable to find work again and have spoken about the hardships they faced, but the public had little sympathy after the physical and mental torture they inflicted.

The UK went back to normal. All plans for a digital passport were cancelled, and vaccinations were not made mandatory, people were able to get on with their lives without fear. Complete body autonomy was granted to all. Funding to the NHS was increased on the proviso that they bolstered their services so that they could deal with any future pandemic. They complied, and many nurses and doctors received pay rises. Terrance disbanded SAGE and a new advisory group was set up, but this time from all communities. Science, health, technology, economic and business, to ensure any future health emergencies would have an overview of how measures would impact all walks of life. All had to be vetted before joining the advisory group, and any who had a conflict of interest would be ineligible to work with the government. It restored trust and within a year Terrance was already at 43% in the polls.

The Emergency Powers Act of 2025 was propositioned, to the shock of many, it meant that the government would be temporarily disbanded with a new cross-party cabinet being stood up in case of a national health, economic or environmental crisis. All party lines would be dropped; Parliament would be able to vote on any emergency measures as independent MPs; and the ability to abstain from votes that impacted seventy million people was removed. Additionally, MPs would be required to attend debates and votes relating to any emergency measures, with proxy votes being strictly controlled and only for those who couldn't attend debates for medical reasons were eligible to use them. The Act was created in a bid to ensure the damage and pain of the Tories was never felt again. It was voted in with a resounding majority.

Just when the economic tide started to turn in 2025, a second global recession caused by the collapse of the European Union occurred. Their handling of Covid-19, along with the rise of nationalist leaders and their insistence on harsher border controls means that more countries wanted to follow the lead of the UK and leave the EU. Trade agreements broke down, and economies collapsed due to the prevalence of the central currency.

The result was most people were working twelve-hour days, some even longer, just to ensure that companies kept afloat and that they could keep up payments with their mortgage. For somebody like myself, working all hours wasn't that difficult, but for those who went into office work the shock was too much to bear. It was no surprise the suicides continued to be one of the largest causes of death in the country, especially for those under the age of thirty. The mental health tsunami was very much real, no matter how much the minister for suicide and mental prevention wanted to bury her head in the sand.

Nobody spoke in the queue, sharing their miserable existence in silence. Many looked down at their phones, probably reading about the horrors abroad. After the resignation of Vladimir Putin due to ill health, a more brutal man took over the reins of Russia. All pretence of democracy ceased the moment he was voted in as president, and he even signed a decree that would stop any future elections from taking place. Still angry at the virus that ravaged the Russian economy, he started to make advancements on the Chinese border. Determined that he would 'expand the Russian empire, and get rid of the cancer of the Communist regime.'

Until recently no inroads had been made on that threat, short skirmishes at the border had been reported but nothing that people feared. That was until last night, when a Russian commuter plane was reported to have been shot down over Chinese territory. Over 750, mainly Russian, souls on board, all killed in an instant. Now the world awaits with bated breath while the Russian president considers his next move. Two countries with a stockpile of nuclear weapons fighting one another, it was unlikely to end well for the world.

Lost in my train of thought I didn't notice I was at the counter until the young teenager called out to me. He used the most hated terminology of mine 'ma'am.' I was not the queen, and could have only had around ten years on the kid in front of me. Instead of picking him up on it I smiled and ordered a black coffee. Anything else was liable to make me be sick.

Small things like queuing for a drink made me grateful to be a non-uniformed officer. There seemed to be a growing trend since the early 2000s in emergency staff being abused for trying to find time to stop for something to eat a drink. It was almost as if the general public expected them to work for twelve hours a day with no breaks to eat and use the toilet. When in uniform I was subject to an abusive member of the public who informed me I shouldn't be buying a sandwich due to 'his taxes paying my wages'. I was content with just ignoring him and going about my business until he decided to spit on me and call me a slut. His demeanour changed when he was hauled up in front of a magistrate and ended up with a criminal record. I remember the tears streaming down his face and the angry words of his wife who decided it was his right to tell us how we should do our jobs. At moments like that I always wondered why I would put my life on the line to protect people.

After I sat back in the car I took a sip and let the warm black liquid slide down my throat, taking the moment to rest my head and shut my eyes. I was grateful for the alcohol still coursing through my veins. Thankfully it meant that the hangover was delayed and, as such, I may have been able to stomach the sight of a suspicious death. With a hangover the size of China, it was likely I would have thrown up over the scene and potentially compromised evidence.

As I sat for a little while longer, trying to compose myself enough to drive a couple of roads down to the scene of the crime, my mind wandered to the stunning man I had left in my bed after a night of amazing sex. Although only a one-night stand, he was the most kind and gentle lover I had ever experienced, while being animalistic in nature at the same time. Normally, drunk sex was sloppy, over quickly, and I found it difficult to get in sync with the other person. But not him, I felt as if we had been together for years; that we knew each other's weak spots and likes. It was, quite frankly, the best sex I had ever experienced.

I finished off the coffee before even contemplating moving off to the crime scene. Although not a cure, it at least made it seem like I was a bit more sober, and would keep me awake for a bit longer. The career I had worked hard to get was in the balance, and being drunk on duty would have likely been the incident that tipped my boss Jackson over the edge. He wasn't the concern though. My direct superior, DI McCarthy, had written me up on many occasions, adamant that I should lose my job for the persistent partying. Much to his disappointment though, anytime it went through official channels he was informed I hadn't broken any rules. At a push, it could be gross misconduct if I had sullied the uniform. But as many didn't know I was a police officer, nothing could be done.

Realising questions would be asked if I didn't turn up soon I put down my coffee cup and pulled away from the kerb. After ten or fifteen more minutes driving it was evident I had arrived at the scene of the crime with the amount of activity going on. The police vehicles were barely visible behind the people crowding around the police tape and the poor sergeant who had been placed there to keep order. I parked my car in the first available spot and opted to walk the rest of the way, knowing that if I accidentally hurt one of the vultures there would be questions about my physical state and potential blood alcohol level.

Slowly I forced my way through the developing crowd of people ahead of me. Some were from the media, others nosey neighbours who wanted a peak at what was going on, so they could inevitably sell their story and discuss how it was such a 'nice quiet neighbourhood' and 'nothing like this had happened before.' With an average of ten violent crimes in the area every month, ranging from assault with a deadly weapon to rape, it certainly wasn't a quiet area. Although this is one of the nicer areas of the city, thanks to the second crippling recession, crime was still at an all-time high.

Some people took offence to me moving them out of the way, believing that they had a given right to be there and find out what was happening. On one occasion I was even called a bitch in amongst the murmurings of discontent. All of which stopped when I produced my credentials to the young officer and I was let through the tape without issue. A wry smile sprung to my face, it was nice to know that they were taken aback by the situation. I went to walk away, but before I could a voice from my past summoned me. A girl the same age as me, but who had taken a different direction in life. Narcissistically, I sometimes felt it was to annoy me.

"Detective Sergeant Rodan. Do you mind telling us what has happened?" she asked. I turned around and looked at the woman. For somebody easily intimidated, the young woman would be rather an imposing figure. She stood 5 ft 10 inches without heels, and a little over 6 ft with them. Her hair was auburn, a colour that very few believed was natural; her eyes were slightly cat-like with a golden tinge to the reasonably-normal hazel colour; she wore a dark-blue, figure-hugging pant suit that showed of the tiny developing baby bump. She was probably around four months pregnant. The woman was vindictive and cold, I always wondered how she could have harboured such lovely and friendly children. I only prayed that this one would take after its siblings.

Her presence confused me. Although the bane of my existence she was an excellent journalist with a reputation for only sourcing out the most lucrative stories to fund her investigative journalism blog. She was motivated by fame and money, and it enabled her to blow the lid on far reaching-scandals around the world. With her attendance I believed this may have been more high profile than originally thought.

"Unfortunately, Bryony, I am in as much the dark as you are. I was just called to the scene. I'm sure we will send out a press release to journalists in a couple of hours, which will give you details that you may need." With that I walked off, knowing that Bryony had a smug smile on her face. Showing her face was her way of making me aware she knew more than I did, and she knew how much it would wind me up.

•

After the run-in with Bryony I wanted nothing more than to get into the flat and find out what was going on. On walking through the large, marbled entrance hall, I made my way to the lift. It wasn't until I stared at myself in the ornate 1930s-style mirrors that I realised I had been in the building before. Now I panicked. The man I had visited here was to do with a case, one that was hopefully going to result in a violent thug in prison. If I had lost the only person who was willing to testify against him, then it was over.

"Hi, Detective Sergeant Rodan, Jackson called me. Could you tell me which floor I need to go to?" I asked the young police officer who had been posted downstairs outside of the lifts. He looked suspiciously at my ID and then back at me.

"Up the lifts, fifth floor. Another guard will be posted outside the door," he stated, before looking forward again impassively. It was the floor that my informant lived on. Not wanting to jump to conclusions I pressed the button for floor number 5 and made my way upstairs. Once the doors to the lift opened, my fears were coming true. I made my way down to the door with the guard placed outside, the one I had visited on multiple occasions over the past few weeks.

Before I was able to confirm my suspicions I was asked to dress in the correct gear. I queried why this did not happen in the foyer downstairs, believing there could have been DNA evidence on the way to the flat. The technician reassured me though that it was common practice, DNA testing a whole block of flats would be difficult to process and would waste valuable resources that could be better used elsewhere. As I placed on the protective clothing, supplied by forensics, I couldn't help but realise how stupid we all looked. It was something akin to dressing like a giant sperm. While walking into the flat, following the trail that the forensic team had left, my gallows humour had turned onto a strange sort of grief.

I was glad I hadn't eaten that morning. Working as a uniformed officer I developed a strong stomach, however, the strong stench of urine and faeces was too much to bear in my hungover state. Had I eaten there was a chance I would have vomited over the crime scene and contaminated the evidence.

The smell wasn't the worst part, nothing could prepare me for the sight ahead of me.

Joseph, the victim, was tied to the bed. As I stared at the naked body my eyes were drawn first to his penis, or the area where his penis should have been, instead there was a hole where somebody had cut it off. He had been castrated. The lack of blood suggested that, thankfully for him, this was post mortem, rather than when he was still alive. Around the hole and his stomach was solidified cum, indicating that he had sexual intercourse the night before. He had a silk scarf tied around his neck that, at first glance, some may have believed was a woman's, but I knew it was from his own collection. His eyes were open in horror and shock, as was his mouth, where a second silk scarf was stuffed inside, an attempt to silence his screams as the life was draining from his body. As I stared at the naked man, my eyes were drawn to the horrific scars on his body. It looked as if he had been tortured into submission, probably during his life working under Marcos. My heart dropped when I saw them, knowing that it was unlikely Marcos would ever face any punishment for causing such a wonderful and intelligent man such pain.

"Did you know him?" Jackson said, as he came up beside me. Although one of the least empathetic men in the country, he was a perceptive detective which enabled him to get high up the career ladder. I knew I couldn't hide the truth and had to come clean.

"His name is Joseph Marsden. I previously questioned him about a theft in the Marcos Vincenzo household. Marcos… was convinced Joseph had stolen around £700,000 worth of jewels and money from him. I investigated but there was no evidence to suggest Joseph was involved." Marcos Vincenzo is a career criminal who I had been after for years. When he was robbed, he specifically requested me to be the investigating officer, some kind of perverse signal that he had influence in the police force and if I didn't play ball there could be consequences for my career.

I only gave Jackson half the truth. All evidence pointed to a theft, and Marcos was keen to point the finger at his employee.

However, what I didn't want to inform him of was that Joseph had shown me a significant amount of evidence to indicate this was a very elaborate fraud scheme. The jewellery was dodgy and he wanted it to be removed from his property. Joseph was going to help me finally get the man who had been involved in so many crimes, until... this. I thought it would be my Elliott Ness moment, being able to bring down a criminal for insurance fraud after all attempts to secure prosecution for murder, rape and child prostitution in the past had failed.

"At least you didn't know him personally. That may have been difficult to explain as you will be leading the case." Yet again Jackson went back to being impassive. It was a job and we all knew not to get too involved or attached. But Jackson had perfected the no-nonsense attitude to a tee. Everybody knew where they stood with Jackson, and he was not the kind of person you'd go crying to over spilt milk. "First thoughts?"

"Well... the way he is laid out suggests a crime of passion. Clearly he was having sexual intercourse just before the incident. The evidence of semen is a clear indication of that." I stopped for a moment, not wanting to go any further but knew I had to. This was a job... that was all. "Strangulation using a scarf is an intimate way of murdering somebody, the person was doing it while they were on top was enjoying the fear and anguish in his eyes. The mutilation of his genitals... that I can't comment on." Pleading ignorance was the best way with the penis. The fact I didn't tell Jackson was because I wanted to hold that card close to my chest. It wasn't that I didn't trust him, it was just that I knew he would warn me off a very good lead and tell me to pursue other avenues.

The penis being cut off and the scarf in his mouth were sinister. Although it looked like a crime of passion, this suggested somebody was trying to send a message. Not only to Joseph, and those he loved, but possibly to their own men. It had one purpose, to silence him and make him less of a man. I believed it was a murder committed by somebody close to Marcos Vincenzo, the problem was going to be proving it.

"Who found him?" I found myself asking. Hoping it wasn't some poor innocent person and he was found by a fellow police officer who was doing a welfare check because he hadn't turned up to work. Jackson took out his notebook and started searching for a name. I knew I was going to be disappointed.

"Her name is Fiona McGuinness. She's Joseph's cleaner, she was due to work today and found him after letting herself in. One of the constables has taken her to an empty flat on this floor to calm down. To say she was in hysterics is probably an understatement." I blocked Jackson out for a moment while I scanned the remainder of the room. With Joseph living in a studio flat I was able to see what was happening. I was perplexed when I didn't see his laptop or phone anywhere. It was highly unlikely they were in the bathroom either. Not wanting to bother the forensic officers I mentally made a note to check whether the items were logged in for evidence in the morning. If not, it was an avenue I could investigate.

"Come on, let's leave the forensics to do their work shall we? I better get back to the station and you should probably go check on Ms McGuinness." As he walked off I came out of my mini trance. Sighing I followed him like a faithful little puppy who wanted to please its master.

•

Fiona McGuinness was not what I expected. When Jackson mentioned she was a cleaner, I anticipated an older woman who just did a bit of cleaning on the side as a way to supplement her pension. She was a glamourous woman, who could have been no older than twenty-five years old. She had brunette hair that was cut into a short bob that framed her angular and slender face; the soft eye make-up she had lovingly prepared this morning was now moist and threatening to streak down her face; her body was slender and she looked elegant in her fluffy, black jumper and blue jeans. She was sitting on a sofa that had clearly been left by the previous tenants. I went and sat down beside her. I nodded at the police constable to signify that they could leave.

"Ms McGuinness, my name is Detective Sergeant Samantha Rodan. I am one of the investigators in this case. I just first want to say how sorry I am for what happened to Joseph and for what you had to witness. As a seasoned officer even I was in shock at the brutality that Joseph had clearly endured, I can only imagine how that must have impacted you." Fiona managed to stifle a short cry as she put the tissue she was holding to her mouth. It was clear she wasn't in a good way, but it was always better to get a statement when things were fresh in the witnesses mind. So easily details could be forgotten or missed at a later date. "May I call you Fiona?" She nodded slightly. "Fiona, I am going to ask you a couple of questions. If you find yourself struggling at any time please tell me and we will stop for a moment. Is that okay?" Another nod of affirmation, I clicked my Dictaphone on and opened my notebook ready to make key notes in case the recording was of poor quality.

"Fiona, can you tell me a little about how you know the victim?" I asked, wanting to start on a less distressing note than the horrendous scene she had just witnessed.

"I started working for Joey about a year ago. He was in need of a cleaner who would be happy to work early hours as he was normally asleep during the day. I had a little baby at the time so the hours suited me and I was hired pretty easily. I would work four days a week for three hours each morning starting at 5am." She spoke in a calm and concise manner but stopped momentarily when she felt her voice about to break. "We got on really well. I had so much in common with him and he had this really fantastic habit of making me laugh. If there wasn't a lot to do we would normally sit on the sofa and just chat about our favourite programmes. He liked spy programmes; he sometimes said his job had an element of tricking people and that's why he enjoyed them." She stopped again, clearly remembering the fun times they had. I decided to move on a bit.

"You say you would spend time with him. Did he ever mention anything about his work? Or if he was dating anybody?" Fiona gathered her thoughts before she answered my question. She was incredibly brave agreeing to do this now.

"I know he was an escort. He mentioned that he would never bring a client back to his flat in case they became too clingy or violent and started stalking him. But he never liked to talk about his job." Again, I patiently waited as Fiona took a break from talking and waited for her to feel like she could continue. "He was in a relationship when I joined. Lovely man by the name of Andreas, but they split up quite soon after. I know he started to see somebody seven or eight months ago. It was strange, Joey was never shy about introducing friends or partners to me but this was different."

"Different how?" I knew I shouldn't have jumped in, but a secret lover was an interesting lead and raised questions. Did he keep the relationship quiet because he was worried about repercussions from Marcos? Or was it that his lover wanted to keep their relationship a secret because he had something to lose. Either way it could be a motive for murder.

"They always met in a secret location, never in the centre of Manchester. They always met in the countryside around the Yorkshire Dales National Park. Apparently the person owns a little cottage there. I know he was quite rich and didn't want to be seen in public with a man." A secret relationship was always a good motive for murder. Especially if one of the parties involved didn't want to be hidden in the shadows anymore.

"Do you have any more information about this secret lover?"

"I know he was younger than Joey. Joey used to talk about how athletic he was. But... unfortunately I really can't tell you much." Fiona looked a little downhearted that she couldn't give me more details. I just gave her an encouraging smile and decided to move on.

"Did he ever mention his family to you? If any of them were still alive?" Partly a fishing question so we knew who to tell about this awful death, partly because I wanted to understand how honest he really was about his life.

"He was alone. Both of his parents died in a car crash when he was in his twenties, not that they were close anyway. They didn't approve of his job. He had a sister, but again she died. She was a junkie, heroin addict. His family life wasn't great growing up apparently. His parents were both alcoholics, and his dad used to… well… pick up prostitutes and bring them back home. Even with his mum there. It was a total mess. He told me they did the whole 'born again Christian' skit, which drove an even bigger wedge. I have no idea how true it was though." Fiona stopped again, she seemed disgusted at what she was telling me. It was a good indication of the mind of Joey though. Growing up with that kind of influence explained why Joey thought working for Marcos was as easy as riding a bike.

"How about his relationship with his boss? Did he speak much about that?" Fiona shook her head and put the tissue to her eyes again. It was evident she was starting to struggle with the questions. I decided it was time to stop the conversation. Seeing a dead body is a horrifying experience even for those of us who are used to it, but for a young innocent woman who just wanted to do her job… "Fiona, you have been very helpful. I think this is enough for today, though. One of the constables will take you home." The young police officer helped Fiona to her feet and led her out of the door. I just sat alone in the room, pondering what my next move would be. I have never sobered up so quickly in my life.

•

"This is torture, mate, my head is banging," Michael stated, as he lifted the weights above him. Alex was staring down at him with a curious look on his face; he was there to make sure that nothing untoward happened and Michael didn't end up with 75 kg weights dropping onto his chest. He had gone home briefly after leaving the raven-haired beauty's house in the morning. Samantha, or Sammi, was her name he believed. On getting back he had a quick shower and downed a very large protein shake, one that made him want to vomit. Since joining Alex in the gym it was clear that he was in desperate need of water. The dehydration was kicking in, and he felt on the verge of passing out.

"Well maybe you shouldn't have stayed out all night then,"

Alex responded in a sober, and cheerful, manner. Even with eight years on him, Alex was able to party all night and come out clean and sober within two hours of sleeping. Michael, on the other hand, was a lightweight, even with an early night or less alcohol, he would still be hungover for hours once he got up in the morning. His low alcohol tolerance was a joke to their team mates, but it didn't seem funny now.

Ten lifts were his limit. He signalled to Alex, and sat up after his friend took the weights away from him. All his movements were slow, and he knew he was acting as if he were a man older than his years. As he sat up, he put his head in his hands, trying to decide if he was going to pass out or not. Deciding leaning over was worse, he sat up and glanced at the news ahead of him and couldn't believe his eyes. For the first time in his life, he was speechless.

"Mikey, what's wrong?" Alex asked, sounding concerned. Believing that his friend was suffering a medical episode and he would need to act fast to help. But when he saw where Michael was looking he realised he couldn't be more wrong. "What's your fascination with Sammi?"

"You know her?" Michael quickly turned his head to look at his friend, and instantly regretted it. An involuntary hiss came from his lips and he grabbed his forehead to centre himself. Alex just smiled broadly.

"Yeah of course, she is the little sister of my best mate. She's a police officer who's been placed on a really high-profile case in the city. How… do you know her?" Alex grabbed the remote and turned up the TV. It was an appeal for the Marcos Vincenzo case, allegedly there had been very few leads and Marcos had put up a reward of £50k for any information. Knowing Marcos it was a ploy. There were strong indications it was part of an elaborate insurance fraud, but he was untouchable and Alex doubted it would be proven. He felt for Sammi having to be the face of the police on TV, he knew how much she hated the limelight and just wanted to get on with her own life. Marcos would have known this would be hell for her.

But that's why he did it, the psychopath that he is.

"She's the girl I met in the club," Michael responded, snapping Alex back into reality. He looked hard at Michael, not quite believing him.

"Sammi... little Sammi Rodan was the girl in that red dress? Mate... wow... I didn't even recognise her, she looked stunning." Alex was surprised, but not because he didn't think Samantha was a stunning girl. Even now, as he looked at her speaking on the screen, he could see how beautiful she was. But she was understated, not wanting others to pay attention to her, preferring to be her natural self. The image of seeing her in the red dress was something different, not bad, but just different.

"Yeah well, she didn't stay in the red dress for long." It was a meek response making Alex sigh in annoyance.

"Come on, mate, do we need that?"

"What... urgh, that's not what I meant." Michael was exasperated as he got up and walked over to the water cooler. Alex followed behind wanting to hear his friend's explanation. "What I meant was I accidentally ruined her dress by dropping her drink down it. She stole my shirt and managed to turn it into a home-made dress. Anyway, this isn't even the point, I wanted to say I had no idea she was a copper." Michael drunk his water quickly, needing to replace the fluid in his body. Alex couldn't help but laugh. "What's so funny?"

"Oh mate, you said you went back to her place, wasn't there any indication she was a copper in her flat?" Alex sniggered as he drunk some water. Michael felt sheepish.

"She had some handcuffs. I thought they may be just something kinky. Maybe I was a bit drunk last night."

"Yes, clearly. Because normally any kinky sex cuffs will have fur on them. But hey, at least you enjoyed yourself. That's the main thing." Michael tried not to smile as the memory of the passionate sex came back to him. She was the most sensual lover he had been with, and he only wished their paths would cross again so that they could have round two.

•

The young reporter stood in the unusually cold March morning with the residents who had gathered. Waiting patiently to see if she would receive any information about what had happened. Normally a murder wouldn't be high on her priority list. Unfortunately, they happened so frequently in the UK that she had become desensitised to such news. But this was a different case. She had received a tip-off that the man who had been murdered happened to live in the apartment of a well-known contact of Marcos Vincenzo, an alleged businessman and somebody Bryony was investigating for her most recent blog post. She wondered if there was some kind of connection.

When Samantha and her boss emerged, quiet murmurings could be heard from the residents around. Bryony's spirits lifted, she was waiting to see if they would come in her direction so she could get some more information, but to no avail. They turned their backs and walked away. Bryony was disappointed but not surprised. She pondered whether she should wait it out to try and gather a bit more information.

That was until the phone call from her husband, one that she was in two minds about answering.

"Hi darling. This is an unusual surprise." Bryony didn't mean to have the malice in her voice, but she knew it was evident. For a few months now she and Lewis hadn't seen eye to eye. It was ever since she had gotten pregnant with their third child. Whereas she believed that another child would enrich their lives, Lewis believed that they weren't earning enough money to afford feeding an extra mouth. In truth, his real concern was Bryony was not earning enough money with her freelance journalism, and was keen for her to get a real job. It was a constant argument, but sadly one that Lewis was unable to back down from. He wanted her to get an abortion, she knew this, but she could never take a life.

"It's to do with work. You've had a phone call from somebody claiming that there has been an attack on somebody outside a club, by a footballer," Lewis replied. None of the sweet talk now, no honey or sweetie. Just straight to the business at hand.

Sometimes Bryony couldn't help but wonder if Lewis had fallen out of love with her.

"Well I'm currently at a murder scene and the man may have links to organised crime, so unfortunately I think a football attack currently has second billing don't you?" She didn't mean to snap but her hormones were all over the place, and in all honesty she wasn't sure she could take anymore. Sometimes she just wanted to curl up at home, eat chocolate and watch TV. But then she wouldn't be able to earn any money, and then Lewis would win his argument about not being able to afford another child. Besides, it was unlikely that the footballer was even that well known. Probably just some youth teamer who had gone out and had a few too many beers before being a total idiot.

"I think you may want to take this one seriously. It's the football golden boy Alex Smith." She hated to admit when her husband was right, however, she knew that if she ignored the tip somebody else could get to the story first. Sighing, she asked for the address of the person who phoned and then walked away from the crime scene. If nothing else comes of it at least she could get a bit of money for a trashy celebrity story, something she was doing her best to avoid and thus far not succeeding.

THREE

I sat in the car with my thoughts for a while outside the police force's temporary lodgings. We moved there after an arson attack by a radical far-left organisation who believed the police needed to be defunded. It was an old 1970s building that looked out of place nestled against the newly built high-rise offices and flats that were swiftly taking over the city. Due to rampant budget cuts it was all the force could afford while our home was being rebuilt. Even then conversations happened about whether we really required an office, and if we should just try and work in a more remote way.

The world went a little insane after 2021.

With my head resting on the wheel ahead of me, I looked out at the rain drops as they fell down the windscreen. I felt sombre, my case against Marcos had died with Joseph. It was selfish, but I knew that without him I was unable to move against one of the most notorious crime lords in the local area; a man who had caused a lot of pain to countless people through his sick deeds. Being able to arrest him seemed so far away. I also couldn't help but feel for Fiona McGuinness, she was too young to have witnessed something so heartless.

Finally, gaining courage, I got out of the car and ran to the front doors, doing my best to avoid the growing puddles in the car park. It had gone from almost freezing to rain in just a few moments, like the typical English weather. It was days like this when people questioned whether global warming, or climate change, was a real phenomenon. UK residents had short memories though, in just a few weeks they would be complaining about soaring summer temperatures and drought-like weather.

As I passed the reception and made my way up the grey mottled staircase, I couldn't help but think about how another coffee would work wonders now. The alcohol was beginning to disappear from my system, however, the hangover was about to kick in. I knew that I wouldn't be able to survive a conversation with Jackson in such a state, but then I also knew he expected me to arrive at his office as soon as I walked in the door. Sighing I continued up to the fifth floor and decided to bite the bullet and see my boss.

We worked in a reasonably small office. There were five desks used by the junior detectives in the force. Those most senior usually shared offices when they were working together on cases, and then they used us on occasion as a pool of resources. Jackson had his own small glass partitioning in the room, which was recognised as his office. He would sit there for hours on end staring at old case files, I could never work out if they were the cases he could never solve or if he was trying to remember what the 'good old days' were like. Whatever he was doing, I'm sure it couldn't have been as important as real police work.

Currently I was the only detective sergeant in the Greater Manchester Police. Although that wasn't just down to budget cuts, part of it was due to the case just over the border. A serial killer who was killing and raping children was on the loose, and it was becoming a high priority case as his victims were now in the double figures. The current count was three police forces and over a hundred officers were all working together in one task force to try and stop the killer before he did any more damage and ruined more families' lives. I had been left behind as I was still working on the Marcos Vincenzo robbery at the time, one he believed should take top priority. The case was trying though, Marcos did not know what had been stolen, and without those descriptions or pictures of the items it was difficult to bring the case to a conclusion.

I knocked on the door and entered Jackson's room, noting that he was not the only one in there. I sat next to the stranger, noticing the cup of coffee in his hands. I knew the drink offer would not be extended to me. It was only those he was trying to impress such as detectives who would be looking to join his team, wanting to give the illusion of a caring boss who you could have a coffee with and tell your problems to, or the higher ranks, as a way to sweet-talk them into putting him forward for an undeserved promotion. I envied the new guy, a warm drink seemed like an excellent way to kill off the pain in my head. It probably wasn't the best start to any relationship that Jackson was going to force on us.

"Samantha, as you know the North York Moors case is top priority. This means that there are very few competent police officers in the local area. I will be unable to take this case due to other priorities, however, I have asked that you take it over with the help of another." Jackson paused for a moment and stood up, walking around the desk to the young man by the side of me. I turned slightly so that he was in view. "This is acting DC Paul Grant. He has been temporarily promoted to detective to support you on this case. It is unorthodox to say the least, however, our hands are tied with budget cuts. As well as Paul you will also have access to one other uniformed officer to help with routine house-to-house enquiries. I am unable to offer more. Is that okay?" It was a rhetorical question; I had no choice in the matter. Unfortunately, I had to take this case, and I would have to have the help of this person who had never been in such a position before. I just smiled and nodded, not wanting to give the game away too early. Jackson seemed pleased and sat down.

"Any questions, Samantha?" he asked when he was back at his desk. I knew what I wanted to do, but knew that the subject would be sensitive. It was easier to be upfront and direct, though, than beat around the bush.

"Not so much a question, sir, but a request? As you know

Joseph worked for Marcos, and was being interviewed as a witness to the jewellery robbery of Mr Vincenzo's house. I would like to speak to Marcos to see if he could shed any light on who may have hurt Joseph?" It felt wrong having to request permission from the boss on how to do my job. I was aware that approaching Marcos about something that didn't relate to his burglary could spell disaster for my career. At first I was convinced that Jackson was going to say no, however, he wasn't an idiot and realised that, if he did, it would just look suspicious. His employer was always going to be the first point of call given his accusations about the stolen jewels. He nodded his head a little, I knew that he was still unsure about the request but had decided to grant it anyway.

"Okay, but be careful. We have had a number of complaints from Marcos, and I don't particularly want another because he feels that we are harassing him. He isn't an idiot, and can pay for some high-profile lawyers." I thanked Jackson and then stood up, knowing that if I remained any longer he would probably change his mind. Paul followed promptly once he realised that this was the end of the conversation with Jackson. Although he hadn't said a word yet I was concerned he wouldn't be able to keep up with the pace.

Although I guess there was only one way to find out.

FOUR

"I know this might be a stupid question, Ma'am, but what is the connection between Marcos and Joseph?" I recoiled at the term ma'am. Something about it made me feel significantly older than I was. It was a term that should only be used for a queen and no others. As I stopped at the lights and flicked my indicator up I quickly glanced at Paul, who was looking at me with large inquisitive brown eyes.

"Okay, ground rules. No calling me Ma'am, I'm only… what… a year older than you at most? Samantha, Sam, or preferably Sammi, will do. We are both novices at the murder game so let's act like equals."

"There are no stupid questions. If there is anything you aren't sure about let me know. I'd rather you ask than make a huge mistake, putting us both into trouble. Those are my only two conditions. Do we have a deal?" Paul nodded his head, it was a good enough indication for me that he was happy with what I was saying. I continued as the lights turned green and I pulled away from the junction.

"Joseph was one of Marcos' prized assets. Both working as an escort and an occasional chauffeur. He worked with him and knew a bit of information about the recent robbery that occurred at Marcos' home." Paul made a couple of notes as I made my way through the streets of Manchester. He paused for a moment, wondering what to say next before speaking.

"But I thought Marcos was a legitimate businessman." I held in the laugh forming deep in my throat, not wanting to seem unprofessional.

"His legitimate businesses are a cover. His claims that he owns a casino and modelling business are to hide the truth. The reality is much darker. He uses the young men and women in his employ as prostitutes, and for his own sick fantasies. He has been implicated in a couple of murders previously, however, no bodies were ever found and all indications that these people even existed has been wiped from the face of the earth. No body, no person, equals no proof of a murder. On top of that he has been suspected of bribing officers in our department, unfortunately we don't know who it is and cannot weed out the corruption. There is even a rumour that he is having an affair with a lawyer, but I am unsure if that is true." I peered over at the notes that Paul was making and smiled, happy that he was taking everything in.

"One other thing, Marcos Vincenzo isn't his real name. He has no Italian blood at all. His name is Brian Poole. He was obsessed with the Mafia culture and believed he would be taken more seriously if he changed his name." I decided it was enough information and settled into focusing on my driving. Paul clearly realised I was going to say no more and opted to just stare down at what he had already written.

We continued the rest of the journey in silence. Eventually we reached our destination. I pulled into a small country road and found my way blocked by two gates and an intercom. Opening my window I pressed on the button and explained my business. I may have been imagining things but it seemed like the woman on the other end sighed and may have even rolled her eyes. I knew I wasn't popular, after accusing Marcos of orchestrating the theft of his own stuff, however, it was imperative to bite the bullet and question him about the death of Joseph.

We were buzzed through the gates, and I began the slow ascent up the driveway. It must have been at least five minutes between the gate and the house. I remembered the property when it was open to visitors and not owned by a notorious criminal.

The driveway used to be beautiful, with colourful wildflowers on the grass verges and trees of reds, yellows and greens lining the way ahead. Now, the trees were there, but due to a lack of care many were dead or dying, having been infected by a number of different diseases including fungal infections and ash dieback; the flowers no longer existed due to the driveway being widened. It was a shame, and showed Marcos' disrespect for nature.

The house ahead was one of the largest in the country. Marcos built it from scratch after his former home mysteriously 'burnt down' which many believed was due to being refused planning permission to tear down the old house. Before it was a beautiful old building that many in the local area were proud of. Now it was large, boring and blocky with whitewashed walls. The windows outside were black, and looked as if they had bars over the top. Leaving many to claim that those inside of the house were being held against their will.

After parking my car out the front I got out. Paul followed not long after.

"Just so you know, Marcos is a bit of a loose cannon and sensitive to the police. Although he doesn't like me, I have dealt with him before, and I believe it would be better if he just continue to hate me rather than us both. Having one police officer on his side may help further down the line and, who knows, he may think he could recruit you into his circle." Again Paul just nodded. I was wondering if he was too nervous to say anything for the moment, and hoped that he would become helpful later on in the case. I didn't think I could handle having him just standing there staring at everything around.

The door opened before we had the chance to knock, a young woman stood staring at us with a mixture of both anger and confusion. She couldn't have been any older than eighteen. Her hair was scrunched up in a messy ponytail, which showed of her large earrings. Other than that all she wore was a bikini, which was blue with white polka dots. In her hand was a Long Island iced tea, with a small umbrella. I was freezing looking at her, the heating must have been high in the house for her to be dressed for the middle of summer.

If I didn't know any better, I would have thought we had just interrupted a party. But this was Marcos, it was likely this girl was just another one of his escorts that he had decided to shag today. He had a reputation for 'sampling' his product, saying it was the only way he could guarantee quality for his customers. They were treated like stock, not human beings.

Without saying a word she turned around and led us through the house, leaving us in the living room where Marcos was sitting. As we walked in he shouted to his cook that he needed another alcoholic beverage, something I'm sure she was thrilled to do after all of her years attending culinary school.

"Detective Rodan, what an unexpected pleasure," Marcos said, as he got up from the sofa. He was tall at around 6 ft 7 inches. His hair was brown and slicked back in a style similar to that of Ronnie and Reggie Kray of the '90s. He wore a thick gold ring on his pinkie finger, and a Saint Christopher with a medium gold chain around his neck. There was a scar above his left eye due to an incident with a former member of staff who wasn't happy with the way he treated her, so she decided to attack him with a glass. Sadly she was now in jail for five years for GBH, and he is still walking around free. Even though she accused him of multiple rapes during the trial.

"Mr Vincenzo. Sorry for disturbing you, we need to have a discussion," I replied, as I sat down on the sofa. The anger in his eyes was evident. He was so used to people being subordinate to him, when he came up against somebody who wouldn't be scared it just made him angry. Especially when that person was a woman, if I was a member of staff I knew I would be punished all night by Marcos himself.

"Are you going to accuse me of orchestrating my own burglary again?" He was clearly agitated. I glanced over briefly at Paul as I pulled out my notebook, noticing he was a little on edge. It made me smile. At least I was able to throw him in at the deep end. Nothing would be worse than Marcos Vincenzo, he was the most vile criminal in the local area and possibly even in the entire country. But unfortunately I couldn't touch him. He was too powerful now, especially with Joseph dead.

"No. This is about Joseph. We found him this morning. He was murdered." If Marcos was shocked, he didn't show it, instead just staring down at his perfectly manicured nails. It was almost like he didn't hear me. After what seemed likes minutes, but could only have been a few seconds, he finally responded.

"I wondered why he didn't turn up for work this morning. What happened?" Cold and straight to the point, an attitude I had come to accept. He didn't see those in his employ as people, just slaves and sexual playthings for the rich. The way he exploited vulnerable men and women who had already had a rough ride angered me, for the sake of Joseph, though, I had to remain calm and level-headed.

"He was strangled." I stopped briefly, questioning if I wanted to mention the mutilation of his genitals to Marcos. I opted to keep it quiet and continued. "We are aware that Joseph didn't have any family, so you were probably the closest person to him. Do you know of anybody who would want to hurt him?" It didn't subdue him, but talking about those in his employment that we knew about seemed to soothe Marcos somewhat. Paul was still sitting beside me with his notepad out, ready to take notes on anything that I may have missed. I was hoping he could enlighten me after this meeting.

"Joseph was very popular with everybody. My staff loved him. He was friendly, always had a big grin on his face. The clients adored him. I never had one complaint from them. He was always happy to do whatever they wanted, regardless of how depraved it was." I could feel Paul next to me tense a little. He clearly didn't enjoy hearing about the man's sex life. I hoped it was the reason anyway and it wasn't anything more sinister.

"Do you know what Joseph was up to yesterday? Any clue about his final moments?" I asked, hoping that we would have somewhere to start. Right now, it felt like we were fish flopping around on the ground with no water source around us.

"It was his night off yesterday. I last saw him about 8pm and he didn't mention what he was getting up to. He was always a very private person. One thing though, is he always loved to go clubbing. I'm sorry I can't be more help." I didn't know if Marcos was being honest or not, the likelihood was that he wasn't. I couldn't help but feel that he wanted to get rid of me as soon as possible. That wouldn't be surprising though, really.

"Thank you, Mr Vincenzo. One last question. Could you tell me where you were last night?" It was like waving a red rag in a bulls face. He was on edge since we got in, but now his rage intensified. Even asking for an alibi was implication enough for him that he was guilty. If I was easily intimidated I would have apologised. However, I wasn't, and it was my job to find out what had happened to his employee.

"I have an alibi, however, I will only supply it once there is some stronger evidence. Now, if you would kindly fuck off out of my house." It was the Marcos I knew. I had rattled him by asking the simple question, made him feel smaller. I stood up from the sofa and smiled sweetly, Paul was walking next to me and clearly tense. He had a lot to learn about this line of work, and I hoped it wouldn't take him too long to do it.

"May I ask... what's going on about my missing jewellery?" Marcos asked as he opened the door for us to leave. I stopped for a moment, even with the knowledge a man had been murdered, Marcos was still concerned about replaceable items.

"Unfortunately, due to the cuts, I have been redeployed onto the Joseph murder. I would recommend you consider hiring a private investigator if you feel your jewels are important." Even when trying to be honest and placate Marcos, I sounded sarcastic. It was difficult to feign interest in a subject matter I didn't care about. He was rich enough to replace his missing jewellery and even admitted to myself it didn't have any real sentimental value. Instead of replying he slammed the door in our faces.

"That didn't go well." It was the first thing Paul had said in a long time. I just gave him a sarcastic look and walked over to the car, gunning the engine to signify we were leaving. After getting in he remained silent for the rest of the journey.

FIVE

She couldn't believe her luck as she sat at her desk staring at the photos that she had just been sold by the Erotica Club in Salford High Street. When her husband rang about the tip she was unsure whether he had lied about the involvement of Alex Smith. Why would somebody so high profile be seen to be brawling in the street? Cameras were everywhere and it was obvious he would be found out. But now she looked at the pictures, it had all that a juicy story would want. If she didn't get them out now, somebody else would get the scoop and it would be too late.

Lewis came up and placed a cup of tea on the desk next to her laptop. She had almost finished her story, and was ready to send it through to any editor who would be willing to pay the highest. If she got it right, she could make a cool £2,500 off this article and pictures alone. Far more than she paid the utter sap who sold them to her. He would have been better off contacting one of the tabloids rather than contacting Bryony. She made it her business to know people around the city, make them aware she was the best person to come to with any story, that she had the relevant contacts. It meant that she would scoop the stories that she wanted early on.

It's why she was such a good freelancer.

"Looking good," Lewis commented, doing his best to be

supportive. Bryony smiled a little but knew it was strained. Their relationship was tough, and had been for a while now. Money concerns were a large part of it, but Bryony thought there was something deeper. She had seen the way he looked at other women during her pregnancy, the casual flirting with the wife of a friend on evenings out together. Their heads dropped close, as if they were both hiding a secret. Or maybe it was what she just wanted to believe as she was questioning whether she loved him anymore. An affair would be an excuse to get out of the relationship.

In reality though, she knew they had to try for the sake of their young children.

"Thanks, darling," she replied, picking up the phone in a bid to try and avoid any awkward small talk with him. Thankfully he walked away not long after she dialled her former boss and mentor at the *Daily Scoop* newspaper.

"Bryony, darling. How are you?" He answered straight away, no doubt with his feet on his desk ahead, looking like a stereotype from an American TV show. The fact that he was originally from America and grew up with that influence probably helped as well.

"Steven, I'm good thank you. Look I want to get down to business, I have a juicy one today," Bryony replied, getting very excited. She knew Steven would give her a more than reasonable price for the photos, hopefully some tips for further stories. It wasn't that she enjoyed writing the trashy celebrity pieces, but it paid the bills and kept her husband quiet. Her heart was in investigative journalism, but only through doing these pieces could she continue to fund the work she loved.

"Hit me then. It'd better be good. It seems to be a slow news day right now. Nothing juicy to put on the front page. At this rate I may need to consider putting the growing tensions in Russia on there and that will just turn our usual clientele off." Although the *Daily Scoop* did deal with serious political matters, such as the Russian conflict, these were normally consigned to the latter pages of the paper. The front page was reserved for more salacious celebrity articles. Bryony was certain Alex Smith attacking a man would be the front-page material that Steven was after.

"I have some CCTV images here from an attack outside a nightclub. Some poor man got attacked…"

"Sorry to cut you off, babe, but… an attack, really? That's even less newsworthy than that murder in Portland Heights." His impatience annoyed her, but it was his attitude to all those who worked with him. If he didn't consider the story good enough from the first couple of words, he would disregard it almost instantly.

"Alex Smith. The man perpetrating the attack is none other than Alex Smith," she replied, getting straight to the point so that he didn't try and cut her off again. She knew his interest had been peaked now. It wasn't everyday they got one of the highest paid footballers in the city attacking a member of the public. It would make the paper thousands.

"Send it over to me now, darling. I will ensure it is in tomorrow's edition. You will receive double your usual fee for this story, £5,000," Steven replied. He was clearly wandering around the room now salivating about what she had given him. The fee was a nice surprise as circulation had been down in recent months, it was surprising print media was still in existence. The news was now more accessible via websites or blogs, so the fact the print media was continuing to make waves was quite surprising. "That suspicious death in Portland Heights, what do you know about it?"

"Well, I believe that the victim may have had a direct link to Marcos Vincenzo. He was one of his closest confidants who knew something about the jewellery heist." It wasn't much information but it was enough to make Steven think for a while. She sat in silence, waiting for the editor to either dismiss her or speak some more.

"I've heard a little more, but I haven't wanted to put it on the front page until it's been verified." He stopped for a moment, leaving Bryony in suspense. "There are rumours that the man in question was one of Marcos' male escorts who had several flings with some, shall we say, in the closet, high-profile men. I'm not willing to put the reputation of this paper on the line for a rumour though." It shocked Bryony to the core. Instantly she went onto the Twitter page and started perusing, wanting to see if there was any information other than what Steven had provided. She needed the story first, if she did then money would be no issue for at least the rest of the year. Thanking him, she hung up and wondered if she would be able to get the scoop on who this man had been in bed with.

If she was lucky, maybe she could earn enough money to take a sabbatical to reconnect with her family. Maybe they would be able to turn things around for the sake of their children before it was too late.

SIX

After a quick stop off at a service station for some fuel, and a refill of our bottled water, Paul took over the driving back to the station. We remained in silence as I sat in the passenger seat, scanning my notes, deep in thought at the details we had gathered, especially with regard to Marcos. It was a gut feeling, but I believed he was either involved, or knew more than he was letting on. The fact that I lacked proof would make things difficult, it would result in a refusal to continue investigating the avenue in fear of aggravating the man.

On arriving back to the office, I set up a whiteboard and collated all the information we had. Most of my colleagues found my method clichéd, preferring verbal briefings with paper documents. For me I found the visual representation of how the case was going kept me on track. As I began compiling what we knew it turned out to be very little. We knew that Joseph worked for Marcos Vincenzo, who believed his member of staff was stealing from him, and that Joseph had evidence to contradict that claim. Additionally we knew Joseph was an escort, who may or may not have had clientele in the higher echelons of society. Obtaining a court order for Marcos' client list would prove difficult so early in the investigation, and it was unlikely Marcos would willingly hand over the names.

Paul had been set up temporarily on Dennis McCarthy's

desk during his secondment. Having him in the office was a refreshing change from the loud, angry presence of McCarthy. From the little time we had together I found Paul to be quiet and thoughtful. Willing to take a back seat and listen rather than say too much. A far different personality from McCarthy who would offer his opinion even if it wasn't wanted. He expected quick results and if he saw a colleague struggling with a case he would tell them exactly who they should pursue. Had he been on the Marcos burglary I have no doubt Joseph would have been awaiting trial for theft as McCarthy would have put together a compelling file to show he was guilty.

I could hear the soft tapping of keys behind me. Paul was tasked with finding out whether Joseph had any long-lost family members, or was alone like many believed. His criminal record was also of interest. I knew it was lengthy and wished to understand links to violent offenders or other high-society criminals.

Other than Marcos Vincenzo of course.

A soft crunch broke the silence of the room, it took my attention away from the board for a moment and I noted that Charlotte Dawkins, one of our uniformed officers, had walked in eating a pack of protein crisps. She smiled just before taking the final one, scrunching the packet into a ball and tossing it in the bin next to her. People took Charlotte for granted on account of her small stature, she was petite at around 5 ft 1 inch and a size 6. Her long, wavy, blonde hair was often pulled back into a tight ponytail to keep it out of the way when on duty; her eyes were soft and a stunning green which most would get lost in. What most didn't realise though, was her brute strength, not only was she an amateur mixed martial artist, but she also taught self-defence classes to vulnerable women who had previously been raped or abused by their partners. She could take down a six-foot man with ease and wasn't the kind of woman you would want to start a fight with.

I gave Charlotte a look of hope as she walked over to her desk, taking off her bulletproof vest and resting it on the back of her chair. She sat down at her desk and pulled out another packet of protein crisps, opening and digging into them. I was jealous of a woman who could eat but never put on weight. After what seemed like an age she finally spoke.

"I'm sorry, Detective. Joseph seemed to be a very quiet person. The neighbours I spoke to said that they liked him, he was kind and friendly. He kept very late nights, but never brought anybody home for the evening. They don't remember any regular partners," Sergeant Dawkins replied.

"And CCTV footage?" Charlotte shook her head as she put her crisp packet down and logged into her work terminal, becoming irritated at its slow speed.

"Hard to believe, but none. The residents demanded that the systems be removed from the building, and the immediate area. They even signed a declaration stating the heavy surveillance was against their human rights." Unsurprising, especially in an area known to house criminals and unsavoury characters. Once Terrance won the election there was a last push to try and give people more freedom and less surveillance. Clearly those in Portland Heights were a part of that movement. Frustratingly, though, it didn't help our investigation.

"Did you manage to follow up with forensics and evidence to see if they logged a laptop and a phone?" Charlotte nodded her head, but the expression on her face was grim. I knew it was going to be yet more bad news.

"Nothing, they didn't find any electronic devices in his home. Well other than the TV." I sighed; it wasn't the news that I wanted. The laptop had the evidence of Marcos' financial fraud, without it the jewellery case was dead. If it wasn't for the mutilation and evidence of sexual intercourse, I would have considered the murder a result of burglary gone bad, however, this was a premeditated and calculated death. Not one that suggested panic after a failed robbery.

I thanked Charlotte for her update and left her to the remainder of her short break. We only had her help for the door-to-doors, with the full investigation falling on myself and

Paul. She was needed back on the beat to give the appearance of visibility. Paul and I would go back at a later stage in the hope of getting hold of those who weren't at home during the first enquiries; or to jog somebody's memory once we had a bit more detail.

"When are we going to go out again, Sam?" Charlotte said, as she continued to crunch through her protein crisps. I wearily looked over at Paul whose interest had now been peaked a little. Charlotte was one of my drinking partners when I wasn't in the mood to go out alone and pick up a guy. She wasn't interested in relationships and enjoyed spending time with female friends, chatting over cocktails and food. It was always relaxed and informal, so much so that we would arrive to work the next morning with blinding hangovers, a habit I wanted to stop. It was rare our time off would sync though.

"Soon, Charlotte. When are you next off work?" I responded, as I unpeeled the orange I'd retrieved from my desk drawer.

"Hmm, so my next real time off is in April. I'll text you and we'll set something up." She stopped briefly and looked at her watch. "Shit I got to go. Speak soon, Sammi." She put her vest back on quickly and ran out of the door after disposing of her crisp packet. I shook my head and turned to Paul, wanting to get back onto the subject of work.

"Well that was a waste of time. I hope you have something more, Paul," I said when Charlotte had disappeared. Paul peered over at me and nodded his head. He then picked up the notes he had made and begun his mini-presentation.

"We were right about the status of Joseph's family. Both of his parents are deceased, and he had one sister who had a lengthy criminal record, drugs mainly, some theft and one assault charge. She was found dead three years ago of a heroin overdose. With regard to Joseph's criminal record, it's all pretty minor. A few soliciting and prostitution charges, all of which stopped once he was in Mr Vincenzo's employ. There was a pretty nasty rape allegation as well, but this was dropped. The man who claimed it, was charged with perverting the course of justice and his trial is still pending," Paul recounted. As he did so I updated the board with all the relevant details. The final thing could be a potential lead, but going from perverting the course of justice to murder seemed a bit of a stretch. I wanted to keep that in my back pocket just in case though.

"When was that rape allegation? And what is going on with the defendant?" I asked, still staring at the board.

"Give me a second," Paul said. I heard the tapping of keys again in the background. "Trial is currently pending and scheduled to be held in September 2028, although this could be pushed back. Defendant is…" Paul stopped briefly while he scanned the rest of the details. "He's currently in custody after he assaulted a young woman. His parole was revoked."

"When was that?"

"It was 3rd February. They're trying to get an emergency hearing to grant him parole again, but no such luck." With that I struck the information from the board, realising the lead wouldn't be fruitful in the circumstances.

I perched on the edge of my desk, picking up and then examined a document of all evidence that had been compiled and removed from Joseph's home. It confirmed that there was no laptop or phone found at the scene. Clearly Fiona was right when she said it had been stolen and it hadn't just been misplaced. They noted that DNA and fingerprint samples had been taken in Joseph's flat, but nowhere else in the building, a caveat was underneath to say that, due to the number of visitors to the block, it would take too long to narrow down any possible DNA matches. I knew the physical evidence wouldn't have been processed yet due to staff shortages at the lab, so there was no point in bothering forensics. At that moment Jackson leant around the door from his office.

"Look guys, you may as well go now. There is nothing else to do right here. We don't really have any tangible leads and you need to wait for DNA anyway. Maybe call it a night and get here bright and early tomorrow." I sighed and nodded my head. The first forty-eight hours of any murder enquiry were always the key, but when there were no leads it seemed pointless to wear ourselves out for the sake of it. I nodded my head in agreement with Jackson and sighed as I stood to pack my stuff up. Paul continued to stare at the computer screen, scrolling through data.

"Paul, are you leaving?"

"Yeah, soon. I just… I just want to try and get up to speed with everything about Joseph and Marcos," he said.

"Okay, well goodnight," I responded, as I picked up my keys and slung my bag over my shoulder. Paul never looked up from the screen and instead just waved me off. I felt bad leaving him, but knew that tomorrow would be a better day.

Or at least I hoped it would be.

•

Exhausted from the previous night, I crawled into bed after brushing my teeth. Sleep eluded me though, and for a while I lay in my king-size bed staring up at the ceiling, imagining the stunning man with his hands around my body again. It was unusual, very rarely did a one-night stand impact me in such a manner, but Michael was something else. Casual sex could be messy, getting into sync with somebody when drunk was a strange experience but with Michael, it was like we'd been together for a long time. Not only did we click in an intimate sense, but also an emotional one and my heart longed for him. I rarely connected with anybody, choosing to remain distant and cold to protect my feelings, but I felt safe in his arms. Leaving this morning was easy, but now I was struggling to come to terms with the loss, and my inability to get his phone number.

Sighing I turned over and hugged the pillow close to me, it wasn't long before a wave of exhaustion finally carried me off to sleep.

SEVEN

The phone ringing was the first sound I awoke to again the next morning. In my groggy sleep deprived state, I went to pick up my mobile before realising the sound was from further away. Initial confusion subsided and I groaned when getting out of bed and walked over to the home phone in its charging dock. Initially there were plans to turn off the technology associated with landline phones to complete a full digital takeover. However, when Terrance came into power he put pressure on BT to reverse the decision, citing the importance of a non-digital solution, not only for the elderly but also for the emergency services. He was successful and the removal had been pushed back to 2035. It proved essential for emergency services, especially for me when my phone stopped working.

"Good morning, Samantha speaking," I said, trying to stifle a yawn. Sleep had eluded me over the past couple of nights and I had hoped I would rest for a little longer, however, it was evident that I was out of luck. I was the lead on the case and there was an expectation I would be available and ready for action no matter the time of day. I couldn't wait to spend a bit of time away from the stress of work.

"Samantha, before you get in, look at the *Daily Scoop*. I think we may have a starting point in this investigation." Jackson left the conversation before I could respond, and I was met with an eerie silence. The sound of shrieking from my alarm clock startled me, putting the phone down quickly I rushed back into my bedroom to look at the time. As my eyes adjusted I noted it was 5am, I often wondered if Jackson was an insomniac, it seemed as if he was always awake at irrational hours of the morning.

On picking my phone up to check the *Daily Scoop* article I noticed that I hadn't charged it. Clearly too exhausted last night I must have fallen asleep without thinking about it. Plugging it in I decided to jog to the shop to buy a paper, giving me a chance to wake up properly and be a little more assertive behind the wheel of the car. Many thought that it was drink or drug drivers who were the biggest issue in road accidents, but approximately 35% of all accidents were caused by driver fatigue and the number was rising exponentially. With more people working longer hours, and wanting to spend what little precious time they had with their family, they didn't consider the implication of getting behind the wheel of the car exhausted. It was a terrifying new reality we were living in.

Passing on a shower, I slipped on some leggings, a sports bra and a loose-fitting jumper that would keep me warm but not cause me to overheat; stuck some change and my house keys in the obscenely small pocket and left the flat.

The streetlights dimmed as the day began to break over the horizon. The sun rose behind the soft, grey rain clouds, causing an orange hue that made the sky look as if it was on fire. The air was still cold in the late stages of winter; frost enveloped the cars and lawns, twinkling in the early-morning dawn. Running with few people around was a nice experience; pavements were free and there were no awkward attempts to weave past other pedestrians. Only one other person was out early, an older man walking a small, fluffy Bichon Frise, he smiled and waved as I jogged past.

Losing myself in my thoughts I continued to run longer than intended. Even with a stressful case coming my way it was the first time I had felt at peace. Since being placed on the Marcos Vincenzo robbery I had suffered with bouts of stress. The pressure to deliver was immeasurable due to the victim; Marcos was seen as a big deal and many wanted to please him, knowing that they could get a foot into his various business dealings as a private security expert. Better pay, and better hours; something many dreamed of after the harsh reality of the police force. It came at a cost though. Marcos owned those in his employee, and kept a tight leash on them through illegal means.

During the investigation Joseph was candid, he spoke of multiple tapes and messages that Marcos used to blackmail his staff into submission. Hours of footage from their clients; their own homes and even their phone messages. It was why he couldn't discuss much in his own home, he had concerns the entire flat had been bugged. Through fear of retribution, he didn't investigate whether this was the case, wanting to show Marcos his loyalty and fealty. I made a mental note to follow up on this claim when I got back to the office.

It wasn't until I ran past a shop I snapped back to reality. The conversation with Jackson came sprinting back to the front of my mind, the necessity to get the *Daily Scoop*. I stopped outside for a moment, wanting to catch my breath. A small bell tinkled to signify a customer as I pushed the door open, and I was received with a warm and friendly welcome.

"Samantha, it's very good to see you," the middle-aged man said, with a smile from ear to ear. I shook the hand he offered as I walked to the counter, and gave him a warm smile back.

"Mr Stones, it's been a while." A former teacher, Mr Stones was one of the most popular at my school. His classes were engaging and thoughtful, still teaching us the syllabus but doing it with a style that very few could mimic. The news that he was made redundant in 2022, at the age of just fifty, was a shock to many. He received a severance package of approximately £35k and, against his better judgement, opened a corner shop which specialised in Japanese cuisine. He hasn't looked back since.

"Yes it has, Samantha. How have you been? How's your sister and brother doing?" he asked with genuine interest. The news of my dad's suicide came through as I was in his class; he accompanied me to the headteacher's office and remained with me while the police broke the news; comforting me through words as I sat numb at the realisation I was an orphan. After requesting the headteacher cover his class, he remained with me until my brother turned up to take me home. I stayed strong until Shaun walked through the doors, and only then did I collapse in a bundle.

His compassion made him one of the few teachers you felt you could speak to, even if it was about embarrassing matters.

"I'm good, work is tough but rewarding as usual." I stopped momentarily, not wanting to discuss the stress I felt in my current role. Leaving it at that, I moved on to talking about my siblings. "Shaun is good. He's a visiting professor at Harvard University and loving Massachusetts, he really adores the American lifestyle. Stacey is flourishing, she is studying a law degree at the University of Sussex while interning at a friend's law firm."

"I'm glad about Stacey. We tried so hard to help her when she was at school, but she was too rebellious and unwilling to listen. Suspending her when she was smoking on school grounds was the final straw, if she hadn't changed her ways she was going to be expelled. Thankfully she finally seemed to come around." I hated to reminisce about our time as teenagers, but it was understandable when the subject of Stacey came up. Until she was suspended she was on a dark path hanging out with a bad crowd. I had found a large amount of stolen goods in her room. Not wanting her to get into trouble I burnt them in the back garden, ensuring there was no evidence and believing I was protecting her, but her behaviour got worse. The suspension straightened her out, and she confided in me she was scared, and angry, that our parents had left us so soon.

Using my limited savings I paid for a child therapist who helped her understand the unremitting grief she was feeling. I only wished I had done it sooner. I sat in on a couple of sessions and it was here I discovered she hated me, feeling as if I had abandoned her for my career. I felt immeasurable guilt, if I hadn't been wrapped up in my own grief and thrown myself into my work maybe I would have recognised her pain sooner. Although the counselling helped her deal with her grief it could never repair our fractured relationship, no matter how much I tried to make amends. At the first opportunity she moved away, and our relationship has been tough ever since.

"Yes, I think I was a big part of that rebellious side. But enough about me," I said, wanting to stop the conversation dead. Talking about my family caused a pang of heartbreak. Even thirteen years down the line, I missed my mother and father. "How are your family doing?"

"Oh well, my eldest got married about a year back and is now pregnant with her first. I'm so pleased for her, they will be a wonderful and loving family. My youngest, she's erm... well her life is certainly interesting. She has made it clear she will be remaining child-free due to the precarious situation on Earth, and has moved onto the Braxton Smallholding, where she lives a fully natural lifestyle. No meat, no processed foods, they all just live off the land." The Braxton Smallholding was a large farm in the Lancashire countryside. Many had compared them to doomsday preppers or cultists, but really they just cared about the environment. Well that was their claim, we wouldn't be able to know the truth as they were a closed, independent community, who didn't allow police officers onto their property. "My wife and I are divorced, my fault, I had an affair with Ms Faraley, your former maths teacher. We are together now." I smiled a little at that news. At school we all believed they had been having an affair, and it looked like we had been proven right.

"Anyway, look at me going on like you have all the time in the world. What brings you here so early?" he asked. I leant down and picked up the paper I needed, glancing at the front cover as I did so, noticing a CCTV image of Alex Smith assaulting our murder victim. My heart sank as I placed it on the counter, my former teacher looked unimpressed.

"Buying this filth, Samantha? If it wasn't so popular I wouldn't stock the rag. All they do is cause chaos and ruin people's lives. I see Alex Smith is the subject of their ire again." I felt like a scolded teenager when Mr Stones made the comment. The only reason these papers survived was the public's nosey behaviour. The fact that they feel owed the intrusive stories because celebrities were theirs to own. Some even believed that celebrities were their best friends, interacting with them on social media as if they had known one another for a long time. It was a sad, sorry, state of affairs.

"I stopped reading that trash after their accusations that his private life was the reason he had lost the country the World Cup." I remembered the story. Rumours had circulated for years that Alex was having an affair with another woman, and his marriage was in imminent danger of ending in divorce. England performed poorly at the World Cup, but the outside influences made Alex the scapegoat. It was a harsh and brutal analysis on a man who could have been struggling in his personal life. Accusations he no longer cared about his position in the team, and required the help of a psychiatrist to overcome his poor performances were below the belt and caused many to boycott the paper in support of their local hero. Not that it seemed to impact sales too greatly.

"Sadly, Mr Stones, I need this paper. The front page could lead to a break in the case I'm leading." Mr Stones sighed and waved his hand in dismissal as I offered him the money for the paper. Feeling bad about getting it for free I opted to transfer it to the guide dogs' trust box he had placed on his till.

"It was lovely to see you, Samantha. Sorry for keeping you too long. Please stop by when you are catching criminals." I smiled and reciprocated his goodbyes before running back to my home, knowing that I should turn up to work soon or be on the end of another Jackson outburst.

•

The light shone through the small gap in Alex's curtains, he peeked out of the soft duvet cover to check the clock in the corner, sighing when he noticed it was only 7am. Still half asleep, he didn't register the noise from his family in the kitchen. His wife had left the house late last night for another of her escapades, so the nanny took over waking the children and getting them ready for school. Alex would normally pitch in and support her, but today it was too much effort. The all-night drinking, followed by an all-day gym session, forced his body to react with exhaustion and want to sleep for multiple hours. On opening his eyes, the room started spinning and he wanted to throw up, likely due to the dehydration that he had barely addressed due to living off energy drinks to get through the day before.

His daughter, Katriona, was her usual excited self. At only five years old school was still fun, it was about developing her social skills and spending time with her friends rather than learning anything too taxing. It was about introducing children to education. His son, Marshall, was a different story, although he excelled at his studies his main bugbear was the belief that he would follow in Alex's footsteps and be an excellent footballer. Marshall, however, had no interest in football, believing that diving and the inconsistency in the implementation of VAR was ruining the game of football. His true love was rugby league, Alex supported him, happy that he just enjoyed sport.

Silence filled the air soon after the front door shut, his children had left for the day. Three mornings a week Marshall headed to the swimming pool with a couple of friends to get some practice in; Alex had offered to get planning permission to build one at their home, however, Marshall enjoyed going to a local pool for his morning sessions. Katriona was heading to her best friend Mindy's home for a bit to watch cartoons before Mindy's mum walked them to school. It was nice for her to get a routine. Alex shut his eyes to rest a little more, hoping that he would feel better once he did. But the peaceful silence in his home turned to chaos when the door slammed open.

"Alex, you get your arse out of bed now," his wife, Katie, shrieked, as she smashed the door shut behind her. Alex sighed, the angry outbursts were becoming common and he was starting to become numb to them. He only wished they weren't loud enough for their neighbours to hear. Although a reasonable distance between properties, there had been a number of complaints to the police; on one occasion they believed somebody was being murdered. Not wanting to make it any worse, he got out of bed and wrapped himself in a soft, blue dressing gown before walking downstairs.

Katie stood in the kitchen, cradling a cup of coffee in her hands as she propped up against the worktop in an eerily calm manner. Her hair was forced up into a ponytail, strands of blonde and purple fell around her face. The lipstick and mascara that had been so lovingly applied the night before was now smeared across her face, and finally, her purple corset top and black lace skirt were a little torn and there was a stain that Alex didn't want to know about running down her side. She looked wild.

"Darling, what an unexpected pleasure," Alex said sarcastically, as he put a pod in the coffee machine and started it up. Before the warm liquid started to pour out he thrust one of their tiny espresso cups underneath. Normally he would join Katie in a proper coffee, but he felt an espresso was necessary. He had an awful feeling about what was going to happen. As he turned his back to Katie he felt a rush of wind past his face, it took him a moment to realise the morning paper was now strewn over the black marble kitchen counter ahead of him.

Not wanting to sink to her level his focus remained on the machine, when done he picked his cup up and swallowed the contents in one fell swoop, allowing the hot black liquid to wake his body up to attention. Only then did he scoop the paper up from the side, ignoring the parts that had fallen into the still-full washing up bowl. Messily he put it together, but the front page was the most important. There he was committing assault. Alex sighed and put the paper back down. He had tried so hard to forget that evening, but the horrific crack as the cheekbone snapped against the pavement was hard to forget. He believed there were no witnesses, but in his alcohol-fuelled mind he forgot about the CCTV everywhere. Privacy was a luxury nowadays.

"What a fantastic look for your career this is," Katie sneered, as she took another swig of coffee. Alex's nostrils flared at his wife's callous comment. "What the fuck were you thinking?" she screamed as the coffee cup left her hand. Ducking at the last minute he managed to avoid getting burnt, only receiving some on his arms.

"I was drunk, he was coming on to me so I pushed him away. Jesus I didn't mean to hurt him!" There was a tinge of sadness in his voice as he remembered the situation. Had his teammates been elsewhere, he wouldn't have reacted as he did. But the pressure of those around, the need to get away from the situation, something in his mind just snapped and he couldn't control himself.

"Oh well, that's fine then. Here we go world, the great Alex Smith decides to assault another human being because he had a bit too much to drink," she screamed up to the sky with her hands in the air. Once she'd made her point she pulled out an e-cigarette from her back pocket and took a drag, the sickly sweet smell of cotton candy filled the room, making Alex feel nauseous. Katie was on another of her health kicks and chose to quit smoking, however, her mood had turned dark and was on the verge of violence.

Unable to contain his anger anymore Alex stalked up to Katie and grabbed his wife by her slender, tanned arms, a colour she only achieved thanks to multiple hours on the tanning bed. He almost spat in her face as he spoke.

"How can you judge me? You pathetic excuse of a woman. What the hell were you up to last night while I spent time with our children? Hey? How old was he this time? Bet he wasn't even legal." Katie sneered and slapped his hands away. She threw down her electronic cigarette and sidled up to her husband, putting her mouth close to his ear.

"Maybe you should be more careful, Alex. You don't want the press to find out what you really are. Do you hear me? I will no longer hide it for you," she whispered aggressively, before picking up her e-cig and walking away again, leaving Alex standing alone in the kitchen. He turned around and looked out the window to the Jumbles Reservoir, just visible through the gate in his front garden. He wondered how far she would go to destroy his career, whether she truly would spill all their secrets to the media in the hope of some money and fame.

Sighing, he went back to bed, wanting to get some more rest before training.

EIGHT

The article written by Bryony now had pride of place on the murder board. Paul was sitting by his desk, looking exhausted. He hadn't left the station until at least 11pm last night, and wasn't too impressed when he was woken up at 6am by Jackson to inform him we both needed to be in the office by 7am. When I mentioned we finally had a starting point to our investigation as he walked in, quite a meaty one as well, his attitude changed quickly. It isn't every day you see an assault in the paper that possibly links to a murder from the same evening. Even though I prayed that Alex wasn't involved in the murder, the idea that he had injured a man was devastating enough.

"So, as you can see we have a starting point. The same night that Joseph Marsden was murdered, he was also assaulted by one Alex Smith." I put a photo of Alex in his footballer gear on the board next to the article written by Bryony. His brilliant white teeth shone out at both of us. It was hard to believe they only looked so good after years of dental surgery. "Now, in this picture, we don't know what happened between Alex and Joseph talking, and Joseph being on the floor. Did you bring up the video as asked?" I said to Paul, he nodded his head and beckoned me over to his computer. The *Daily Scoop* had very kindly offered the full CCTV footage of the attack, showing that the tabloid media had no consideration for normal people in such a circumstance.

I crouched by his desk as he played the grainy CCTV footage. Even with advancements in technology, CCTV could still be a difficult watch. Many public systems had the cheapest models due to budget cuts, and a percentage of them were either poorly maintained or damaged by vandals. Private CCTVs were normally a little better quality, but not always.

"So, Alex pushed Joseph over when he got too close to him. Joseph then smashed his face against the kerb. I'm surprised he didn't black out." I said as we watched the short clip for a second time. Even without sound I could imagine the crack of Joseph's jaw and cheekbone as he fell. The distress he felt when he realised he had probably broken a bone and lost a couple of teeth. My heart sunk, he'd spent his final hours in fear and pain. The video had finished for a second time, Paul went to play it again but I shook my head and stopped him.

"Come on, I think it's time to go discuss this with the person who sold the footage." I remarked as I walked back to my desk. Paul decided to shut off the computer and shot me an obscure look.

"And who would that be?" He pondered, not realising that I had an intimate knowledge of the area where this image was shot. From the camera angle, and the buildings in the background, I knew it was one of my favourite haunts, even though the reputation of it was a little sketchy.

"Come on," I said, as I picked up my coat and walked out the door, deciding to take my word for it, Paul followed me not long afterwards.

•

My thoughts returned to the CCTV as I weaved the pool car through the streets of Manchester City Centre. It played over in my mind like a broken record; the way Joseph went up to Alex, as if there was familiarity there; the way Joseph folded over when he was pushed; the clear break in his cheekbone as he hit the floor; and the droop in Alex's shoulders as Joseph got up and ran away.

I felt there was something more to the story, but couldn't quite put my finger on what it may be.

Not wanting to dwell on it while we were still at an early stage, I opted to bring Paul out of his silent trance.

"Why are you here, Paul?" I said, as I clicked the indicator up and turned the corner, only to be met with another wall of traffic. As I put the handbrake on and glanced over to see him looking back at me perplexed. "As in, how did you get to be my colleague for this murder? I mean you must have really pissed somebody high up to be stuck with me." In my career I have been considered a loner, forcing all my colleagues away due to my recklessness and attitude. It was an unfair assessment, but made things easier for me. Working alone suited me, nobody to worry about if I put myself in the line of fire; a focus on how to investigate my own way. At times the solitude did hurt, but I kept it quiet by remaining busy.

"I'm looking at promotion and my boss thought this would be a good learning opportunity. So I volunteered." As I put the car back into gear I had to stop myself from laughing. I was the last person to mentor somebody, he would find that out soon enough.

"Just like the police force. Put one inexperienced copper with another and see the carnage that happens," I responded, finally unable to hide my amusement and started to laugh.

"Well, what about Charlotte?" I stopped laughing and gave him a puzzled look, hoping that he would understand I wished for him to elaborate. "Isn't she formerly a detective sergeant who worked on a couple of murder cases before? It's not like we have no experience with us."

"You've done your homework, Paul. Or at least you've spoken to Jackson about us." I looked over at him as we sat stationary at the red light. "You are right. Charlotte was previously out of uniform. She led a domestic murder case, a man who was beaten to death by his wife. She was adamant she was also a victim, but all evidence pointed to her being the sole aggressor. It was one of her biggest accomplishments nailing her."

"So what happened?"

"She just wanted a change of pace. She never quite felt like she belonged and found the non-uniform life unfulfilling. She wanted to go back to uniform. Jackson told her she was mad because she was on the fast track for promotion but she's happy. Anyway, she won't be with us any longer, we could only have her for door-to-door enquiries" I couldn't tell Paul the truth that her reason for going back to uniform was Jackson. Charlotte, although prone to enjoy a drink and spending time out with me, was a straight and narrow police officer. She had her suspicions that Jackson was not and didn't want to be taken down with him. I could see Paul nodding his head from the corner of my eye as I looked up at the mirror, checking to see if the car behind was going to put some distance between us. It didn't seem as if they were. Paul spoke again, this time to change the direction of the conversation.

"Where are we off to then?" he asked, looking down at his notebook, pretending to look through the notes he had made from the morning. Too focused on the road I almost forgot to respond, only when I stopped at yet another red light did I remember to.

"Erotica Club. It's where the CCTV camera images were coming from."

"How did you work that out?" Paul asked, looking back at me in a shocked way. I smiled softly again as I put my car back into gear.

"It's one of my frequent haunts," I responded, at that moment deciding I didn't want to speak anymore I flicked the CD player on in my car and turned the volume up. Paul got the message and sat in silence, staring out of the window. We ignored one another the rest of the journey.

•

I pulled up next to the Erotica club and buzzed down to the security office. They always had somebody around, whether it was a member of the bar staff or a security guard ensuring that there was no funny business when the owner was not around. Luckily, today, the owner was on duty, a man who I was keen to speak with about the CCTV images being leaked. Normally I wouldn't directly accuse anybody of such an act, but I knew this man and it wasn't beneath him to go to the media rather than the police, especially when the rich and famous were involved.

"Deacon, how's it going?" I said, pushing my way past the owner of the club, not waiting for an invitation to enter. He remained silent and held the door until we had finally made our way downstairs. In his fifties, Deacon was an unremarkable man to look at. He stood the same height as me, shorter than an average male. He was balding and took the decision to shave whatever remaining hair he had on his head, wanting to take control of his looks. He wore small, round glasses that seemed to just fit on the tip of his nose –making me wonder if they were a fashion statement or necessary for his eyesight. He was large in size, mainly due to his insistence on working-out to keep his body in peak condition, but age was starting to catch up with him and he was developing a small beer belly.

"You know who I am, Deacon, however, let me introduce DC Paul Grant. We would like to ask you a few questions," I stated, as I sat on one of the tall stools next to the bar, staring around the club. It was certainly a different feel when there weren't humans everywhere trying to gyrate on each other to try and find some kind of connection with a stranger. The club had a reputation with many believing it was a cover for a sex club, and from looking at the décor one could understand why. It was covered with sexual imagery, including attractive people in sexually suggestive positions; chains and whips were available for use on the walls, some of which I had used myself in the past and lastly BDSM handcuffs hanging from the ceiling could be seen. On a night out, the handcuffs were normally filled with young people getting a buzz from being touched by strangers, I could see why it had the reputation of a sex club.

Deacon clearly wasn't keen on engaging in our conversation

and was showing his boredom by moving stock around behind the bar, loudly putting them down so the glass bottles tinkled as they hit one another. It was clearly a way to stifle the conversation, however, I persisted.

"Two nights ago, somebody in your club witnessed an attack and saw that it was caught on CCTV." As I flipped my notebook, ready to take anything important down, I heard a crash of bottles. Stunned I looked up to find the broken box lying on the floor close to the bar, alcohol was already starting to seep out. I silently wondered how much money he had lost in stock from that box. Deacon stared at me with rage-filled eyes. From the corner of my sight I could see Paul ready to jump and restrain the man if there was any hint of movement towards me.

"So what? You think I sold those photos to the press? Is that what you're here to accuse me of?" Instantly he was on the defensive, normally the sign of a guilty conscience. Calmly I continued.

"Photos? I'm unsure what you are talking about? We're just here to discuss a possible assault, we haven't heard anything about photos." Paul looked at me warily while Deacon looked sheepish, he knew that his little outburst was an admission of guilt, that he was the one who had spoken to the press. He sighed and sat down next to me.

"I've made a right moron of myself. Ask away." I stopped and instead beckoned Paul to continue, wanting to be the one taking the notes. He pushed himself off the wall he was casually leaning against and made his presence known.

"Would you mind telling us what happened that night, sir? What did you see?" Paul started off with a reasonably solid question. And it was good to see he was being respectful as well by still calling Deacon 'Sir', something that I didn't have the energy to do. I couldn't help but smile a little as Deacon recounted the story.

"It was the night that Joseph normally took off, a Tuesday. I never understood why it was his night off. Anyway, he's a regular in the bar and was always very nice to all my customers. That night he stopped briefly to speak to my bouncer, and was possibly even flirting a little with him." He paused for a moment, wondering if he was saying too much, but instead decided to continue. "When he was talking to my bouncer, a group of lads came up. I was counting door money at the time, so didn't notice who it was. But I do know that Joseph was minding his own business and had not engaged with them. Some derogatory remarks were being made and I heard a bit of a commotion. It was the last I saw of him."

"Thank you. After this happened, when did you decide to look through the CCTV?" He was good, solid and straight to the point. I knew I was going to enjoy working with Paul, I preferred colleagues who didn't beat around the bush.

"After I shut the club I spoke to the bouncer, he told me that Joseph had been assaulted and looked pretty upset. It was then I decided to go through the CCTV, with every intention of sending any tape to the police."

"But you didn't?"

"No... I admit I didn't."

"So at what stage did you decide to sell the CCTV images to Bryony Penn-Seaman, the reporter who wrote the story?" Deacon became crestfallen at the question. In an ideal world, I would like to arrest him and ask these questions down at the station. Scare him a little so he didn't do it again. However, with a lack of police resources, it would be irresponsible of me to haul him down the station when he didn't know Joseph was dead.

"As soon as I saw the attacker was Alex Smith, I admit I got greedy. My club is not having a good time at the moment, what with the recession, and I thought the extra money would help." Money, always a motive, this time used to sell out a friend and stalling the start of a murder investigation. Each second counts and that CCTV could have been vital just after we found Joseph's corpse. Instead we spent a day chasing our tails, wondering how we would even start the investigation. I knew it was best to come clean.

"Deacon," I said, getting off my perch to walk around the club a little. Paul went silent and leant back against the wall to allow me to say my part. Deacon patiently waited for me to finish my sentence. "Joseph was found dead in his home after the assault. We believe that he may have been murdered. I want you to think carefully, did you see anybody follow him?"

Deacon remained in stunned silence for a moment, unsure what to say at the revelation that one of his best customers had been murdered.

"Dead? Oh dear… oh poor Joe. He was… sorry, Detective. I really didn't see much. Honestly. If I did I would tell you. Joey was so nice and everybody loved him. I feel so guilty selling those photos now." Normally I wouldn't have been sold on the empathy route. But I believed that Deacon regretted his actions. He sat down on the bar stool looking a little broken. Deciding that pressing him for more details wouldn't yield anymore results, I put my notebook away and wrapped up our conversation.

"Deacon, one last thing, would you be willing to hand over the CCTV from the night of Joseph's attack?"

"Uh yeah, of course. Let me download it for you and I'll get one of my employees to drop it down to the station." His voice was barely a whisper now, completely different from the usual loud, booming voice I was used to.

"Thank you, Deacon, it will really help with our investigation. I can only apologise for the way you had to find out about Joseph's death. If you can think of anything else, please don't hesitate to call." I handed over my business card with the randomised crime number that had been assigned to Joseph's death. He nodded his head and we made our way to the exit.

"He seemed genuinely upset," Paul stated, as we left the club and walked over to the car. I nodded my head, opened the door, turned on the ignition and pulled out into the road. Not looking over to Paul, feeling bad about the way I had broken the news of Joseph's death to Deacon. One of my biggest flaws, as pointed out on multiple occasions by my superior Dennis McCarthy, was my lack of empathy. A flaw which reared its ugly head again today. I didn't consider the implications of what I was saying, just wanting to get the truth out as soon as possible. It was clear

Deacon considered Joseph a friend and valued customer. Yes he made a mistake but he didn't deserve to be hurt with the news.

"Yes, I believe he was. But now, we need to go and find out what happened and why Alex pushed Joseph away like that. Time for a little football trip."

NINE

I drove over to Manchester Red Energy's training ground. During the Covid-19 outbreak of the early 2020s finance in football started to dry up. When seasons went behind closed doors; stars experienced major pay cuts; football teams had to repay season ticket holders for their lost games; staff had to be furloughed and, in many cases, sacked and finally TV money had to be paid back to companies around the world. It had a devastating impact on football and the sport that people had loved for so long. It was only with the help of large corporations' backing that some teams managed to survive. Red Energy, a large energy conglomerate from the United States, wanted to invest in an English football team. They decided to do so in Manchester and created a new identity, Manchester Red Energy. They were unpopular from the start.

All the way there, Paul didn't say a word, instead looking down at his notes and reading through them. Still feeling guilty with our conversation with Deacon, I was happy to have a bit of peace and quiet. I also wasn't sure how to take Paul. He was a bit of an enigma, and I struggled to come up with conversation topics. Although with most of my colleagues I'd be happy to discuss their personal lives, I didn't feel he would be so forthcoming with his own. He seemed like a closed book. We had only been working together less than twenty-four hours, I hoped it wouldn't be the case for the remainder of the investigation.

I parked up outside the training ground and got out of the car.

"So how do you want to do this?" I asked my colleague quietly, as we stood by the car. With us both being novices at the murder game I valued having his input. Cynically, it was so that if anything went wrong we would both go down. A harsh thought, however entirely reasonable when working in such a cut-throat environment.

"I think we should split up and interview the footballers who were there separately, other than Mr Smith who we should speak to together. We will hold back that this has become a murder investigation until the end." I agreed with Paul, it was the best way to go through with the interviews. If they knew it was a murder enquiry they may try and hide key details of the evening, in the incorrect belief that they were helping Alex, when in fact they were just perverting the course of justice.

We walked up to the players' entrance of the training ground. I had already phoned ahead to tell them to expect us, and that it was regarding the article in the *Daily Scoop*. I requested that they remained quiet about our visit, not wanting the players to discuss the assault with one another and get their story straight. I needed their honest assessment of the night as it happened, and discussing it with one another would make this difficult.

We were met at the door by the female coach of Manchester Red Energy, Tanja Safina, a Russian-Scottish former women's footballer who had to retire aged twenty-six when she was involved in a horrific tackle that damaged her anterior, posterior, lateral and medial knee ligaments all at the same time. She spent at least eighteen months trying to get back to fitness, only to be too worried to get back on the pitch and play football. I still remember the pictures of her on Instagram lying in bed with her knee swollen to at least twice the size with black and purple bruises all the way down her leg. Now aged thirty she was in possession of all of her coaching badges and was second in command to Fernandes, the manager. There were rumours that a team in the south wanted to sign her up as their full-time manager. But she didn't seem to be interested in moving. If she did opt to move into management though she would be the first female manager of the men's game in Britain; it wouldn't be down to equality either, just pure ability.

"Detective Rodan. Detective Grant. A pleasure to meet you both," Tanja said, without any real enthusiasm as she shook our hands. When I phoned ahead I had spoken to her briefly, and knew that she wasn't happy about us disrupted their training to discuss the assault, especially as it was only a couple of days before a big game. It wasn't until I mentioned that the assault had now turned into a murder enquiry did she relent. I hoped she had informed Fernandes we would be turning up at the end of training for a murder investigation.

"Thank you, Miss Safina. May I ask if you have discussed why we are here with Fernandes?" I enquired. Tanja just nodded her head and turned around, beckoning us to follow her. We did so, and entered a room with a number of footballers staring at us, some looking very angry, others very confused. I wasn't looking forward to this.

"Thank you all for staying behind. I really appreciate it," Tanja said, I found it incredible how they all just stopped talking and listened to her straight away. She was clearly well respected. I just wished that I could get to a level like that in my career. "I would like to introduce Detective Sergeant Rodan and Detective Constable Grant. I will now pass you over to Detective Rodan to discuss what this is about."

"Thank you," I said, stepping forward. I could see what most of the men were thinking, that I was the junior in the investigation. Even in 2028 there were still the same unconscious biases that women were inferior to men. I wasn't concerned with these though. "As most of you have probably seen in the *Daily Scoop* this morning there was a very unfortunate picture linking an assault on a man to players in this club. Now… I'm not here to make any arrests, just to establish the facts of what happened. Then a decision will be made on how to proceed." I paused for a moment, many of the footballers were looking unhappy at what

I was saying. I just continued, knowing that I was going to be highly unpopular regardless of what I said. "Again, thank you all for staying. However, I only need those who were either in the photo, or out that night, to remain behind. The rest of you can go."

There was a collective sigh of relief as players got up to leave, picking up their bags and murmuring to one another as they walked out the door. I quickly scanned the faces of those who remained sitting. They seemed displeased, but keeping this at the training ground meant we would remain away from the prying eyes of the media for now. I turned to Paul and beckoned him away from the men.

"We will interview Alex last. I want to understand what happened from his teammates first. I will take the lead on the interview, but we should both be there." Paul nodded in agreement. Although he was the more junior colleague I wanted him to feel as if this was a partnership and that he could question my tactics if he felt it was necessary. I called the player closest to me to begin.

•

"Look, the guy was coming on to Alex. He was clearly a queen. He saw Alex and decided he wanted a piece of it. Alex was understandably not very happy and pushed him away. It wasn't like he meant to hurt him," Wesley De Jong said, as he sat in front of me in Fernandes office. It was a small room that seemed to be an afterthought in construction. The walls were filled with white boards that had game tactics on, this was evidently his space to tinker before sharing with the team. The resident Manchester bad boy was not impressed that we were here upsetting his friend and investigating what he saw as just a push to the floor. It didn't matter that it was GBH. I hoped he would change his attitude when he found out the truth that the victim was in fact dead.

Although I wasn't sure with Wesley.

"I mean how would you feel if some dyke came on to you?"

The comment snapped me out of my thoughts and my rhythm. Originally thinking my next comments would be about the murder investigation. Instead I answered Wesley's question.

"Well, considering I'm a lesbian it wouldn't really bother me." It wasn't true but the look on Wesley's face brightened my day. I had in the past experimented with women when I was finding my sexuality, but it didn't take me long to realise I was definitely heterosexual. Now that Wesley had decided to remain silent, I dropped the reason we were really there.

"Mr De Jong, please be aware this is no longer an investigation into an assault. This is a murder investigation," I responded. There was an angry look in his eyes as he stared at me.

"And you think Alex murdered him?" he asked aggressively. Although I hadn't implied we thought it was Alex, this was clearly what he had taken from my comment.

"I'm just trying to establish the facts of what happened that night," I replied, hoping to placate him. He still seemed angry but calmed down a little. I was slightly concerned when he started to flex his hand as if he was trying to stop himself from lashing out. "Can you tell me where Joseph went after the assault?"

"He walked off. Well… he ran off crying down the road. Nobody followed him. None of us followed him. He was alone. After that we went into a club and didn't really think much of it." I wrote it all down, and dismissed Wesley, in all honesty I wasn't sure I wanted him in the room for much longer. He was vile, however, it wasn't until he went to leave that I realised just how much of a vile person he really was. "The queer probably deserved it. He was clearly out that night to try and get a piece of arse. Maybe he tried it on another bloke, but the next person wasn't so forgiving." He shut the door on me, I stayed for a moment, wondering how anybody could be so closed-minded. Although the term 'queer' had been reclaimed by certain sections of the LGBTQ+ community it was clear that some still used it as an insult.

I was looking down at my notes when I heard the door open, not thinking much of it, I just continued to write while speaking to the unknown figure who had just walked in.

"Sorry, I will be with you in a second," I said, not raising my head to see who had come into the room. I jumped a little as the door slammed shut, the message was clear and I finally gave the person attention. I wasn't happy with the result. "You?" It was the only word that came into my mind when I saw Michael standing ahead of me – the man who I never thought I would see again after our night together. He looked furious, and understandably so. In our first meeting I was vague about my real job, and remember telling him I worked in business. After sneaking out in the morning I didn't think we would see one another again. Silently, I chastised myself, how could I have missed him in the dressing room? Maybe an acceptable mistake when there were thirty other men in there, but not when there were only eight.

"What the hell are you doing here?" Michael asked in a low growl. I just sat and stared at him. It wasn't looking good for my career. Not only was I hiding that Alex was a childhood friend, but now I had to pretend I didn't sleep with somebody linked with him. It was a dangerous game I was playing.

"I'm working. You never told me you were a footballer?" It was a weak response. I didn't have the moral high ground in this situation. I deliberately held back I was a police officer, knowing that we didn't have a stellar reputation in the world now.

"Well at least I didn't outright lie! I never got the opportunity to tell you what I did because you were too busy trying to rip my pants off. But you claimed you worked as a business consultant." Michael's voice was raising in pitch as our conversation continued. It was evidence that he was becoming irate. I prayed nobody would hear the conversation, Paul, knowing the truth, would be a certain way for me to be removed from the case effective immediately. I was compromised, and securing a conviction could be seen as unlikely.

"Look, keep it down. I don't think we need to let everybody know that we slept together the other night," I replied through gritted teeth, trying to get him to be a bit quieter.

"Why not? Maybe they should know?"

"It's none of their damn business, now sit down and calm it!"

I ended up shouting at Michael, I didn't mean to, but preservation mode had kicked in. I didn't want to get thrown off this case due to past indiscretions. He followed my instructions and sat on the chair opposite, glaring at me in silence.

"Thank you. Michael, I am sorry for lying to you. Believe me when I say I regretted it the next morning. I don't like lying to people." A knock at the door stopped me in my thoughts. I wanted to discuss what happened further but my job came first. Michael would have to wait. I called for the person to come in, knowing it would be Paul. He popped his head around the door.

"Samantha, I am ready to go ahead with the interview of Mr Smith." I signalled I would be there soon by waving my hand at him. Once he had left the office I turned my attention back to Michael.

"I really have to go, but I want us to talk about this. Just not here, somewhere a little more private," I said, as I got up from the chair. Just before I got to the door, though, Michael grabbed my hand and kissed my palm lightly; I longed for him at that moment and wanted to kiss his lips. But I managed to stop myself, we would deal with that later.

•

Paul was located in Tanja's office next door to Fernandes. I was surprised to find how spacious it was, with excellent views of the five perfectly manicured green pitches. There was a lot of pressure on teams to adopt Astroturf, but Manchester Red Energy were one of the few that refused to move in this direction. On Tanja's walls were pictures of her during her playing career, she was one of the most successful female footballers to play for England. Not only did her honours include five league wins; a champions league and a World Cup; she also won the Ballon D'Or on three occasions. It was a sad day when her injury forced her into retirement.

Paul was sitting behind a large, plain desk, with Alex sitting opposite looking like a naughty schoolboy, I sat down beside Paul and looked over to a perplexed Alex as I placed my notebook and Dictaphone on the desk.

"Mr Smith, my name is Detective Sergeant Rodan and this is Detective Constable Grant. We would like to ask you a few questions. Do you mind if I call you Alex?" He nodded his head and I clicked the Dictaphone on. "Alex, we have been made aware of an assault that took place on the 7th March on a Joseph Marsden. I would be grateful if you could just tell me what happened."

"Erm, okay," Alex started, before stopping briefly to retain some kind of composure, "I was out with some of the lads for a few drinks after a football match."

"Could you tell me who you were with?"

"Of course, Wesley De Jong, Michael Parkes, Hakeem Lewis, Justin Johnson, Ricardo De La Rosa and James Sutton." Alex stopped for a moment and then continued. "We started off in Club Mexicana, I had probably around five or six drinks, and then we decided to move on. Michael stayed behind because he met a young woman." Thankfully Alex didn't mention it was me, and just continued with the story. "We decided to go to Pulse, which was past the Erotica club. As we were walking past, Joseph walked up to me and was attempting to flirt with me. I was trying to give him hints that I wasn't interested, but… unfortunately, he tried it on. I just wanted him to leave so I pushed him, but he tripped and his face smashed against the kerb." The lack of emotion was what surprised me in Alex's story. He spoke almost robotically, giving the impression that the statement was rehearsed.

"We have a witness that says Joseph never came on to you? In fact he was minding his own business and you and your friends approached him," Paul interjected. Alex's eyes darted around the room as he quietly processed his next move. I watched his body language with interest, noticing his hands as they played with the button of his shirt. It seemed like minutes before he responded.

"I was pretty intoxicated, maybe I am misremembering. I know Joseph was walking towards me and I pushed him away. I believed he was coming on to me."

"Did you know Joseph?" I cut in before Paul was able to continue his line of questioning. I wanted to try and make the interview personal by naming the victim again. It was slight, but I noticed the hesitation before he went to answer the question.

"No… I didn't." Alex shifted uncomfortably in his seat and looked to the floor as he answered my question. The anxious movements and refusal to look either me or Paul in the eye suggested he was conscious of the fact he was lying to us and didn't feel comfortable doing so. I considered prying a little more by calling him out on the lie, but felt being honest would be the best way to reveal the truth.

"Alex, there is something we need to tell you. Less than six hours after this CCTV image was taken Joseph Marsden was found dead. We believe he was murdered." For a moment, Alex just stared at me in complete shock, unable to process the information I had just given him. Then slowly, tears started to fall from his eyes and the calm façade broke.

"No… this can't be happening. This… it can't be true." He sat with his head in his hands, sobbing uncontrollably. It was an unusual reaction, especially for a person he claimed not to know. We hadn't informed him he was under investigation for murder either and, even if we had, we would have expected anger rather than raw grief.

"Alex, please be aware we aren't accusing you of murder," I stated, in the hope that it would calm him down. It didn't seem to work though. He seemed to be inconsolable, as if his heart had shattered at the news. Turning off my Dictaphone I turned to Paul. "Paul, I think we need to stop the questioning. I will go speak to Tanja and see if we can get Mr Smith home." Paul nodded his head as I slipped out the door to find Tanja. She was in the team dressing room alone, not wanting to leave until we had vacated the premises.

"Tanja, Alex is in a lot of distress. We have finished questioning him, but he is in no fit state to drive home. Would you be happy to take him?" There was a look of concern on Tanja's face but she nodded her head. I thanked her and turned my back, hearing her footsteps not far behind me as I made my way back to Alex and Paul.

"Tanja has agreed to take Alex home. Paul, I'll meet you outside by the car." As I spoke, Tanja popped up behind me. I let her past to go to Alex, who was still in significant emotional distress. She bent down to his level and spoke to him in a gentle voice, rubbing his back lightly as a way to calm him. Alex's breathing was becoming shallow as the wracking sobs grew louder and more pronounced. Tanja put her arms around her colleague and stared at me coldly. Paul had already left and I was clearly overstaying my welcome. I turned around and left swiftly, grateful at being able to get away from the emotional scene before of me. As I went to walk down the corridor I remembered Michael, walking back, I opened Fernandes' door, happy to see him still sitting where I had left him.

"Look Michael," I begun as I closed the door. "I want us to talk. But you have to understand, if what happened between us comes out in this investigation I could get thrown off the case and lose my job. My career is already vulnerable, and this could help tip it over the edge. Do I make myself clear?" Putting it straight to him was the best option, lying would only worsen his feelings towards me. Although I generally didn't mind how people felt, he was different. My body and mind urged for him to like me. Michael nodded his head and ran his hands through his hair, as he did so it hit me how sexy he was. I was fortunate that he walked up to me in the club that night, it was a memory I would cherish.

"I understand, but I don't want to leave it like this. I want to talk about everything." When I started to protest he didn't let me and continued. "Please, Samantha, I know it's only been two days but I haven't been able to get you out of my mind. I don't believe in love at first sight but I in holding on to something special." I knew I couldn't say no now. It was clear that Michael wanted to spend more time with me to see how our relationship could develop, and I longed to spend more time in his arms.

"Okay, I have a house in Darwen," I said, grabbing my

notepad, writing down both my address and phone number and handing it to Michael. "Meet me at 8pm there. Very few people know I own it so privacy won't be an issue."

"Perfect, I'll bring dinner," Michael replied with renewed energy, I couldn't help but smile when his face brightened as he looked down at the paper. I blushed a little.

"Okay, I'll bring dessert then," I responded as I got up. He stood also and hugged me tightly. I leant into his warm embrace, wishing I could just remain there all day. He moved away from me slightly and cupped my head in his hands, then leant down and kissed me tenderly on the lips. It felt wonderful feeling him close to me again. After a minute I wriggled away from him, smiling and looking up into his eyes. "I'll see you later, Michael," I said softly, before moving away and leaving him in Fernandes office.

TEN

"That was a weird reaction wasn't it?" I said to Paul, as he started to take a sip of water. We leant against the car, enjoying the soft yellow sun beating down on us and the cool and crisp March air. The sky was a flawless blue with no cloud in sight. From the location of the training ground we could see the rolling hills of Lancashire in the distance. I watched with interest at the new wind turbines that were installed in a bid to move the country onto more renewable sources of energy. The turbines had divided the residents, some claiming they were an eyesore, but others believing they were necessary for our planet's survival. For me I just enjoyed watching them lazily spin during days of little wind, like today.

I popped a couple of cashew nuts in my mouth as I was waiting for him to respond. At times it could be difficult to take a break get food while on a case, especially with time-sensitive cases such as murders. Because of this I would have a small reserve of nuts or dried fruit in my car. It wasn't the best way to sustain myself, but helped me get through hunger pains.

"Absolutely," he responded, putting the lid back on the bottle and tossing it back onto the passenger seat of the car through the window. "Normally, when a person is told about a murder, they can become quite defensive. I expected Alex to be telling us we were wrong and he would never kill a man, but that…

I didn't expect that." He stopped a moment and stuck a piece of chewing gum in his mouth, we all had our own ways to get through the hunger. "Although he denied it, the reaction he had would suggest he knew Joseph quite well. It is possible he even cared about him."

I continued to chew on my cashew nuts as I considered Paul's words. He was right. I thought back to all the reactions I witnessed informing people of their loved ones passing. The emotions were raw but they ranged wildly. Some stared in silent shock, their brain unable to process the news they had been given; others angry, yelling that we must have made some mistake and we needed to check again; some in denial, believing that they would see their loved one again. But the one that broke me most was the moment you could see a person's heart shatter at the news; the uncontrollable crying and wailing at the knowledge that they had lost the biggest part of their life and things would never be the same again. The final way was how Alex reacted, like a man who had lost somebody very dear to him, it wasn't a reaction you would expect from a stranger. I wanted to dig deeper at the time but it was clear Alex was in no state to continue answering questions.

"I think you're right. We need to look into this further. We need to go back to Portland Heights to see Ms McGuinness to see if anybody recognises Alex." If there was a link between the two I hoped that those who knew Joseph, or lived closed to him, would be able to verify it. Seeing Alex so soon after was not a viable option, I wanted him to calm down before speaking with him a second time.

"Well… Fiona lives in one of the closes off Ordsall Lane which is on the main Trafford Road. So I think we should go there before we move into the Salford Quays area." Paul nodded his head. I walked around the car and got into the driver's side while he settled into the passenger's side of the car. He put on his seatbelt as I pulled away for the short drive to Ordsall.

•

Ordsall is an inner-city suburb of Salford located opposite Salford Quays. Not many outside of Manchester are aware of it, but it was known for its small historic house nestled in the middle of large high-rise buildings and small semi-detached houses. I indicated and turned into Ordsall Lane, and then down Robert Hall Street. Sad to see the growing decay of the area that had worked so hard to move away from its unsavoury image.

I pulled into Whimberry Close, a pretty little area with a number of semi-detached properties. As I drove slowly down the road I couldn't help but notice the number of properties with large gates and walls, all of which had spikes on. Historically, Ordsall had a poor reputation, recording one of the highest crime rates in the country in the 1990s. However, a large scale regeneration project, and years of private investment, brought the area slowly away from this reputation. With the improvement in school facilities it was becoming a more family-orientated area. It was a shame then that since the recession there had been an upturn in burglaries. With so many people losing their jobs some felt desperate and like they didn't have any other options they would end up stealing for a living. Those who had property were just trying to protect their own.

I pulled up at the end of the close outside the only detached house in the area. Originally semi-detached like the others, a large fire took hold a few years ago which resulted in both properties collapsing. It was believed that it was because the original owners didn't get planning permission for the property and decided to take matters into their own hands. It was surprisingly more common than most people realised and very rare for those who did it to get caught. Arson was difficult to prove at times. Once the old property was taken down the new one was built and sold for a huge profit. The developers ended up retiring at around forty years old, it was okay for some.

After positioning my car close to the gates of Fiona's home, I pressed the button. After a couple of moments, I buzzed again, making sure that there was nobody home before leaving. As I was about to restart the engine the intercom crackled into life.

"Who is it?" the soft voice of Fiona replied.

"It's the police, Fiona, may we come in," I said quietly, not wanting her neighbours to hear and get the wrong end of the stick. Having lived beside some nosy neighbours as a child I knew what it was like to have people constantly questioning every visitor who came to your home. I was unwilling to put Fiona in that position. She buzzed the gates opened and I proceeded to drive through slowly and park up.

As we got out of the car and locked it, Fiona arrived at the door. I took her in as we made the short walk over to her. It was clear she was still upset about Joseph, her eyes were a little puffy and red from crying recently, however, she was more composed than on our first encounter. She had her hair up in a small ponytail and gone was the fluffy high-end cashmere sweater. Instead she wore a large shirt that was two sizes too big for her and jeans, both covered in paint. She smiled politely as we arrived at her door.

"Detectives, sorry about the mess. I was painting in my studio. Would you like to come in?" She moved out of the way to let us in. The entrance had a large open hallway which went high to the second floor; attached to the ceiling was a large chandelier that must have been around ten foot long and six foot wide. The stairs were marbled and went up both sides of the hall. Fiona led us through a large, mock-Georgian archway into the living room where she sat on a plush, expensive sofa. I sat on the armchair and Paul elected to stand. The decorations wouldn't look out of place in a large mansion or historic house.

"Would you like something to drink?" Fiona asked, as we got comfortable, both Paul and I shook our heads. I didn't want her to make a fuss over us and believed our visit would be short.

"You paint?" Paul asked Fiona. She smiled brightly. I was taken aback by the young woman and her different persona. If she was struggling with the after effects of finding Joseph's body she was hiding it well, the sign of a strong person.

"Yes, just for myself and my family though. Watercolours mostly. That painting just over the fireplace, that's mine." I turned to look over the large wood-burning fireplace. The painting she directed us to was excellent and of a place I had fond memories of, Jumbles Reservoir in Bolton. Before our move to Darwen we had originally lived in Lees Cottages on the banks of the reservoir, mum would sit out and feed the ducks, making friends with every new person who was out for a walk. Often we would come home to hear stories about a new person she met. Her friendliness was infections and people just felt comfortable in her company.

"It's wonderful," I said softly, before changing the subject abruptly, I could feel tears welling up in the corner of my eye and wanted to push the tinge of sadness away before I lost control. "Fiona, do you know who this man is?" I asked, as I handed her my phone with a picture of Alex.

"Yes, that's Alex Smith the footballer. Why do you ask?" she responded, as she handed back my phone. Alex was well known in the community and even those who didn't follow football knew who he was, I would have been surprised if Fiona had said no.

"Yesterday there was an altercation between Joseph and Alex outside a club. After speaking with Alex, we now have reason to believe he may have been known to the victim in some capacity. Did you ever see Joseph with him, or did he speak about him?" She looked a little shocked at our line of questioning, but this passed quickly. She thought hard before responding.

"No, as I said before, Joseph never gave me the names of his clientele. Although…" Fiona stopped for a moment.

"Please Fiona, any information you have may be helpful."

"There was a day when his relationship was new, he was really excited about going away for the weekend as he said they didn't normally have a chance, and he did accidentally slip that his name was Alex." It was a possibility that he was talking about Alex Smith, but with 60,000 people with a variation of the name Alex in the UK, and 800,000 with the name Smith, it was difficult to verify. It was enough to continue with the lead though.

"Thank you, Fiona, that is very helpful information." I was about to ask a follow up question when she cut me off.

"Are you saying Alex could be gay?" She couldn't stop herself from asking. I looked over to Paul, there was a slight shake of the head, so miniscule only I could notice.

"We are only trying to establish whether there was a prior relationship between Joseph and Alex before their altercation outside of the Erotica club. We are looking into the possibility they may have been friends," I answered diplomatically. She nodded her head, content with how I responded. I then continued with my own question. "I just have one more question, it's a stretch but any details you may have will be helpful. Do you recall the last time you saw Joseph's laptop or his phone? We didn't find either item when we were logging evidence from his flat."

"You wouldn't have. A couple of days before, Joseph mentioned he had a break in, his laptop and phone had been stolen but everything else was left untouched." It was not what I wanted to hear.

"Why didn't Joseph report the items as missing?"

"He didn't want to. He was worried, but wouldn't elaborate why. I didn't press him though. It wasn't my business." It was still possible the burglary was nothing to do with the murder, but two incidents in such a close period of time was unlikely to just be a coincidence. Realising Fiona couldn't help us anymore I wanted to leave the young woman to forget this sorry incident.

"Thank you, Fiona, you have been extremely helpful. We will let ourselves out," I said, after getting up, she smiled and nodded her head. Paul followed me out of the room and house without saying anything, waiting until we were back in the car.

"Do you think she could be talking about Alex Smith?" Paul commented, as I turned on the engine. I shrugged my shoulders after putting the car into gear and pulling out of the driveway.

"It's possible, but Alex isn't the most uncommon name. I think we should still go to Portland Heights to see if they can place him at Joseph's flat. If so, we may eventually be able to find that link between them," I responded.

"You don't think… he killed him?" I sighed, we were sitting at red traffic lights to take us from Ordsall into the Salford Quays.

The fact that Alex was my friend made me want to believe in his innocence. I had known the guy since I was five years old, when we moved to the UK from Romania. He was my brother's best friend and confidant, a surrogate son to my mother. The idea of him being a potential murderer was something I didn't want to come to terms with. I had to remain objective though. If it was indeed the case that Alex had a personal relationship with Joseph, and he had lied to us, I had to consider the possibility that he may have had some involvement in his murder. Innocent people tend not to lie to the police.

"I don't know, let's just get going shall we." It shut down the conversation. I wasn't interested in speculation, just wanting to find out cold facts. Paul sat back in his seat and remained silent, looking through his phone and feigning interest. It was clear he wanted to say more, I continued to focus on the road.

Pulling up outside Portland Heights, you wouldn't have known a murder had taken place recently. Less than twenty-four hours after, the tape around the building had been removed, as had the police constable. I was surprised, although police resources were low, I believed they may have attempted to show some visibility in the area, especially one where there was no CCTV.

I looked up at the building in frustration. Standing there, I realised how valuable the uniformed resource was. At twenty-five stories high with six flats per floor we were looking at 150 door knocks. A tall order, but necessary for the case. Part of me considered the short cut of just focusing on Joseph's neighbours, however, valuable witnesses would be missed that way. It was possible somebody may have spotted Alex entering or leaving the building.

That was if he did indeed know Joseph, and visited him. From the conversation with Fiona though, Joseph liked to keep a low profile and didn't have many visitors to his home.

As we stepped into the building we were met by the doorman, remembering my conversation with Charlotte about how the residents of Portland Heights had hired him instead of having

CCTV in place. I either missed him yesterday or he had been asked to leave the premises while the initial murder enquiry was taking place.

"Hello, may I help you?" he said, as he stood from the small desk that had been tucked into the corner. He was a young man, only around sixteen years old, he had probably left school and this was his first job. He wore thick black rimmed glasses and had brown hair loaded with grease, likely he hadn't washed it in a while. He was tall, closer to 7ft then 6ft and his face was full of acne. I walked up to him and smiled charmingly while pulling out my card.

"Hi, my name is Detective Rodan and this is Detective Grant. We are here to speak to the residents about the murder the other evening." For a moment he was a little hesitant, but not long after he regained his composure.

"That's okay, please go up," he responded. I walked over to the lift and punched the up button, Paul came and stood beside me.

"So how should we do this, divide and conquer?"

"Six flats on each floor, let's just do three each," I responded, he nodded his head. We got in the lift and punched in the first floor. I would have felt lazy not taking the stairs if the flat had any. It was a flagrant health and safety violation for any property to not have stairs in it in case of emergency, but somehow Portland Heights was built without them. The argument of the building company was that the built-in fire suppression system would ensure that any fires would be contained quickly and efficiently. There was an overreliance on technology, nobody had considered the consequences if there was a fault. People would die. The residents have continually voiced their concerns but nobody was interested. Although I empathised with the residents, they all choose to live in Portland Heights even with this increased risk. They knew the building wouldn't have an evacuation stairwell and still bought properties and, as a result, paved the way for more buildings to be built in a similar fashion.

I just prayed it wouldn't end up another Grenfell Tower.

We didn't have much success, either residents weren't in or they blankly stated they hadn't seen Alex before and slammed the door in our faces. All was looking lost until we came to Joseph's floor. We opted to leave it last so that we didn't give up too early in our searches. Thankfully we were in luck.

"Yeah, I've seen him around. He came to see the queer down the hall a few nights back, couple of days before he was found dead. Making a huge racket as well, pounding on the door and demanding that the fag let him in. Walked off after the queer wouldn't answer," his neighbour stated. The language was starting to anger me. Unfortunately homophobia was still a prominent part of society. It was disappointing, love was complex and, as long as it was between two consenting adults within the confines of the law, it shouldn't matter what somebody did in the bedroom.

"Could you tell me what he was yelling about?" I asked, trying my best to ignore the man's insufferable comments, I wanted to get as much information as possible before going for the jugular.

"I dunno, he just wanted him to come out. Something about not being able to just leave his wife, that's all I really got. But he left after the little fag wouldn't answer. Nothing else happened after that. Fucking give up my season ticket if it turns out Alex Smith is a poof. Don't want anybody like that playing for the team I support."

"How about the night that Joseph died? Did Alex visit him that evening or was he visited by anybody else?" I asked through gritted teeth, doing my best to ignore homophobia for a moment. Although it was becoming increasingly difficult.

"No idea, wasn't here. Was around a girlfriends house," he said with a wide smile, showing his yellowing teeth. "I'll be honest. I'm glad the queer is dead. The place is better without him." That unnecessary addition to the conversation was what made me snap at that moment.

"Alright, sir, I understand, you don't like gay men, you are fully entitled to hold that opinion, however, I am also entitled to put a stop to it. If you continue with this hateful language I will arrest you under the Hate Speech act of 2026. I will then hold you for thirty-six hours without charge, making sure all your friends and neighbours know that you have been picked up for being a narrow-minded prick. Do I make myself clear?" He slammed the door in my face, I turned to Paul who was standing beside me and shrugged my shoulders.

"I guess he didn't like my comments. Let's go." We left the block of flats and made our way back down to the car.

ELEVEN

"I hate people like that," I said to Paul, as we sat in the car staring out at the raindrops falling on the windshield. It was unusual for me to lose my cool, but abuse sent me over the edge. Our world would be so much more peaceful if people could just accept each other. But differing political, social and religious views just made that impossible. As such it would always be the case that racism, sexism, religious intolerance and homophobia would always be a part of our lives. I believe in people's right to have an opinion, but once that opinion turns into hate speech, then we fall back into a cycle that the world doesn't seem to be learning from.

I would be surprised if within the next five to ten years another Hitler was on the horizon. The human capacity for hatred never ceases to amaze me. It just seemed to be a never-ending cycle.

"So what now?" Paul asked, at the exact moment Jackson rang. I sighed as I saw his name pop up on my mobile. Knowing that he was likely to be angry, I didn't want to answer, but I knew that I had to.

"Sir, I have to apologise for the lack of updates," I said right away, hoping it would cool his temper, but I was mistaken.

"What the fuck, Samantha? Surely you can't still be following this Alex lead?" I just stared over at Paul and rolled my eyes, it was common that he wouldn't expect us to be out actually checking anything out. Also very typical from Jackson, I wouldn't be surprised if he thought we were just slacking off at a coffee shop, chatting about our lives rather than investigating the murder.

"Well sir, the Alex lead has turned out to be more than we thought. His reaction to Joseph's death was... unusual to say the least."

"How so? Did his reaction seem to indicate he was guilty?"

"No, I don't think so, sir. It was the reaction I would expect from somebody who had just lost a loved one, like a partner or a family member. We had to stop our questioning because he was inconsolable, and we were unable to get anything out of him." I could almost hear Jackson's smug smile on the end of the phone, no doubt he felt that we now had a prime suspect in the murder. I was obviously not keen to jump to that conclusion.

"We are going to go back to speak to Alex again, hopefully he has now calmed down a bit."

"That's fine, Samantha, just keep me informed. I want to know how this case is progressing and don't like how you keep going radio-silent on me." Before I had the opportunity to respond Jackson hung up on me.

"Knob," I whispered, the comment elicited a laugh from my colleague, I smiled at him and started the engine of the car. "Time to go see Alex again."

•

Unlike most footballers for Manchester Red Energy, Alex lived in a quiet area of the Bolton countryside, close to Jumbles Reservoir. Most of his colleagues lived in the infamous 'golden triangle' area of Cheshire. One of the most affluent areas in the North West. Alex's home was quite modest in comparison. It was still larger than most, and probably had more rooms than three houses combined, but it didn't look too ostentatious. As we drew closer, the road was becoming almost impassable, it was obvious that people were here to try and get a piece of the action. As we pulled up we could see the media camped outside of the house. Obviously hoping to get more of the story of the assault in the papers. I just hoped that they hadn't caught wind that this was linked to the murder in Portland Heights. I would rather they found that out through the proper channels, and not through rumours on social media. It was becoming more and more difficult though. People liked to talk, and all it took was a discussion with a neighbour, or a witness of the assault.

I pushed my car through the media scrum slowly, they moved with urgency but it didn't stop them banging on the car in an attempt to get me to speak. I ignored them and focused on trying to get through safely without causing any injuries.

"Detective Sergeant Rodan to see Alex Smith," I said on the intercom. I angled the car close to the wall, meaning no unnecessary questions. A couple of journalists were knocking on Paul's side, but he respectfully ignored them. A security guard arrived and led us through the gates, after we were safely inside, he pushed back the hoard. I left the shouting crowd behind and parked up in front of the house.

As we stepped out of the car the door opened. Alex Smith's wife, Katie, stood there. She looked the same as when I last saw her ten years ago, many would think she was still in her early twenties she looked after herself so well. A little older than me, her stunning blonde hair was down past her lower back. There were flecks of purple in it, which would look tacky on most, but made her hair look slightly more beautiful. She was wearing a soft red jumper, clearly cashmere. Her skirt was black and slightly longer than I expected. When we walked up, her face was like thunder. Although I could understand her anger, it was misplaced. We didn't make the media aware that Alex had been involved in an assault, it was their decision to camp outside the house.

"Samantha Rodan, how dare you show up on this doorstep after what happened at the stadium? Do you have no empathy?" I was ready to defend myself from a potential physical attack, my hands were poised on the cuffs at my side, ready to restrain her if necessary. My fears were unfounded though when Alex turned up and subdued his wife. She stormed back into the house, saying no more. To satiate my curiosity I turned around to see the media reaction. Many had gone silent, some were desperately scrabbling down notes, others trying to make sure they had got the moment on their cameras. It was at that moment I decided enough was enough, and went to the radio in my car.

"This is Detective Sergeant Rodan. Any officers available please come to Horrobin Lane near Jumbles to remove a number of media officials who are disrupting the peace." There was an acknowledgement from a nearby colleague and I left the car again. I felt guilty having to get colleagues involved in such a situation. I was a believer in a free press, however, when it was at the cost of somebody's mental health something had to be done. I turned around and went back to Alex, even from a distance I could see the unimaginable pain in his eyes. I knew this was going to be an uncomfortable conversation.

"Alex, thank you for seeing us again. Are you sure you are up to this?" I asked, as we walked into his home. I was eliciting genuine sympathy; Alex was a man I had known since my childhood and as such I knew he was a sensitive person. He nodded his head and led us through the hall and into the dining room. Seats had already been arranged for us. Alex sat opposite Katie, with Paul taking a seat next to her. I moved my chair so it was at the head of the table wanting to have visibility of all parties.

"I needed to talk to you about all of this. It's been on my mind a lot." His voice was choked, I had reservations that he would make it through this interview. "The reason I collapsed at the stadium was I knew Joseph... Joey well." He paused for a moment to come to his senses before continuing. I waited with bated breath. "He and I were in a romantic relationship for the past six months. You see... I am gay." Paul just made notes while I sat staring at him in shock. This was the man who told my older brother all of his secrets, a man who was a known gossip, and I never knew the truth about his sexuality. He had hidden it for so long. Not that it mattered to me at all, but it was an amazing revelation. An England international and one of the greatest footballers of his generation, the revelation of his sexuality could be historic. Paul noticed I had been stunned into silence and cleared his throat before speaking.

"You are aware of this, ma'am?" He turned to Katie. She looked solemn as she nodded her head.

"Katie and I have an arrangement. We married to hide my sexuality from the media and the fans, and my wife can do whatever she wants. As I can too," Alex continued. I think he knew what we were going to say next as he continued speaking. "Marshall and Katriona weren't conceived naturally and are a product of IVF treatment. I have never slept with a woman in my life. I have always known I was gay, but I am too scared to come out in public."

"Why?" I said, not even sure I was really speaking the question was so quiet. Alex put his hands through his sandy-coloured hair and sighed. I had to admire him somewhat, he was doing incredibly well not to fall apart considering the man he was in a relationship with had been murdered, and their last words were full of anger.

Unless he, of course, was the killer and this was all an act.

"The fans. They can be… unforgiving. How many footballers survive after coming out of the closet in England? Almost all wait until they have retired or retire straight after? I know I'm not the only person, but I also know that… I have no support. None of my colleagues will know my struggle, and I just don't think I can handle the hate that will be thrown my way." It was now that he finally descended into tears. I pulled out a packet of tissues from my pocket and handed them over. It was something that had played on his mind his whole life. I couldn't imagine how difficult it was hiding who he was to the world. I didn't wish that on anybody.

"Alex… you did a brave thing telling us this. Now we need to discuss your relationship with Joseph. Do you think you can handle that?" I replied as softly as I could. I knew that Katie was going to react, but again Alex cut her off. He nodded his head. Although distraught he knew the importance of his statement in finding Joseph's killer. No doubt he wanted to do everything in his power to bring him to justice. I clicked on my Dictaphone and placed it on the table ahead of us. "How did you meet Joseph?" It was a simple question, the answer to which I was both interested to hear as well as hoped it would give me more of an idea as to how their relationship started.

"Well, it's slightly embarrassing. But I want to be totally honest. As such a public figure I've never been able to meet men in the normal way. Dating websites and approaching a man in a pub or club would result in a newspaper article outing me. So, for a while, I had been using the services of a… well a pimp by the name of Marcos Vincenzo." He stopped for a moment to allow me to write some notes. "He used to give me a few different guys. Then I met Joey and we just… clicked. It wasn't just about the sex with him, he was kind, intelligent and I found myself just talking to him for hours. Every time I went back to Marcos, I would ask for Joseph, wanting to be with him almost all the time. At first I thought he wouldn't feel the same, I mean it's a job for him, I'm sure he met many people who became obsessed with him. But he confided in me, told me he wanted out of the life and to settle down with another man, with… me. We took our relationship further and we became a couple."

"How did you take this, Katie?" I asked, turning to her.

"Well, I guess I was annoyed to begin with. But I knew that Alex was gay before we got married. So I was happy for him in the long run. Joseph made him happy, and for that I was grateful," Katie replied, as she reached over the table and squeezed Alex's hand. He stared at her with either a small smile or grimace, it passed quickly though.

I had to admit I was learning a lot from the body language of Alex and Katie. It was an undeniable fact that Alex was uncomfortable around his wife. When she touched him in comfort, he flinched a little and was unwilling to look into her eyes. It was clear the empathy she showed was forced.

"How were things between yourself and Joseph?"

"They were good. We were in love I'd say. But that night, I

regretted it so much. We were out with my friends and I knew if I didn't get rid of Joey he would just keep coming up to me." Tears were welling up in his eyes as he spoke. I just tried to remain focused. "I felt so guilty after it happened. I kept ringing him to try and apologise but he wouldn't answer his phone. I knew I had hurt him more than ever."

"I'm really sorry for your loss, Alex. I have to ask this final question, and please don't take this as me accusing you. I need to ask for my job." He wiped away the tears in his eyes and nodded his head in acknowledgement for what I said. "Can you tell me where you went after the attack on Joseph?"

"I went to one of the clubs with the guys and then came straight home. I came in at around 4am," he replied, avoiding my gaze. His lack of eye contact suggested to me he was lying about his movements. We would be able to verify this as time went on. If he was innocent, though I couldn't understand why he would lie.

"Can anybody else verify when you came home?" I responded. Katie looked like she wanted to smack me. Her face was like thunder. She couldn't understand that I was only doing my job.

"Yes, I heard him come in. When he did I turned over to check the alarm clock. It was a little after 4am." When Katie responded I thought I saw doubt in Alex's eyes, but it was gone in a second. It was almost as if he didn't want to get his wife in trouble. I just hoped that we didn't find out later that she was lying to save somebody she cared for.

"Alex, thank you. Again I am so sorry for your loss." I stopped momentarily when Paul received a text in the background. He looked at his phone and then turned it off, paying attention to us once again. "I am going to be honest. This will not be the end of it. I have no doubt there will be other questions that we will have for you. Unfortunately we have to be thorough in the investigation."

"No, it's fine Samantha... Detective. I want whoever did this caught and brought to justice." He responded as he stood up and led both myself and Paul to the door. We briefly shook hands before he shut the door firmly on us. I had a feeling, although he obviously cared for Joseph, he would not be happy with us probing into his personal life.

As we walked to the car Paul pulled out his mobile to check through his messages. I opened the car door, as I did he put his phone away and diverted his attention back to me.

"Jackson wants us to go and brief him on the developments. He's also told me he's angry that the medical report is not back yet," Paul stated. I just rolled my eyes. Him and me both, but I couldn't make them go any quicker. Half the staff would be dealing with the Moor case, and an active serial killer of children is more important than what we are working on at the moment.

"We should go back then. I guess we have left Jackson waiting for long enough." As I got in the car I was glad to note the journalists were no longer around. It was a satisfying sight to see that I had won, but I knew they would come back when they find out the truth.

TWELVE

"Hope the waiting was worth it?" Jackson's tone was sarcastic as we walked into his office. I knew he was unhappy, but it was right that we followed the lead at the time before giving a thorough update. As long as we were investigating the case. Evidently he didn't feel the same way...

"Yes sir, it was. We have now found the whereabouts of Joseph Marsden in his final hours," I responded, wanting to get to the point so we didn't need to spend any more time than necessary in Jackson's office. "As you know he was in a physical altercation with Alex Smith, the striker for Manchester Red Energy, before he was murdered. We have since found out that Alex and Joseph were in a romantic relationship." Jackson baulked at my response. Although a reasonably tolerant man I knew he had some homophobic streaks in him. He believed in peoples' right to love whoever they wanted, but also disagreed with marriage being opened up beyond heterosexual relationships, claiming it damaged its sanctity. He was an active part of a 'revoke the gay marriage act' pressure group, so deeply entrenched were his beliefs. I challenged him on a number of occasions but he refused to acknowledge my views. Although LGBT+ rights had come a long way, intolerance was growing in some sections of society.

"That's a very interesting revelation, Samantha. I have to admit I didn't expect that," he stated. I just looked at him and then back down at my notes, not wanting to get into a discussion that may result in me losing my job.

"We spoke to Alex and he confirmed he went clubbing, arriving home at around 4am. He attempted to ring the victim several times but couldn't get through." I stopped for a moment to allow Jackson to intervene, but when he didn't, I continued. "We also visited the owner of the Erotica club. Deacon confirmed he was the man who sold the images to the press, however, this was before he realised Joseph was the victim of a murder. He confirmed Alex went to a club and Joseph ran off alone but doesn't know where he went. He has agreed to bring down the rest of the CCTV for us to view, see if we can find where Joseph went."

"That's good. At least you have got somewhere. We know where Joseph was in the hours preceding his death, although we don't know what happened in the interim period. We obviously need to find out what happened in that time. Have you got anything from the coroner yet?" Jackson asked. He was now walking slowly around his office. He stared over at the murder board in the adjoining room for a moment, like a man possessed. I was slightly afraid of what he would say, especially as Marcos was on the board. Something he told me not to do.

"We have had no word yet, sir. We are hoping they are able to talk to us in the next couple of days." He nodded his head and sat back down behind his desk. He didn't seem annoyed, an unusual development as he would become easily frustrated when cases didn't move at a pace.

"Good… we will have to wait for that." He looked at his clock briefly and then back at us. I didn't even notice it was beginning to darken outside. It had been a long day yet, in a way, I felt like it had gone very quickly. "Look it's late. We can't do much more now. You two might as well go home and start again tomorrow." Both Paul and I thanked him and we left his office.

"You know, I think it would be beneficial if we make a plan of action for tomorrow," Paul said, as we walked back to our desks. I nodded my head in agreement, it was always good to be on the same page with a colleague, especially during a high-pressure murder case.

"So... what do you think, Paul?" I asked, sitting down at my desk. He sat down at his and stared at the murder board for a moment before responding.

"At the moment Alex is our best lead in this case. We need to establish if there were any problems between him and Joseph. I think it would be worth talking to his football agent. Mainly to understand if he knew about Alex's sexuality and if so whether there were any problems between them." He paused for a moment; I nodded my head encouraging him to continue. "Then the pathologist. We need to know the circumstances of Joseph's death and whether they could link any suspect to the crime scene." When he finished I remained silent, wondering if there was anything we had missed.

After deciding there wasn't I responded. "Right, we'd better get moving. We are going to have an equally long day tomorrow. Get a good night's sleep this time," I said, as I jumped up from the chair. Paul gathered up his bag and put on his coat. We said our goodbyes as he headed out the door. I intended to follow soon afterwards, unfortunately Charlotte's arrival scuppered my plans.

"Sammi, how's it going? Some guy called Deacon brought this in, said it was to do with your case," she said, offering the USB stick to me. Although Deacon did say he was going to bring the CCTV footage in today, I hoped he would be delayed or forget. I sighed a little, I couldn't ignore the footage now I had received it. Time was ticking and my personal life should have been on the back burner. Charlotte could clearly see my reluctance to remain behind and examine the footage.

"Look, I'm happy to stay behind and go through this if you want. I could do with a bit of overtime," Charlotte said, as she put the USB stick on her desk.

"You sure?"

"Yeah course. I don't have anything going on. And I wanted to put some money aside for a new motorbike, the extra money would do me good," she responded, going to sit down. Knowing that Jackson wasn't a fan of overtime I signalled to Charlotte to wait and check her intentions with him. After a couple of seconds he nodded his head in agreement, I was elated at the fact I could leave.

"He said it's okay. Fill your boots." She was in the process of pulling out the 'dirty' laptop. It was an item we used when we were in receipt of USBs, DVDs or file attachments from the public. The intention was to ensure we didn't end up exposing the computers to a cyber-attack. It worked, without it we would have been infected by a virus on multiple occasions costing the police force millions to fix. Charlotte stood briefly and I took this as my opportunity to give her a hug. "Thank you for doing this."

"Yeah well, I wouldn't want to get in the way of love," she responded. I jerked back suddenly, without meaning to. Charlotte smiled at me and winked before sitting down and logging into the computer. I knew she was wasted in uniform; her perceptiveness was something we missed in non-uniform and I hoped there was a situation where she could come back. Sadly I didn't think that would be until Jackson left.

"Night, Charlotte," I said, picking up my bag and making my way to the door. She just flicked her wrist, clearly engrossed in the CCTV video she was looking at. I would have to discuss Michael with her one day.

THIRTEEN

I pulled up outside the small terraced house in Darwen, not far outside of Blackburn and part of the same political area. The house was pitch black, as it had been for the past decade; the 'For Sale' sign hung off the increasingly rotten boards, with a little time it would fall off; the paintwork outside was chipped from the battle with cold, wet and snowy weather. As I put my key in the lock I wondered if it would work, fearing that it may have rusted over since it was replaced after a break-in. Thankfully, the neighbours heard the commotion and scared them off. Although nothing valuable was housed, I still didn't enjoy the idea of somebody picking through the last items my parents owned, it made me feel sick. As I turned the key I was pleased to hear the click as it opened, thankful that I didn't have to call a locksmith this time.

The inside looked like a scene from a ghost story. Ever since the tragedy me and my siblings very rarely come back and the home is essentially abandoned. Much of the furniture remained under dust sheets, anything of real value had been removed and put into storage. I tried the light switch, and was unsurprised when it didn't work. Faulty wiring was common, and we didn't have the time or inclination to keep up with the repairs.

I set to work with the battery-powered lamps and candles, to give us some light; large, fleecy blankets would be our heat source and giant cushions would be our chairs for the evening. Although the furniture was in good condition, I knew seeing it again would bring back the grief for my lost parents. Not long after I had made the living room comfortable there was a knock at the door, if it wasn't Michael then likely a neighbour coming to check all was okay. I was thankful when I opened the door and it was my expected guest.

"I bought some amazing Southern-American food. Do you realise how far I had to go to get this?" Michael said, as he walked into the house. I found his Southern-American drawl sexy and surprisingly relaxing, I would be happy listening to him speak for hours.

"There's a shop just two roads away from here," I replied, laughing, as I took the carrier bag. He smiled, showing his perfect white teeth. It was nice for us to start off on a good note, I had my concerns after the argument at the ground that tonight would be a disaster. Instead of being able to discuss what happened as adults, I had fears we would be angry with one another. Maybe my past relationships had clouded my judgement somewhat though.

"Damn, you caught me. Have to try harder next time," he said, looking around the room. I could see an element of concern in his eye as he examined the furnishings. I hadn't informed him the house wasn't used, just handed him the address at the ground. In retrospect, it may have been best to tell him, however, I didn't get the time. For the moment he stayed silent, instead just finding a large soft cushion to sit down on.

"Sorry about this. As you can see I don't really have plates… so containers it is," I said. I was glad that he was sensible and brought food that could easily be eaten without plates. I handed him over one of the blackened redfish and dirty rice and begun to dig into the other one. It was divine. Although I was a little disappointed that he hadn't picked anything more cultural to his society. I would have liked to try Jambalaya or Shrimp Creole. At least the food he brought was safe.

Maybe for another day…

"This is lovely," I said. The greasy flavours being prominent in my mouth. Michael was digging in like he hadn't eaten for a week. Being a footballer that doesn't seem likely, but a diet of protein-rich and non-fattening foods would make any person hunger for grease and fat when it came around. He smiled at me as he dug into another piece of redfish.

"Thank you. I'm glad you like our cuisine. I was a little apprehensive about bringing fish as many people don't enjoy it. I'm really pleased to see you do," he responded with a disarming smile. I smiled back. Being in the company of somebody I didn't consider a work colleague was an enjoyable experience. My difficulties in maintaining friendships and relationships often meant I was a bit of a lone wolf. If it wasn't for Charlotte and her insistence that we should spend time together, I felt I would have nobody. For the most part, it was something I had accepted and didn't dwell on too much. On occasion though, I felt a pang of regret that I didn't have a firm friendship group I could fall back on.

Raising a sister from the age of sixteen would do that to a person though.

"I thought you said you owned this property. It seems a little abandoned," Michael said, bringing me back to reality. I sighed and shifted on the cushion, feeling the discomfort in my injury-riddled knee as I did so. I swallowed the redfish in my mouth and put the container on the floor beside me.

"Yes, well... it's a jointly owned property. It was my parents when we were growing up. But they died. My mum when I was fifteen, and my dad when I was sixteen," I responded, in a small voice. Even a decade on the pain was still raw. The death of my mother was one I had grown to accept, in the years she was ill I spent as much time as possible making lasting memories with her; visiting our favourite museums and art galleries, travelling around the United Kingdom; spending the summer in Romania together. My dad, the unexpectedness of it, broke me.

"I'm so sorry, Sammi, I didn't know," he responded. I just smiled and shook my head.

"It's fine, you weren't to know. It's not the kind of bombshell you drop on a guy who you've met for a one-night stand," I said, not wanting him to feel bad about bringing up my parents. "The house has been abandoned for years. My mum died of cancer when she was just thirty-six in 2017, she was Romanian. She had been ill for some years so we were able to make lasting memories with her. My dad put the house on the market not long afterwards. But it never sold. When he couldn't take living here any longer he killed himself." Feeling my voice start to quiver and tears in my eyes, I paused for a moment, not wanting to cry in front of Michael. He smiled encouragingly, after being alone for so long being able to bear my soul to another person was a wonderful feeling. I just hoped he wasn't scared off by the baggage that came with me.

"After that I was left with a younger sister, Stacey, only eleven when it happened. My brother, Shaun, upped and abandoned us as well. He was twenty and had just started at Oxford University. I spent a couple of years working various retail and waitressing positions just to make ends meet. Thankfully, my parents had paid off the mortgage, so I only needed to worry about food and bills. When I turned eighteen I applied to become a police officer to provide for my sister and myself, and that's been my career ever since. I moved out of this home when my sister went off to university, but… I've never had the heart to properly move forward with the sale or renting it out." Michael slid over and put his arm around my shoulders, I let my head fall onto his chest, it was at that moment he circled his other arm around me, pulling me closer. His touch was a comfort, I felt safe in his arms.

"Oh Samantha, that must have been so hard for you growing up. I can imagine it must be difficult to get close to people having a childhood like that."

"I think it definitely shaped the way I act around people today. I had my sister, but my brother had pretty much disappeared on me. I have major abandonment issues, which obviously makes it difficult for me to really build any meaningful relationships."

"I'm sorry for dragging this up, Sammi. I don't blame you for acting this way."

"Hey. No apologies. We didn't come here to talk about that anyway." As I looked up into his eyes I could see them swelling with relief. Wanting to put him at ease again I decided to change tack. "Tell me a bit about your family. I would like to hear a bit more about you."

"Well, I'm from New Orleans in Southern America. My mom is an established lawyer, she specialises in homicide. My dad's a doctor. I have a brother and a sister, both have gone into academia. And I'm the only footballer in the family." He stopped a moment and then continued. "My parents are proud of me in a way. They know I earn significantly more money than the lot of them, and afterwards I want to go into sports psychology. Mental health is so often forgotten about in sport and I just want to help my colleagues when the time is right. I have a degree in sports psychology, and sports science, I gained that on a scholarship." The way he spoke indicated he was nervous – fast and without real pause. The comment about his education intrigued me. Footballers, rightly or wrongly, have a cruel reputation for being stupid. The common misconception being that most would focus on sport over their studies. However, more often teams were now supporting children through education, wanting them to have the skills and knowledge to have the intelligence off the pitch as well as on it. I did often wonder how successful this really was in most cases, but it seemed to be the case that Michael really cared about his education. Having a successful family probably helped.

Hearing about his family made me yearn for my own.

"Tell me a bit about your brother and sister?" he said, bringing the conversation back to my family. It was heartening to have somebody who wasn't scared off by my tragic life. It was why I was so closed to most, often when I mentioned my parents dying and my role as a surrogate mother people would get strange and try to shut down the conversation. But Michael... he seemed to care about what I was saying.

"Stacey, she's a smart one. She's currently down in Brighton studying for an MA at the University of Sussex, while working at a family-friend's law firm. We don't have the best relationship, she erm… resents me a lot. Feels like I wasn't there enough for her when she was growing up. It was hard, although she was old enough to understand why I had to work she wasn't mature enough to deal with it. I wish our relationship was a bit better but, it is what it is.

"Shaun, he's fantastically intelligent. He's a visiting professor at Harvard, seconded from Oxford University. He has about two years of his tenure there left. Although he abandoned us, our relationship is a little better. I guess I've always been closer to my brother because of my sport interests anyway. You could argue I'm the underachiever of my family academically, a bit like yourself. My parents would have been proud of me though, giving up my dreams to give my sister a good life. Even if she didn't see it like that," I responded, accidentally going into more detail than necessary. I just hoped it wouldn't be enough to scare him away.

"How old are they both then?"

"My sister is twenty-two and my brother is thirty."

"Twenty-two… so you are… twenty-seven?" Michael looked a little shocked. I just nodded my head though. I had been told in the past that I looked young for my age. Many were shocked when I told them I had been with the police force for nearly a decade. It was a common misconception I was straight out of university and from the fast-track programme. It didn't take them long to realise how wrong they were.

"Wow… I'm only twenty-one. You're a cougar," he teased. And then, completely unexpectedly, he kissed me hard on the lips. I couldn't do anything but kiss him back. "I don't know why, Samantha, but you bring something out in me. Something… I just like being with you." He kissed me harder again. My mind was yelling at me, telling me I should ask him to leave and that getting close to him was a bad idea. But my body was taking over, and I leant deeper into the kiss. We were both so consumed with one another we forgot the dessert I had brought.

FOURTEEN

The combination of rain hitting the window in the dawn, and a small leak dripping onto my cheek, woke me from my slumber. In my confusion I wondered if my upstairs neighbour had left a tap on, causing their flat to flood down into mine. However, when my eyes adjusted to my surroundings I realised I was in Darwen, the leak was coming from a small crack in the window that I had, somehow, managed to position myself under during the night. It was only when turning over and putting my arm out did I notice Michael had already left. Disappointed, I sat up and stretched my arms, spotting a note on the dust sheet of the chair ahead of me. My mind could only wonder where he had found the pen and paper. Curious, I stood and wrapped the sheet around myself, so I could have a quick peak. My heart fluttered, I prayed that it wasn't a goodbye-forever-letter. Even though our evening had gone well, my heart still struggled to trust another's intentions and I couldn't help but feel they may abandon me.

> *I didn't want to wake you up, Sammi, you looked so peaceful.*
> *I had training today so had to go earlier.*
> *Don't forget me and let me know when you want to meet again.*
> *Lots of Love*
> *Michael xxx*

My heart lifted, there was no doubt in my mind that I was developing strong feelings for Michael. It wasn't love, I didn't believe in love at first sight, but my affection for him was deep. I hoped it would continue to grow, even though I hated to admit that I enjoyed having somebody in my life.

The good feeling was short lived when I lay back against the cushions and picked up my mobile and switched it on, the portable charger doing as intended to bring the dead battery back to life overnight. The time was a little after 6.30am and I had several messages and missed calls from my colleagues. My brain was alert and ready to deal with the coming storm.

On scanning my messages, I could see that none of them were good. The majority were from Jackson. I was not in the frame of mind to deal with his anger yet and scanned further down the messages, hoping to see one from Charlotte with some news from the CCTV checks. When there was none I decided to ring her.

"Morning, Charlotte speaking. Who is calling?" she asked with a yawn, clearly too tired to check this out for herself before picking up the phone. I wondered how long she had been working through the CCTV footage last night. Had she only just got home? If so, I felt bad getting in contact with her after such a late night.

"It's me, Samantha." I could hear her shift a little in her bed in the silence.

"Sammi, what time is it, babe? I swear I've only just got back home?" I could imagine her right now, sitting up in bed, her hands rubbing the sleep from her eyes. My guilt was starting to rise.

"Sorry, Charlotte, Jackson has been trying to get hold of me this morning and I think it's bad news. Did you find anything on the tapes?" She exhaled briefly before responding, I knew she wouldn't be providing me with good news.

"Yeah, erm... sorry, babe, there was nothing. After Alex pushed Joseph he ran off and the lads walked in the other direction. Sorry, nothing was caught." My heart dropped. I wanted a lead, one that would take the heat of Alex for a little while. But it wasn't to be, I knew Jackson would want the Alex lead investigated further.

"Thanks, Char, Sorry for waking you. I'll leave you to sleep." She muttered a short goodbye before putting the phone down. For a moment I sat and flicked through the messages from Jackson, finding the courage to ring him. When on an investigation he wanted all his staff to be contactable at all hours of the day, a rule I have broken for the past couple of mornings. He was unable to contact me each morning, my phone had conveniently been dead, something he would claim was an evasion-tactic on my part. I knew he would bide his time though, waiting for the moment to strike about my insubordination.

I only hoped I would solve the case before any of this happened.

Wanting to get the situation over with I punched in Jackson's number and started the call. "Good morning, sir," I said in a voice that was unintentionally laced with malice. Normally I did my best to keep Jackson on my good side, but this morning I didn't have the strength.

"Great start to your case, Samantha. Not only did you find out your victim had been assaulted through the paper, now somebody seems to have leaked there may be a connection with that assault and the death in Portland Heights. I thought you'd dealt with that bitch?" I breathed heavily at the comment. The 'bitch' in question was Bryony Penn-Seaman, although the bane of my existence I still didn't have the power to stop her from creating speculative articles. Living in a democracy, freedom of speech was still very much a thing and I was unwilling to censor a woman who had not crossed the line with her reporting... yet.

"Jackson, I don't know what you're talking about." I genuinely didn't. When I flicked through the messages I found vague references to newspaper articles, but on checking through the internet I couldn't find anything of relevance. Only the article from Bryony from the previous day. It was why I choose to ring Jackson instead of make my way into the office.

"Of course you don't, because that would indicate an element of competence on your part," he responded with a sneer. I felt my hand flex into a fist. He wasn't wrong though, but there was a way to say it. My mind had been elsewhere for the first couple of days of the investigation and I hadn't given it the full attention it deserved. I acted unprofessionally when Alex came out as gay and froze up during our conversation leaving Paul to pick up the slack. Then, on the same evening, I put my personal life ahead of trawling through CCTV imagery, leaving Charlotte to do the dirty work even though she was no longer there to support us. It was time to stop all distractions and do my job.

I knew it was the only way to exonerate Alex for this crime.

"Sir... I'm sorry."

"Oh sod off with all of that, Samantha. Just get in, I have left the *Daily Scoop* on your desk." He hung up on me without a goodbye. I knew I needed to get back as quickly as possible. I got myself dressed under the large blanket, not wanting to feel the cold air against my naked flesh. Once I was clothed I started to clear away the rubbish into a bin bag I had brought with me. I thought about clearing up the cushions, lamps and blankets, but there was no harm in leaving them in case I wanted to come back to Darwen for a bit of peace and quiet. I opened the door and walked to my car, throwing the rubbish into the backseat after I unlocked it and dialling Paul.

"Paul, it's Samantha..." I said as I opened the door of my car and slid into the drivers seat, before I could continue he cut over me.

"Jackson got in touch. I'm already on my way to the station," he responded. It was frustrating how bad he was making me look in just a couple of days, but at the same time I was glad to have a partner like him who I could rely on.

"Look Paul, I'm going to be there in an hour or more. I have something to do this morning." I didn't want to admit I hadn't been home all evening and needed to go for a shower and change my clothes. It may have been my imagination but I could almost sense the judgement from him at the comment. His voice betrayed nothing though.

"It's okay, Sammi. I'll see you when I see you." With that he hung up. I plugged my phone into the satnav and typed in my postcode. It was saying that I would arrive at my destination in forty minutes. In my head I did a calculation, accounting for the speed of my car, my driving ability and the blue light, that I would be utilising, I believed I could push it down to twenty minutes if I managed a steady pace of 70 mph.

"Guess I better get going," I whispered to myself, before starting the engine, checking the road and then pulling out from my parking space.

•

An hour after leaving my family home in Darwen I was pulling into the police station car park. I still was unsure how I would explain the multiple speeding violations on my way to Manchester, but it was something to worry about another day. It was only after walking through my front door that the musky smell from my ruined clothes hit me. I had the right idea swinging by my place for a shower and change of clothes, realising that turning up in the same, damp, clothes as the night before would only raise suspicions.

I ran up the stairs to our floor and composed myself before walking through the door. When I pushed it open I scanned the room, finding only Paul sitting at his desk and the door to Jacksons' office firmly locked. I peaked through the window and was relieved to see he wasn't there.

"Where's Jackson?" I asked Paul, without the pleasantries. He looked up from his computer desk and around the office. Obviously he was too engrossed in what he was doing to notice he was the only person there. I was surprised when he was able to offer an answer to my query.

"Something about the Marcos case. They have a lead and he wanted to talk to him about it," Paul replied. I left it at that and sat at my desk. As far as I had been made aware the robbery case had been put on ice, the murder of Joseph taking precedence due to staff shortages. I was surprised to hear that Jackson had opted to take this over, surprised and a little suspicious. In reality Marcos had his crime number and could claim on his insurance, maybe Jackson just wanted to make it look a little bit more legitimate?

Not a friendly way to think of my boss.

As promised a copy of the *Daily Scoop* was sitting on my desk, I picked I up and recoiled at the headline. It was bad, not only for Alex but for me also. It was obvious that the media were going to pick up on the fact I was both at the murder scene and Alex's home.

> **Is Alex Smith a suspect in a recent murder?**
> *Alex Smith, footballer for Manchester Red Energy, was questioned last night in connection with the murder of an unidentified person two nights ago. Mr Smith, thirty-one, assaulted the man the previous evening in an altercation. A witness also places Alex at the man's flat on the evening before the attack...*

I slammed the paper down onto the desk and almost screamed. It was obvious which of Alex's neighbours had gone to the papers. I was, however, surprised he hadn't mentioned that Alex seemed to indicate he was in a relationship with Joseph, though. My anger quickly shifted to Bryony, she had been informed time and time again to stop speculating. Not only did it open up people to abuse and harassment, it made convictions much harder when it came to the trial. At this stage though, she hadn't done anything illegal and had just pushed the boundary so far. In a way I hoped she would go over that boundary one day.

"Sammi, I've spoken to the pathologist. He's telling me that he should be ready for us by 1pm today. I've informed him we need to have any information he can give us as soon as possible." He paused a moment and looked back down at his notes. I just sat at the desk and stared over at our board. "I've phoned Alex's agent. Had a bit of an ear bashing, but he's agreed to see us and discuss his client. We are due there at 9.30am." It was only 7.30am, even with the rush-hour traffic I envisaged no issues making it on time. As I sat staring at the paper ahead of me I felt a pang of hunger, and a craving for caffeine.

"Shall we go grab a coffee and something to eat?" I said to Paul. He looked up and nodded his head.

"Sure, let's head to the canteen," he answered, getting up from his desk with his wallet. I shook my head and grabbed my coat.

"No chance, I'm not drinking that piss water and eating salmonella toast. No, let's go to Giovani's. It's pricey but worth it." Giovani's was an independent coffee shop in Manchester that, for me, sold some of the best coffee in the city. The price was an issue though, not wanting to spend my wages on business, I only went once or twice a month. Today was one of the days where some Giovani's coffee would perk me up.

"Okay, I'll drive," Paul said, as he picked up his car keys. I was grateful for it. I still felt fatigued from my night with Michael. His stamina certainly wasn't in doubt, he could go on for ages if he was left to his own devices. Most blokes had a limit, but I was struggling to find his.

After leaving a short e-mail for Jackson to say what our next steps would be I walked out the door and followed Paul, who had already left to go to his car. A conversation with Alex's agent was not something I was looking forward to, and I felt a strong coffee would be essential beforehand. He had a reputation for being a hard man to deal with, slightly high maintenance in a way. On many occasions people have claimed he was a bit of a diva. In a way, I could understand it, being agent to some of the best sportsmen and women in the country. But he was just an agent, they come and go without a second glance. He has just managed to stay there for a lot longer than most.

We hit heavy traffic almost as soon as we left the station car park. Roadworks ahead, yet again more cycle lanes being placed for the overly cautious Greens who now had more of a stake in the council. Since their election onto the council, they have made a push for more sustainable transport in Manchester.

Conveniently forgetting that with buses, trams, and trains, there was already a wide range of sustainable transport options in the city. That didn't satiate their needs though, and they managed to push for a city-wide referendum about the inclusion of more cycle lanes. With the large student population in the city concerned about the environment, it was an easy win for them. Now cycle lanes were being installed where the road is wide enough, causing more pollution through significant traffic jams. The Greens declared it a triumph and even won awards for their push for sustainable transport, most of the people in Manchester hated them and didn't see the point in them.

Paul threaded his car through the traffic. Both of us remained in silence, neither knowing what to say to the another. I was in my own head, furious that a woman I knew was trying to insert herself into the case again by writing spurious articles, and Paul... well I wasn't sure what his problem was. I know I was late for work, but that didn't impact him in the way he believed it was.

Not wanting to poke the bear, I rested my head against my hand and just watch the world go by as we made our way to the coffee shop.

•

Forty minutes later we had parked up in a side road close to one of the Manchester University buildings, close to the Manchester Natural History Museum. Although permit parking only, it was rare for a traffic warden to be around these parts. It was not a lucrative area for ticketing and as such the council left it alone for the most part. Even if a traffic warden turned up I would just wave my badge at them.

We were both tucking into our breakfast and coffee. I went for a bacon bap and a latte, whereas Paul bought a normal coffee with soy milk and a vegetarian sausage roll. Other than discussing what we would like to order we hadn't said a word to one another since leaving the police station. Just as I was taking a bite into my bacon bap, Paul started a conversation.

"Look, it's none of my business…" I stared over at him and wondered how he could continue that sentence. He was going to ask a very personal question, which would exactly be none of his business. I let him continue, though, out of pure interest. "But why do you insist on coming into work hungover and exhausted when you know your bosses are waiting for you to slip up? Jackson and McCarthy are looking for any reason to demote you now." I chewed on the bite in my mouth and took a sip of my latte, using the time to centre my thoughts before responding. It didn't work.

"Did Jackson talk to you about me?" I asked, possibly a little too defensively. He shrugged his shoulders as if not wanting to get his source into trouble. Rather than worrying about it I responded. "You're right Paul, it is none of your business. But as you are my colleague I will answer," I said begrudgingly, before taking another sip of my latte, leaving him to wait a little before I continued.

"It's about enjoying the things that make me happy. Seeing my parents die so young made me realise that life was for living. And that's exactly what I do. I enjoy meeting new people, partying, attending events. I work in a potentially dangerous job. A man or woman who's angry, maybe with a knife, could cut my life short? So why is it so bad to spend the time I am alive enjoying myself? Jackson and McCarthy can make all the comments they want but the undeniable truth is I am a hard worker. At the start of my career, I was first through the door in the morning and last out in the evening for my shifts; I had one of the highest arrest records as a uniformed police officer; I was handed a commendation for protecting my colleague in the line of duty. I am a good detective and my personal life shouldn't have any bearing on that. I'm not hurting anybody with my actions, I'm just getting pleasure out of what little time I believe I have left," I responded. Paul stared down at his coffee and slowly nodded his head. I doubt his opinion had changed, but I hoped he would see my side of the story. During Covid, every fun part of our life was completely stripped away by the government. Living had become worthless.

I wasn't willing to let my life be so hollow again. Some may claim that my refusal to settle down and my insistence on having fun meant it was, but I didn't see it like that.

"Okay well… be careful, Sammi. I happen to like you, but I haven't been here long and have worked out that there are those out to get you."

"I think I can take care of myself, Paul," I responded, hoping that I was right. Thankfully it was the end of the matter though. We finished our breakfast in silence, not knowing what to say to one another yet again. The only sound in the car was the swallowing of our food. I was frustrated that Paul had asked me the question. It was unnecessary and I hoped it wouldn't harm our working dynamic and get in the way of solving the case.

•

The agent's building was located in Deansgate, only a couple of minutes drive away from where we had parked up for breakfast. After our disagreement I decided to walk, wanting to clear my head and get away from the judgemental silence that had enveloped the car. Paul informed me he would meet me there and drove off. I didn't understand why I had to justify my actions to anybody. Although I was known as a bit of a party animal, I always remained on the correct side of the law. Yes, at times, my attendance may have been questionable. However, even if I turned up to work late, I usually worked later than many of my colleagues. Whereas most would only work forty to fifty hours a week and then go home, I was commonly working up to seventy. To prove to myself and my superiors that I was capable, and willing, to stretch myself and be the best at what I did. Although I had slipped over the past few days, I knew it wouldn't take long for me to rack up the hours again.

Distracted by my thoughts I made it to the building in no time at all. It was one of the modern, large, blocks of flats in Deansgate. Directly next to the tram station and opposite the train station, it was a perfect location for those who didn't drive.

I met Paul in the car park and we walked up, still in silence. The agents office was situated at the top of one of the highest points in the city. I have heard him in interviews claim it was because he enjoyed heights and did his best thinking at an altitude, whereas I believed it was because he liked to look down on everybody like they were mere ants. My assumption was the one I instantly preferred to his.

The guard at the door stopped us on our way in, and wasn't too happy when I waved my badge in his face. He still couldn't, or wouldn't, believe that I wanted to have a discussion with somebody in what had now become an exclusive part of the city. It wasn't until he spoke to the agent that he let me up and, looking at my watch, I was surprised to see we were in fact late. I was unsure how as we had left ample time to get from the university. Obviously I was more lost in my thoughts then I had realised. I knew it would irritate the agent, I did, however, hope it would work to our advantage. He was a man who liked to be in control of a situation and would not have anticipated our tardiness. Maybe it would throw him off guard and make him sloppy in his answers.

The office was like something out of a film about Wall Street, windows were ceiling to floor height and his furniture was sleek and black. The desk ahead looked larger than both mine and Paul's put together, with the floor being a dark burgundy colour. On each wall were bookcases, again floor to ceiling height, with numerous editions of sportsmen and women autobiographies and biographies. The agent was sitting at his desk, back to us, with a trail of smoke coming from the top of his head.

"Detectives, you're late." I couldn't believe the audacity of the comment, and was about to respond when Paul cut in.

"Please accept our apologies, sir, we were held up," he responded, in a cool and calm manner. I continued to stare at the back of the chair, wondering if I could bore a hole in it with my eyes. Probably hoping for a bit too much though.

"No need to apologise, please sit," he directed, finally turning around. He was fifty, maybe even sixty now, his hair was clearly dyed in an attempt to conceal the signs of ageing; there was not a line on his face anywhere, a sign that he had been having Botox for a while, and his suit was something for a much younger man, a model I would say. When he smiled, his teeth were perfectly white, and clearly not his own. No doubt a number of implants to ensure that he went to the grave feeling his age, rather than looking it.

"Thank you for agreeing to see us, Mr Danvers. My name is Detective Sergeant Rodan, and this is Detective Constable Grant. May I start by saying, sir, that your client is in no way a suspect in this murder investigation." He tensed a little, but then relaxed when I mentioned Alex was not a suspect. "As you are aware, the media are highly unforgiving, and as soon as they put two and two together they made an assumption. We just wanted to talk to Alex about his relationship with the victim, and that's why we are here now. I assume you are aware of his… identity?" I paused before choosing my words, as the wrong ones could have been career ending for Alex. Had his agent been unaware of his sexuality, he may have reacted poorly and dropped him.

Although I didn't see a situation where he would drop his greatest cash cow.

"Yes, of course. I have been ever since I signed him. I was the one who told him to hide it," the agent responded, as he stubbed out his cigarette. I just stared in anger and annoyance. I couldn't understand the logic of telling a man to try and hide who he really was for his career. "I thought that it would be difficult for him to establish himself as a gay teenager. So I advised him to hide it. You can think what you like of me, Detective, but ultimately I am a businessman, and that means I need to understand our business. I knew for a fact that English football was not ready for a gay footballer," he protested on seeing the frustrated and questioning look on my face. I turned to Paul and indicated he should ask the next question, wanting to cool off a little so I didn't say something I'd regret.

"Did you ever meet Joseph? Or did Alex keep his relationship low-key?" Paul asked. It was an interesting question, one that would establish how open Alex was about his relationship to those around him.

"I never actually met Joseph, but I knew they were in an intimate and loving relationship. Alex was careful, he never went anywhere with Joseph where he would be recognised. I believe he has a small cottage in Yorkshire somewhere and that's where they would meet. I just let him get on with it though. As long as it wasn't in the public eye I wasn't interested."

His response didn't sit right with me. For years he had controlled every aspect of Alex's life. The team he played for, his media appearances, interviews and even hiding his sexuality. I had a hard time believing then that he would be uninterested in Alex's relationship with Joseph, especially if it would result in him losing his greatest asset. I thought he would meet him once to impress on him the importance of being careful when meeting with Alex and keeping his sexuality a secret. To just act okay with it seemed unusual.

Maybe I was just reaching for something that wasn't there, though.

"Although you never met him, were you aware of any issues between Alex and Joseph?" Paul continued, I decided to let him take the lead while I observed. Often actions spoke louder than words, and many people were unaware of the small indications they gave off when they were anxious or lying. That's why body language experts are now becoming an important part of the CPS's 'toolkit'. Many videos of interviews now have to go through these experts before any decision is as to whether charges will be made.

"Well, I know that Joseph was not happy with being 'the other man', so to speak. I think he wanted the relationship to be more out in the open. Of course, Alex pushed back on this because of his career. I think that caused some friction between them," the agent replied. I could tell from the way he was speaking that he was the one who wanted Alex to hide Joseph. I was curious to understand if he would be open about his sexuality if this man wasn't dictating his life.

"Finally, we have to ask you this… do you have an alibi the night of the murder?" Paul asked. I was shocked at the question. We had not discussed whether he would be a suspect before this meeting and I was unsure if it was wise to ask him for an alibi. The agent baulked a little but seemed content to provide us with an answer.

"It's… embarrassing. I was with somebody that night." He paused a moment. Sighing he announced who his alibi was. "Katie Smith. She and I have been seeing one another for about a year now. Alex knows about it, but… yeah my alibi is my client's wife." It didn't add up. When we spoke with Alex he informed us he'd arrived home at 4am, something that Katie had verified. Before I was able to push the matter his phone rang, he looked at the number briefly before answering.

"Alex… is everything…" The agent stopped speaking, concern etched in his face. I couldn't hear exactly what Alex said but it was clear he was distressed. "Alex, calm down, I'll send around the detectives," he said, looking over to us, I nodded my head to indicate we would go over. "Yes, they're here. Yes I will send then. Yes… okay… no, I understand. Calm down and rest." The agent put the phone down and turned back to us. It was evident that things had escalated with the news article being published this morning. No doubt that he was trapped in his home with an army of media outside.

"Alex is really upset. He's had to skip training today because the media are at his home and the stadium. He's really stressed." I thanked the agent for his time and said our goodbyes. I wanted to get to Alex as soon as possible and see how we could support him.

As we left the office I couldn't help but wonder about the agent though. Something about his demeanour just didn't sit right with me. The lack of interest in Joseph was the first major red flag, and then his convenient alibi which seemed to suggest Katie was lying about Alex being home by 4am. It was also a well-established rumour that Katie preferred the company of younger men, teenagers to be exact, men who had only just become of legal age. She was careful enough to ensure all her conquests were over the age of sixteen, however, there were still some very questionable grey areas when it came to her.

"Let's go sort out Alex then shall we?" Paul brought me back to reality as we walked out of the office block. I nodded my head and got into the passenger side of the car as he unlocked it. I hoped the situation wasn't too bad outside of Alex's home.

•

When we arrived, I was shocked to see the number of people who had taken over the road. Not only media, but an assortment of others who I can only assume were protesting. Somebody had managed to find his home address and people had arrived with the intention of harassing him and his family. Uncaring about the fact he had a young child and teenager. Additional security had been hired to keep them back; people with banners calling for his sacking from Manchester Red Energy; and screaming murderer at him. My heart sunk, Bryony didn't care about the consequences of her articles. All she cared about was making a living, the fallout wasn't her concern.

I decided to phone Jackson to see if we could get any uniformed police to deal with the issue. I knew his initial reaction would be no, but believed I could bring him around to my thinking that Alex was currently being harassed. Arguably if we did nothing, and this situation escalated and put Alex in harm's way, we could be investigated by the IPCC. Something I wished to avoid.

"Sir, it's Samantha," I stated the obvious, I was calling his mobile which had my number on. Not wanting him to respond I decided to continue as quickly as possible. "We have a situation at Alex's house, I need at least one constable to deal with it."

"Samantha, you know we can't afford it. With the case going on over the border we are running thin. I can't see anybody agreeing that helping one footballer is a good use of taxpayer's money. Especially when he can get security in to support him." I knew he wouldn't want to play ball. Although I saw his point, the security would only be able to offer so much protection to Alex. I decided to try and different tactic.

"Okay, sir, I understand. But please remember, this has happened because we spoke to him about an assault that turned out to be a murder. I will go in and inform Alex we won't be helping with his problem. You never know, maybe he'll be kind, maybe he won't take us to court for getting his name all over the paper. But… if somebody was to…"

"Okay, okay, Samantha, you've made your bloody point. I'll send out a constable. You go and tell Alex that we will make sure his precious house is safe." He put the phone down on me, I smiled in jubilation. After this I told Paul to drive at those outside Alex's house. Although he seemed reluctant at first, he changed his mind after the look I gave him.

It shocked me that we got through without hitting anybody. I had the urge to arrest several though, especially the virtue-signalling idiots hitting Paul's car and claiming we were part of the problem, trying to silence their views by forcing them out of the way. Others, claiming they had a right to be there, harassing Alex and urging for change in football, which they saw as a homophobic institution. I ignored them, knowing that stooping down to their level would only result in more anger.

We got through the gates with no followers thanks to the extra security guards. Katie was the first to greet us in her usual friendly manner. In a way I couldn't blame her, but then I also could as it was clear she was not really in love with Alex. All she wanted was his money, and also the fame of being a WAG.

"You utter bastards, how the hell could you do this to him. Claim he was a suspect in a murder?" She screamed at me and Paul. The media behind were getting very interested, not wanting to be on the front page of several papers tomorrow, I ushered her in quickly and slammed the door behind us. I was furious, she was treading on dangerous water.

"Firstly, Katie, we never spoke to the fucking media, alright?" I responded, almost snarling at her, she shut up quickly and looked down at her feet, sulking like a small child. I knew I shouldn't have sworn while on duty, but I was having a bad day and her berating me for something I was not guilty of set me off. "We would never claim that Alex was a suspect. That was all Bryony's fault; she decided to create that statement."

"I knew it." The voice was that of Alex. He had walked down the stairs without us noticing. He was a man that was haunted by all that was going on, and I couldn't do anything but feel sorry for him. This had all gotten away from us too fast, and it was destroying his life, it was possible his career would be over as well. "I knew that little snake did it, she has it in for me again." I wasn't quite sure what he meant by again, I wanted to ask him to elaborate but instead choose to ignore the comment. I would circle back round if necessary later on in the investigation.

"Alex, we are going to get rid of them. I have let my boss know that there is no other option other than removing them from outside of this property. It isn't correct that you have had to deal with this," I replied sincerely, Alex smiled and nodded his head. He seemed a lot calmer now with the reassurance. Katie was still staring at me like I had grown a second head, it was how she looked at most women, though, and I didn't take any offence to it. It was just her as a person.

"Thank you, Samantha. You really are one of the good ones." My phone beeped with an incoming text message, I quickly had a read through and realised it was the news that we were looking to hear. We finally had the pathologist's report. I put my phone away and looked back at Alex and Katie.

"Sorry Alex, we will need to go soon, but before we do, I just have a quick question for you, Katie, if that's okay?" She looked startled as I addressed her, but nodded her head in agreement. I continued. "When we spoke with you yesterday you confirmed that Alex arrived home at 4am on the day of Joseph's murder. However, this morning Mr Danvers informed us he was with you at this time. Could you just confirm your movements for us?" I saw Katie's eyes shift a little to the right, most body language experts would suggest this was because she was formulating a lie. She took a brief moment before responding.

"Of course, Detective. He is correct we were together, but we were together here. As Alex and I have an arrangement I can bring men back to the home. But only when my children are out of the house. That evening they were staying at their grandparents." It was convincing but looking at Alex even he seemed to doubt her words. I wasn't sure who was being protected now, whether it was Alex or Katie. But this would be a conversation for another day. I wanted to get back to the matter at hand.

"Thank you for confirming, Katie. Sorry, Alex, but we really need to go. Will you be okay?" I asked, he smiled and nodded his head. Dragging Paul out the house I informed him we were needed at the pathologist's office, and that he had some news for us. I only prayed it would help in our case.

FIFTEEN

Autopsies took place in a small bungalow-type medical facility on the outskirts of the city. It was inadequate for the number of suspicious deaths that occurred in Manchester, however, with cuts to the police force and a depleting economy it was something that was worked around. It was normal for bodies to be stored in hospital morgues for extended periods of time and moved when an autopsy was needed. It wasn't the most efficient way of working and petitions had been set up to have a new autopsy centre built in Manchester, but with funding running low it wasn't a high priority.

The pathologist stood beside the recently sewn-up body of Joseph Marsden, who finally looked at peace now they had shut his eyes and he no longer had the scarf in his mouth. It saddened me, I had spoken to him on many occasions over the course of the Marcos' case and he seemed a friendly man. Now here he was, on an autopsy table, after being murdered by an unknown assailant.

It was a waste of human life and I hoped I could give him the justice he deserved.

Darren, our pathologist, stopped what he was doing and looked up at us. He smiled and shook both of our hands. Many people who had met Darren were instantly charmed by his good looks and strong jawline, once you got to know him, though, he was a bit of an arse. On many occasions I had to reject his sexual advances over a drink. I was just glad that Paul was now here to back me up as we listened to the results of the autopsy, at least I thought he was, until I looked over to him and saw a very green face.

"Are you okay there, Paul?" I asked with concern. It wasn't a good look for a police officer if he couldn't stand the smell of an autopsy room, especially one who wished to go for promotion.

"I'm fine, just… never attended an autopsy before," Paul stated.

"Well, you're not attending one. We are just here to receive the report." My response was a little blunt, but he needed to get a stronger stomach when it came to death. I turned back to Darren and smiled, wanting him to think I didn't despise being in his presence. "If you'd like to proceed, Darren?" I asked sweetly, he nodded his head and complied instantly.

"Cause of death is pretty self-explanatory. He was strangled. With his size, I would have originally estimated a man or very strong woman, however, after the toxicology findings I noted that he had actually been dosed with Rohypnol." Darren paused for a moment while I processed the information. The date-rape drug? It seemed strange, however, if it was somebody very small who commit the murder then they may have been unlikely to do it without the additional help of the drug. "His penis was cut off post mortem, hence the lack of blood around the wound. I don't understand the significance of that.

"He sustained a fractured eye socket, fractured jaw and the loss of a couple of teeth. Likely caused by his face hitting the kerb when he was pushed to the floor." I made a note of it. Realistically, Alex should be done for assault, but with the victim now dead, it was unlikely the CPS would want to waste the time bringing charges, and the murder was now the priority "We found a towel at the scene of the crime with a lot of blood on it. We did a DNA test to verify it was Joseph's blood. Likely from the eye wound he sustained before death."

For the first time since we arrived Darren walked over to

the body, I duly followed as it was a sign he wanted to show us something. Paul stood back, looking unwell. Part of me wanted to give him the opportunity to leave the room to get a glass of water, but I knew that listening to the outcome of the autopsy would be invaluable experience for him. It's only by getting through these situations he would build up that resistance.

"I found skin flakes under his fingernails, we should be able to get DNA from it. Now… this may not be from the murder though, as I also found evidence of sexual intercourse just before his murder. Unfortunately I couldn't get any DNA from this though, the semen was Joseph's, it seems a condom was used and the contents were poured over Joseph, it had been removed from the scene before we arrived. I looked down at his fingernails, and wondered whether he had managed to get us some evidence of the murderer. I doubted we were that lucky, though.

"Anything else important?" I asked. Darren shook his head and smiled again. "Well, if there is anything then please give me a call as soon as possible."

"If you can get any DNA samples from those who came into contact with Joseph in the days before his murder, we may be able to get a hit on who he may have scratched," Darren suggest. I nodded my head. We only have two people who we know definitely came into contact with Joseph. Getting Marcos to hand over his client list may be invaluable as well and lead to more avenues of investigation.

I thanked Darren and grabbed Paul to take him out of the medical facility. I think we needed to let Jackson know about everything.

"Paul, I want you to go and discuss the case with Jackson. I will go back and get a DNA sample from Alex to determine whether he was the person that was scratched, and then will head back to Marcos to pick up a client list. Will you be okay?" I asked. Paul meekly nodded his head. I wasn't convinced though. "Take me back to the station and then I will grab my car." He nodded. When he went to open the door I noticed that his hands were shaking and he seemed a little unsteady on his feet. Sighing,

I grabbed the keys from his hands. "You know what, I will drive," I said, pushing him round to the passenger's seat of the car before getting in myself and driving off.

•

Michael sat in silence in the dressing room while his colleagues joked around him. He couldn't understand how they could be happy when Alex's life was collapsing around him. Not only was he their leader and teammate but also, for many, he was one of their closest friends. Always there to help others when they needed them the most, yet none seemed bothered he was missing because of such a horrendous allegation.

The room quietened down as soon as Fernandes walked in. It was strange, although he was disliked by all, he commanded respect whenever he walked into the room. As a manager, he was extremely talented and had won multiple trophies with some of the best teams across Europe. His ability to deal with people was poor though.

"Everybody. As you have probably seen, Alex has been outed as a potential murder suspect. Now, these allegations are completely unfounded. I want everybody to support Alex through this until we have more information as to what is going on. Can we do this?" Fernandes asked. Everybody looked at one another and started murmuring, it wasn't until Ricardo cleared his throat and went to talk that everybody go silent again.

"But what about long-term? I mean if Alex did do this, and I'm not saying he did, we were with him when he hurt this guy, could we be seen as accessories to murder? Did he die because of the injuries he sustained?" It sounded like Ricardo was ranting, but all those who went out with Alex that night nodded in agreement. Michael kept his opinions to himself. The problem with Ricardo was, he played the 'caring teammate' when he was out and about and on social media, but when it came to reality he only looked out for number one. It wasn't the first time he had distanced himself from a colleague whose private life had been trashed in the paper.

"We don't know, Ricardo. But we need to show a unified front. Train as usual, spend time with Alex outside of the team. Make him feel like he isn't going through something traumatic. We are family here, and many of us have known Alex from a young age. He needs our support the most now," Tanja interjected, much to the annoyance of Fernandes. Ricardo remained silent, and many just murmured non-committal responses. Michael was worried. He knew what Ricardo was truly like, he would sell his own grandmother for an extra £1, so wouldn't think twice about doing the same to Alex.

He just hoped that he would be proven wrong.

•

Bryony sat at her desk, admiring her latest piece of work that had become yet another sensation. She was the first to work out that there was a link between the suspicious death and the assault on that random man. She had seen Samantha at both crime scenes and decided to dig a little. It was Joseph's neighbour who provided the evidential link, as he had seen Alex at Joseph's a couple of nights previously. Meaning that their meeting outside of the club wasn't coincidental like many in the media believed. The *Daily Scoop* didn't hesitate to run the story when she said she had corroborating evidence.

She sat staring at her screen, wondering what she could do next. The money had been nice, but if she earnt more she could buy a second property to rent out, giving them a steady source of income and the ability to solely focus on her investigative journalism blog. She didn't like the scandalous articles that she put her name to, however, it was the only way she could continue doing what she loved. Her phone rang, bringing her back to reality, she couldn't believe her luck when she answered.

"Hello, is that Bryony Penn-Seaman?" A man with a timid voice said on the other end of the phone. Bryony's heart lifted, she didn't exactly know why but had a good feeling about the call and what was going to happen.

"Yes it is, may I ask who's calling?"

"My name is John Young I was interested to read your article about Alex in the paper. I thought… maybe we could discuss things a little further." Bryony became excited. She hoped this was the missing link between the assault and the murder. If it was the money could set her and her family up for life. No more tabloid journalism, and back to proper investigative journalism. Enabling her to gain back her credibility as a serious journalist, not some kind of hack.

SIXTEEN

The silence was almost deafening outside Alex's home. Gone were the media rabble, we were back to the tranquillity of Jumbles Reservoir. I was pleased with the outcome of the police turning up, but did wonder how they were so effective in moving them on. I spotted the solitary marked car tucked away in the corner of the road and made my way over to it. Just as I did, a walker came past with his dog, smiled and said hello to me. I reciprocated in a friendly manner. Once he left I knocked on the window of the marked car.

"Hey Sammi," Charlotte said cheerfully, as she wound down the window. She was half way through eating a cake. I looked at the food enviously, wondering how she could eat so much and still retain her perfect figure. I nodded my head in acknowledgement to her young colleague sitting beside her who was reading a magazine, clearly bored of his assignment. Although I didn't know his name I could place where I had seen him before, it was outside Joseph's house, pushing back the throngs of the media and residents as they tried to get a peek of what was going on. He seemed uninterested in his job then too.

"Hey Charlotte. Did the media give you any trouble?" I asked. She looked at her young colleague who shook his head and went back to the magazine.

"Had it all covered. Well... apart from the one woman who

had to be restrained and taken back to the police station by one of our colleagues. But apart from that all good." After finishing her sentence she forced the remaining cake into her mouth.

"That's good then. Can I ask something though, Charlotte?" She nodded her head, still chewing away. "Aren't there any other police officers in this city? I swear it's just you and him that I always see."

"Ah maybe we're just the best, Sammi. Isn't that right Leo?" The man sitting next to her just looked up passively, not saying a word. A second later he went back to his magazine. "Okay, well maybe it's just me. Anyway, you'd better get in and chat to Alex. Are you okay if we leave?" I nodded my head and Charlotte started the engine. It didn't take long for her to be out of there and no doubt back to patrolling the streets.

Instead of pulling my car into the drive I just walked over to the gate and pressed the button. A moment later I was let through. Concerns that I may have been harassing Alex had entered my head, but right now he was the only lead in the case. I hoped that continuing down this avenue would open up new ones, but at the moment it was looking unlikely. As I walked to the front door it opened, I was initially elated to see Alex standing there but my attitude quickly changed when he spoke.

"Samantha, I would say nice to see you again but we both know that isn't true," Alex said sarcastically, I just ignored the comment and decided to walk into his house. I knew this wasn't all him, and that his wife probably had something to do with his sudden change of attitude.

"Please believe me when I say I am sorry," I said to Alex with the utmost sincerity. Alex was a person I loved and respected from a young age. He was beloved by all in my family and became a second brother to me. I didn't want him to feel ill of me for doing my job. "I wish I could just leave you to grieve in peace. What you have been through is devastating and it must be so hard to properly process what happened. But you have to understand you are the only lead we have at the moment and we need to follow this through until we can rule you out as a suspect." Alex went quiet and nodded his head, I sighed a little.

"I don't expect you to be happy with this but I need to take a DNA sample to eliminate you from our enquiries. Are you okay with that?" I asked softly.

"Yeah...,sure. I know you're only doing your job. I'm sorry." I smiled softly at his response. He took me into the dining room so that I could take a DNA swab. He sat down on the chair while I removed all of the equipment that I needed. After putting on my gloves I took a swab from the inside of his cheek. Thankfully it was a painless and non-intrusive procedure.

"Alex, I just wanted to ask. Did Joseph ever talk to you about other clients? Or trouble at work?" It was going to be a painful question, but I hoped that Alex would be able to stomach answering it. It's not easy when you know your boyfriend is sleeping with other people for money. Alex must have really loved him to ignore that fact.

"We tried to stay away from the subject. But recently he was getting really upset. He said that… Marcos, his boss, was trying to make him go and sleep with women as well. Which generally he didn't mind, Joseph was bisexual," Alex clarified. I was surprised to hear it, but let Alex continue. "But he told me that there was one woman who kept asking for him. She was very aggressive. Joseph would come back with bruises and scratches all down his body. Almost like she had beaten him up. He even informed me that she threatened to kill him at one stage." The tears that were in his eyes made me stop asking questions. Nothing else really was important, it was unlikely that Alex knew who this client was, but maybe I could find out who the mysterious woman was from Marcos, if he was happy to let me look at his client list.

•

Paul sat opposite Jackson as his boss busied himself with sending one final e-mail from his computer. He didn't feel comfortable being here alone and wasn't happy that he had been left to discuss the case. He was concerned it was Samantha's way to get rid of him so she could work alone for a little while. Maybe he had offended her this morning when prying into her personal life. He made a note to not do it again.

"So, tell me what is going on?" Jackson asked, no nonsense, straight to business. A far cry from the welcoming man on his first day who offered him tea and small talk. It was now, Paul realised, that side of him was for show. Paul looked down at his notebook, ready to discuss with him the case. But Jackson put his arm up to stop him from speaking; he looked back at him very confused. "No, I mean… tell me what is going on with Samantha." Paul just stared for a moment, wondering what Jackson's game was, but he decided to use this time to get his troubles out of his system.

"Samantha, she's a very good colleague to have. Knowledgeable, and…" Jackson yet again stopped his young detective and decided to tell him his own concerns. He knew that they would be there all night if he let Paul go ahead and continue in the vein he was going.

"Look Paul, I'm going to be honest with you. I'm concerned about Samantha." He stopped for a moment to savour the look on the young detective's face and then continued. "Samantha is very single minded. She is likely to want to go for Marcos over this murder. Even though the chances are he is innocent. They have a history together; you see Samantha's dad used to use some of the 'young women' in his employment after her mother died. She feels that Marcos used her father's grief to his advantage, and it was only once he could no longer afford company, he cut him off, leading to his suicide." Paul remained in silence for a moment. He could only nod his head at what he was hearing. He wasn't sure what to say. Samantha did seem a little single minded, but he didn't think she would deliberately mess up a case for a grudge that she had. Surely?

"Well… sir, so far I would like to confirm that things seem to be going… fine." He didn't know how else to respond. Samantha seemed to be on the level, she was intelligent and engaging; an excellent police officer and seemed extremely loyal. He wasn't sure she deserved the third degree she was getting.

"May I ask where she is now?"

"She's getting a DNA swab from Alex and then…"

"Yes?"

"She plans on visiting Marcos to collect Joseph's client list." Jackson grinned sardonically at the last comment. He knew she wouldn't be able to resist going down the Marcos route.

"Thank you for being honest with me, Paul. You may go now." After Jackson finished, Paul walked out of the room. He sat at his desk, pretending to look at the paperwork around him but instead keeping an eye on Jackson's office. After a few moments he noticed Jackson grab a phone from his desk, Paul was able to get a glance at it quickly before he turned around. It was a very cheap phone, likely a pay as you go that had very little internet connectivity with no location settings. It was strange, why would a detective chief inspector need a pay as you go phone unless there was something to hide? Due to the positioning of Jackson and the phone, Paul was unable to see what he was doing, but he deduced it was likely checking through messages.

He had seen enough and decided to leave the room.

•

"What do you want, Detective? Don't you have anybody else to bother? I'm sure Alex knows more about this than I do anyway," Marcos snarled at me, as I stood at the front door. I was taken aback initially but regained my composure. I was determined to get Joseph's client list and wasn't going to be distracted by his jibes. I believed that Alex was completely innocent, and I hoped the client list would give me a new avenue to investigate. Hopefully, somebody who would have a good reason to murder him. "I would let you in but… I still haven't got the stink from your last visit out of the carpet."

"Don't worry, Marcos, I'll be brief. If you would ask your members of staff to send through Joseph's client list. That will be all." I turned my back on him, signalling the end of the conversation, however, I knew that it wasn't for Marcos. I stopped when I heard him clear his throat and waited for the comeback.

"Sorry, Detective. Don't you need a warrant for that?" he remarked in a calm but smug manner. I turned around and looked back at him, wondering how to play this. In most cases I would avoid threats when dealing with him, however, I felt that in this case it would be the only way for him to hand over what I wanted.

"Of course, Marcos, but… shall we be frank for a moment? You know if I come back with a warrant, you will have to hand over your entire client list; every single person that has ever used your services, no matter their status in society." I paused for a moment for effect and then continued to accentuate my point. "Any police officer, lawyer, judge, criminal, you have on that list will come out in my investigation. It will be one of the biggest scandals in Manchester, and you will lose your credibility as a man who can protect his clients' interests. Right now, I just want the list of clients for Joseph Marsden. Any man or woman who used his services. If there are any who are in the public eye, I will do my best to protect their names and reputations. That is all I am interested in, and I hope we can come to an agreement that will allow me to view those names." Marcos was taken aback at how forceful I was with this situation. He smirked a little and nodded his head.

"You know what, Samantha, if you didn't work for the scum in blue I would almost respect you. My assistant will e-mail over a list by the end of the day." With that he slammed the door in my face. I turned and walked back to the car, elated in the knowledge that I had got one over the most hated criminal within the North West. In a way I was also disappointed, I wanted to drag his name through the mud and those of his clients.

Maybe another day.

SEVENTEEN

I made it back to the police station later that afternoon, wanting to square a few things away with Paul before retiring for the evening. I was an early riser and trying to work late didn't cut it for me. By 6pm I was usually tired and just needed to rest and unwind. If I remained on high alert for too long my work and my judgement became impaired and I became too focused on one thing. Something I didn't want to happen in this case.

As I walked into the office I was accosted by Paul, who pulled me into one of the meeting rooms without saying a word. I had concerns that he took me aside to scold me and take me down for leaving him in an awkward position. I was ready to defend my actions

"Do you know what kind of phone Jackson owns?" He spoke in hushed tones, concerned somebody may hear our conversation through the walls. I was confused by the question. Why was he so concerned about the phone Jackson owns? Were we now questioning our own colleagues in this investigation? Wanting to understand more, I played along.

"Erm, he has an iPhone, latest model," I responded; it was the only phone I had seen him with at least.

"Have you ever seen him with a small pay as you go phone? Unsure of the make but it's cheap, probably only about £15?" I was perplexed. Even if he did have a pay as you go phone, why was Paul so interested in it? I have known of many colleagues who would have a second phone; some who wanted to have a cheap one to hand so they didn't put their expensive new phones in danger when out on patrol. Others who had one for the purposes of speaking with informants, so that their numbers couldn't be traced by their criminal friends who they were ratting on. Maybe it was wrong, but I didn't see the big deal about a second phone.

"No. What is this about, Paul?" I asked forcefully. He went silent for a moment and looked intensely into my eyes, as if trying to understand what was going on in my soul. I felt a little uncomfortable and just wanted it to end.

"Nothing... erm... I just... no it doesn't matter." With that he got up, opened the meeting room door and walked back to his desk. I stared, blinking and wondering what that random conversation was about. I eventually got up and walked back to my desk, glancing into Jackson's office and noting he wasn't there. Not wanting to bring up anything, I just logged into my e-mail account and started to check through my message, wanting to see if Marcos had made good on his promise of sending over a client list.

There was nothing. Maybe I was expecting a little too much to have an answer within an hour, but I wanted to get trawling through these names as soon as possible. I shut down the computer and picked up my bag.

"I'll see you in the morning, Paul," I said, as I walked out of office. He just waved goodbye, engrossed with something in his e-mail. There was something strange going on, and I was keen to know what. I hoped I would find more out in the morning.

•

My flat was not an area where I wished to be at the moment. Too many of my colleagues; media personnel and my friends knew of its location, and I didn't want the possibility of an impromptu visit. I needed some time alone. Sitting in the dark all night wasn't an option, some of my lights were motion sensor and just walking from the living room to the kitchen for a drink could set them off. Instead, Darwen was the best choice. Only Michael, Alex and my family knew about the property. The solitude was something that I wanted most right now. Yes, the property was barely habitable, but I was willing to overlook that just so that I could get my thoughts in order and be alone. The case just seemed to be falling apart in front of me, and I wasn't entirely sure how I would swing it back in my favour.

I sat on the cushions that I had left from my evening before with Michael, drinking a large glass of wine from a bottle that I had just opened. Some would claim I was an alcoholic, that I had a dependency on alcohol and couldn't get through a day without a drink in my hand. Those people would be wrong. Yes, I enjoyed alcohol, and probably drank a little too much on occasion, but I wasn't dependent on it. Most of the time I wouldn't touch the stuff, only in cases of extreme stress did I grab for the bottle.

There was a knock at the door, in my heart I knew I didn't want to answer it. I just had a gut feeling that it was going to be a conversation I didn't want to have. But something compelled me...

"What the hell are you doing?" They were the first words Michael said as the door opened. I sighed and moved out of the way, he walked in and I shut the door behind us. I took another swig of my wine as I sat back down on the cushions. Michael remained standing for a bit. "You're destroying a man's reputation." It was at that moment I couldn't control my emotions and I choked out a few tears. He saw this and came and sat next to me.

"Oh Samantha, please don't cry," he whispered, as he kissed me lightly on the head. "I'm sorry, I didn't mean to make you cry." It was obvious he was close to Alex and he felt the man's reputation was taking a hit. I didn't know how to stop it though, no matter how much I wanted to, I didn't know how to change what was going on.

I also knew it would get so much worse if the truth about his sexuality came out.

"No, it's not you, Michael. It's… Oh I don't know what to do." I managed to eventually choke out through the tears and racking sobs. "Alex is such a decent guy and I feel like this investigation is destroying his life, and on top of that I could be harming my own career. People already think I'm a laughing stock, with the nights out and one-night stands. If I mess up this case, or if I'm taken off it, I might be out of a job and Alex could be in jail for a crime he didn't even commit." I continued to cry into Michael's chest, his strong arms around my body. Neither of us said anything further, we just sat close to one another until I'd exhausted myself into a deep sleep.

EIGHTEEN

When I awoke it took me a while for my eyes to adjust to the morning glare. After rubbing away the sleep, I realised I was on the floor of my Darwen home again, tucked up under one of my fleecy blankets. I looked around while yawning and noticed I was alone; Michael had likely left for football training already. I hoped he had no ill feelings towards me after last night. Although I've suffered with PTSD and depression since a teenager, I did all I could to keep my emotions in check. Last night I couldn't remain strong. I was scared that he would think terribly of me because of what happened to Alex. It was strange, I had never cared what a man thought about me until I met Michael. Even though we had only spent a short time together I knew he was a person I could make a future with. I just hoped this case, and the media interference, didn't drive a wedge between us. It was obvious he was close to Alex and I was determined to protect our friend.

I spent a little bit of time laying on the cushions, flicking through my phone and adjusting to the day ahead. Once I felt more awake, I got up and made my way into work.

•

Bryony read through her latest article on her laptop, thrilled with its contents. She had been up all night writing it in the hope she didn't get pipped to the story by another journalist. Her conversation with John had been enlightening. They had met at a pub late last night and spoken over a few drinks, non-alcoholic for her of course because of her current condition. At first it took a while for John to speak, wanting to just discuss mundane topics such as the environment and politics. But a few drinks brought him out of his shell, and he told an unexpected story about a man universally loved across England.

Rather than the kind hearted husband who was devoted to his wife, John painted a picture of a troubled man who was secretly having a gay affair as a teenager; one who had threatened those who knew to silence through physical attacks; and had coercively controlled his wife into hiding his secret by threatening her with divorce and refusing to pay for their children if she did speak out.

Bryony was hooked, she couldn't believe everything that John was telling her. When he finished, she didn't speak for a while, trying to regain her composure. When she finally broke the silence all she could do was ask how he knew all of this information. His response was startling.

John was the man he had attacked when he found out, through pure chance, that Alex had slept with another man. He beat him so viciously that he required surgery on his jaw to fix a break. Undeterred he spoke to Alex's wife and informed her what had happened, and was surprised to find she already knew. Not only that but she confided that Alex had threatened to make her destitute if she dared to speak out. Bryony had heard enough, she informed John that she would write the article and would pay him 10% of what she received from the paper. He was happy with the arrangement and left it at that.

She knew the story was gold and would complete her week. She was expecting a large payday, and she knew who would be happy to provide it.

•

Paul was already at the station when I arrived. I scowled on noticing the Marcos robbery file in his hands. I was frustrated at the idea that Jackson may have asked him to review it as part of the Joseph murder. I wanted to ask what he was doing but knew it wasn't my place to do so and decided to keep quiet.

"Samantha, you have a message on your desk," Paul said, not looking up from his file. I looked down at the small post-it and saw the name Bryony. Instantly I knew I didn't want to have a conversation with her and threw the message in the bin. After taking my coat off and hanging it up, I went back to my desk and logged in to my e-mail to see if Marcos was a man of his word. The top e-mail was from his assistant, I was glad he followed through with his promise and I didn't have to get a warrant. It was an arduous process and would have tipped Jackson off to the fact I still believed there was more to investigate than Alex.

I opened the file and quickly skimmed down the names on the list, hoping to find somebody of note who may want to harm Joseph but it looked to be a dead end. All the people listed were either not of interest, or had already been very public about their lifestyle choices and had even been photographed with Joseph on dates out on occasion. It was another dead end. Disappointed I sighed and stared intently across the other side of the room.

"What happened to Joseph?" I said quietly. It was enough to peak Paul's interest and he looked up from his file. It didn't take him much longer to put it down and pay attention to what I was thinking.

"What?" he asked, standing up and picking up the file from my desk. I smiled a little, but not enough for him to notice.

"Joseph, we have interviewed all these people and nobody knows where he actually went after he was pushed to the ground," I said, looking through all of the statements that we had collated from Alex's team mates, as well as what Alex himself said in his own interview.

"They were all quite drunk though, can that be the reason why?" Paul said. It seemed like a convenient answer. Unless paralytic it was unlikely that their alcohol intake had a bearing on how they viewed this incident. It was traumatic to see somebody injured in such a way. An event like that would stay with you.

"I don't know. If I saw a man fall to the floor and crack his jaw the way Joseph did I think I'd remember every detail, regardless of my alcohol intake. I'm concerned there was something else but drink in their body." It wasn't a matter I should be speculating about, but it all seemed very weird. Maybe they had been drugged, maybe it wasn't their fault. Or maybe they had been celebrating with cocaine. Many players were known to have done that since the FA became a bit lax after the legalisation of drugs act of 2025, as long as it was in private and didn't come up in drugs tests, they turned a blind eye to the majority of drug use. It was an act that police despised, and for good reason. A number of previously very dangerous people were able to appeal their sentences and were back on the streets dealing again.

And then people like Marcos were able to continue with their criminal acts without being held truly accountable.

I looked down at my phone when it started to ring, noticing it was the pathologist with the DNA test results. I had a feeling of dread in the pit of my stomach that I would soon be speaking with Alex again.

"Samantha, it's Darren. I hope you are well," he said, as I picked up. Normally when Darren wanted to talk about our private lives he would start a conversation in that way, but I wanted to get down to business and find out the results of the DNA test.

"I'm fine, Darren. We're a little busy here, so if you could get to the gist of what is going on." I didn't mean for it to sound so harsh. But I found the man to be a creepy pervert and just wanted to get off the phone with him as soon as possible.

"The skin flakes below Joseph's fingernails are a match to Alex Smith's DNA." I sighed in annoyance. It was the news I did not want to hear. I was unhappy with the fact that I would have to tell Jackson that we had a match. "This doesn't necessarily mean he murdered him though, it could have happened outside of the club. If Joseph grabbed onto Alex in any way, maybe he accidentally scratched him." I was glad that Darren was trying to make things a little better, but it was still looking bad for Alex. A secret gay relationship; an assault caught on CCTV and now the fact his skin flakes were found under the fingernails of the murder victim.

I hoped something else would happen to make this whole week a bit better.

"Thank you, Darren. If you have more information then please get in touch with me," I responded, before putting the phone down. Paul was back to examining the burglary records at his desk. "The skin underneath Joseph's fingernails does belong to Alex Smith. We should probably go back to him and see what's going on. See if there is more to the story." Paul put down his file and nodded his head.

"Okay, Samantha, do you want to drive or shall I?"

NINETEEN

Michael felt the ache in his leg after another gruelling training session. With only one day to go until the next game, many managers would go for non-contact light training to avoid injuries. Fernandes was a different breed of manager, pushing his players to the extreme until matchday. Today consisted of watching their opponents matches to understand their style of play; then afterwards two thirty-minute 11v11 matches with both sets of players taking on the role of Manchester, and then their opponents. It was good preparation but questions about whether players could be overprepared started to rear their head, especially after a run of five losses.

As Michael sat, massaging some cold cream into his aching quads, he noticed Fernandes ask Alex to come with him. Many of the team stopped as their captain trudged after their manager, they all knew it was a bad sign to be called in after training. After the door closed there were murmurings about what the conversation would entail. But Michael refused to partake. He wasn't interested in gossip, only hearing from Alex what was going on when he was ready.

•

"Alex, how are you?" Fernandes asked, trying to sound as

though he cared about the situation. It was false though, Alex knew his manager well and knew it was all a show. In reality, as long as the players personal lives didn't impact their playing ability, Fernandes couldn't care how they were doing. He was there to manage them, the well-being element was delegated to Tanja and the sport's psychologists on the payroll.

"I'm fine, Fernandes, just keen to get on with training and focus on the game tomorrow," Alex replied, he noticed a hint of scepticism in Fernandes eyes, but it disappeared as quickly as it had arrived. Alex knew the rest of the conversation was going to make him angry.

"Alex, with everything going on, we were thinking that maybe it's a good idea if you didn't play until this situation is resolved. Both for your own mental well-being and the club." Alex did what he could to remain calm, and just stared hard at Fernandes, trying to work out what to say to him without getting himself sacked. Just as he was about to speak, though, he was saved by a knock at the door.

"Sorry if I'm interrupting," I said, walking in on the conversation between Fernandes and Alex. Although the former looked angry, the latter looked both worried and relieved. I made a mental note of that. "Sorry Fernandes, I'd be grateful if you could give us some space." I knew it was rude as I was throwing him out of his office, but there was nowhere else to discuss this delicate matter with Alex.

And there was no way I wanted Fernandes in the room to hear it. I wasn't willing to out Alex, especially to a man who had a hold over his career. Once he shut the door, I shut the blinds to the room. Not wanting a teammate to walk past and see us. I spoke as quietly as possible.

"Alex, we found your DNA under the fingernails of Joseph. Mind telling me how they got there?" His expression was deeply troubled, but he remained calm. I admired him a little. With his personal life falling apart, he managed to retain a composure that I envied.

"Yes, I... briefly went back to Joseph's before I went home.

I wanted to try and apologise for what I'd done, but he was so angry at me and lashed out. I reached out to comfort him but he thought I was going to harm him again and he scratched me on the arm. I've been covering it up with the help of Katie ever since." He pulled up his undershirt and showed the scratch up his arm. I was surprised we didn't see it before, but then remembered we had only ever seen him with a jumper on. The revelation accounted for some of the timeline between the attack and Joseph's death, but not much. It also raised more questions than answers, and I was starting to wonder if Alex was innocent in all of this.

"Why didn't you tell us before?" Paul asked, as he stood in the corner, his voice laced with judgement. Alex looked to the floor, not wanting to give either of us eye contact. He knew it looked bad for him. He was officially the last man that we know of to see Joseph alive, and as such is now the most credible suspect in the murder investigation. Currently though, I wanted to keep speaking to him as a witness as, if he was guilty, he would be more likely to screw up now, rather than if we took him into a police station and interrogated him for ages.

"I was genuinely scared. I had just been outed for Joseph's assault. Is it too much of a stretch to imagine that I would be arrested for his murder if the police came knocking?" I could understand his theory, but withholding information during a murder investigation was a serious offence and could have still landed him in jail for at least ten years, or an additional ten years if he was guilty.

"I understand but... if you cared about Joseph you would have been honest from the start." Until then I had never seen Alex angry. I believe the words that irked him were 'if you cared about Joseph'. It was clear that he cared about Joseph, unless he was a very convincing actor. He did his best to keep his voice as low as possible, remembering where he was and the implication of talking about his sexual orientation too loud.

"If? If I cared about Joseph?" Alex said, in a low tone, his teeth gritted together. I slunk back a little and just watched

Alex direct his anger at Paul. I didn't want to be linked to this comment. If there was going to be a complaint made, I didn't want to be involved. "Listen here, Detective, I loved Joseph. He was kind and thoughtful, and didn't care that I was a footballer. All he cared about was me, and I loved him. I absolutely… loved him." He didn't break down, I believe he was too angry to do so. Paul didn't say anything, instead just looked over to me. I didn't know why I was the one he looked to help for in the situation, it wasn't my doing.

"Look, Alex, please let me apologise for my colleagues bad choice of wording. I would say he didn't mean it, but I don't think that's the truth. I believe he may have meant every word of it," I said. Paul could not mask the anger on his face when I looked over at him, clearly thinking that my comment was a betrayal. I turned back to Alex though, I was not done yet. "You have got to understand our position though, Alex. You have lied to us since the start of this investigation, and now you've put yourself high on our list of suspects.

"You claimed that Joseph came on to you when you pushed him away, that was a lie; you claimed you and Joseph had no prior knowledge of each other, that was a lie and now you have lied about your movements after that attack. So please, for Joseph and for this investigation, start telling us the truth." Alex looked down to the floor like a scolded schoolchild, I turned back to Paul who now looked impressed at my words to Alex. I continued. "Now, tell me what happened when you went to see Joseph."

"Okay," Alex responded in a small voice. I turned on my Dictaphone while he recounted the last time he saw Joseph. Part of me was hesitant to believe he would be truthful now, but I wanted to give him the benefit of the doubt. "When Joseph opened the door, he did everything he could to shut it again on my face. He was crying and yelling that he didn't want to see me. He was scared."

"Did he have a reason to be?" There was a brief flicker of anger in Alex's eyes, but it subsided quickly.

"Of course not. I just wanted to explain why I pushed him

away, that I felt awful and never intended to hurt him." Tears were starting to form in Alex's eyes, he looked away in embarrassment. "I just wanted to help him, get some medical help for his wounds. But when I tried to get into his flat, he scratched my arm and slammed the door on my face. I tried to reason with him through the door but he threatened to ring the police. So I left."

"And that was the last you saw of Joseph?" He nodded his head slightly. "Did you see anybody else at his flat?" Instead of responding he shook his head. "Alex, could you just confirm for the Dictaphone that you didn't see anybody outside of his flat?"

"Detective Rodan, I did not see anybody outside his flat when I left. I was the last person to see Joseph alive," he responded, staring intently in my eyes. Thanking him, I clicked off the Dictaphone and we said our goodbyes. I knew that this would only end in one way, and that was with the arrest of Alex. Especially now he confirmed he was the last person to see Joseph alive. I needed to prove this was not the case.

TWENTY

As we arrived at the door of our office a feeling of dread entered the pit of my stomach. The loud, booming voice of my superior was the cause. I pushed open the door to find Detective Inspector Dennis McCarthy back from the Yorkshire Moors case. He was recounting his story to a couple of fresh-faced fast-trackers, regaling them with details of the man they had arrested for the murders. A young man just twenty years old, who was found with child porn on his computer. They arrested him and he confessed to the murders. The fact that he had learning difficulties, though, did not sway them to reconsider whether he may be telling the truth about his guilt.

That was McCarthy for you, wanting the fastest and quickest answer. I didn't argue with him, knowing that my opinion wouldn't be wanted. As he continued to speak out a desk clerk walked into the room and came over.

"Detective Rodan. There is a man here to see you," he whispered, I looked over to Paul and indicated that we needed to go. "He's in interview room 1 for you." The desk clerk walked back out and I went to follow him.

"Where are you going, Detective? You might learn a thing or to about closing off a case," McCarthy said, not looking in my direction. I paused briefly and wondered if it was worth poking the bear and being rude. Instead deciding it was best to be respectful.

"Sorry, Dennis. I need to go, it's to do with our case," I replied. McCarthy studied me for a moment and then waved his hand, indicating he was happy for me to leave. Paul followed quickly behind.

•

As we walked to the interview room, I wished I had taken the time to ask the desk clerk the purpose of our guests visit. Walking into a meeting blind was a bugbear of mine, especially during this investigation. I'd had one too many shocks and didn't feel I could handle any more. I opened the door to the room, finding an unassuming man in his mid to late thirties sitting at the table, staring at us with dark brown eyes. I studied him with interest as I shut the door behind myself and Paul. He looked familiar but I was struggling to place where I had seen him before.

"Good Afternoon, my name is Detective Sergeant Rodan and this is Detective Constable Grant. You asked to see us?" I said, sitting at the table. He leant down to pick a bag off the floor, although I was certain he had been searched on entry, I was still poised and ready to protect myself if this wasn't the case. I was surprised when he pulled a laptop and phone out and put it on the table in front of us.

"I think you have probably been looking for these." I looked down at Joseph's technology in disbelief. The small purple laptop, identifiable by the chip to the top right corner; and his blue phone with the tell-tale crack down the middle, were both sitting before of me. I knew they wouldn't have any use in the murder investigation but they could help me nail Marcos. I thought they were lost forever. I came to my senses and tried to maintain a calm and professional voice.

"Who are you and where did you get these items from?" It was a little blunt, but there wasn't any other way to ask it.

"My name is Aaron Jefferson, and I stole these items. Joseph hired me to." I was a little confused. I looked over to Paul who was equally perplexed by the statement.

"Joseph hired you to steal his own property?" I said slowly. Aaron nodded his head and recounted his story.

"I've known Joseph since we were teenagers, we went to school together and remained good friends into our adult years. He came to me recently begging for help. He had concerns he was being stalked and believed it was to do with the Marcos Vincenzo robbery." I saw Paul shift a little in my eyeline but ignored it. "He wanted me to fake a burglary and steal his laptop and phone. He told me the evidence on there could convict Marcos and bring about an end to his criminal empire. I was happy to oblige."

"But why didn't he just give you the phone and laptop?" I knew I should have been making notes, but in my haste to get away from McCarthy I had forgotten my notebook. The camera in the corner of the room would be recording the interaction.

"It needed to look real. Joseph had concerns that a hand off of the items would put me in danger. If they had been stolen by a professional burglar the data would be 'lost' as they would wipe both the phone and laptop before selling." Aaron stopped for a moment; it was then I clicked where I had seen him before, he was a suspect in a major bank heist. Due to a lack of evidence, though, he was never pursued. "Joseph told me if anything happened to him that I should come to you, that he trusts you implicitly. When I saw he had been murdered I knew it was the right time to come."

I stared at the laptop and phone, giddy at the fact they had made their way to me. Not only could it bring an end to Marcos, it could also prove that he had a motive to murder Joseph. This evidence could change so many lives.

"Aaron, thank you for bringing this in. We won't pursue charges…"

"No, please. You have to arrest me," he responded cutting me off mid-sentence. "Marcos has people everywhere. If you have that laptop and I am not under arrest they will know the information is still there. Just please keep me in."

"It's okay, Samantha, I can deal with this. You go and get the laptop into evidence," Paul chipped in. I could sense the doubt in

Aaron's mind. He was informed only I could be trusted, and now my colleague is jumping at the chance to get me out of the room. Against my better judgement, I backed him.

"Don't worry, Paul is one of the few I trust." Aaron seemed to relax a little. I picked up the laptop and phone, and left the room swiftly.

•

As I left the interview room I came face to face with Jackson; leaning against the wall opposite with fury in his eyes. It was inevitable that everything would catch up with me when I didn't bring Alex in for questioning. Not only was there evidence of his DNA under Joseph's nails, but he admitted he had lied to us throughout the investigation. It was more than enough to arrest him and get a warrant to search his property.

"Samantha, I need a word with you, now," he said in a brusque voice. I looked down at the items I had been handed, not wanting to deviate from my plan of going to the evidence room after the words of Aaron.

"I'm sorry, sir. I need to get this into evidence straight away." It was like waving a red fag in front of a bull. Jackson's nostrils flared and he curled his hands tensely into a ball. I knew I was now treading on dangerous water.

"Now, Samantha," Jackson shouted, as he pushed away from the wall and stalked off down the hall. I considered ignoring him. Aaron's warning seemed legitimate, and I had fears as to what would happen if I didn't log the laptop and phone straight into evidence. But Jackson needed my attention and going about my own business could be worse for me in the long run.

•

I took a seat in Jackson's room, placing the laptop and phone ahead of me on his desk. Feelings of dread entered the pit of my stomach. I knew this conversation would end badly, likely with my suspension. Although he was unaware of the intricacies of the Marsden murder, Jackson would be aware we had found DNA evidence linking Alex to the crime scene. The fact I hadn't acted on that and brought him in would be enough for Jackson to take action and remove me from the case.

"Samantha, care explaining to me why we haven't got a suspect in custody?" Jackson said. He was surprisingly calm at the moment. But I knew it wouldn't last, he felt that Alex was guilty in this case and wanted a quick result. If we arrested Alex it would be a huge notch on his belt. And the subsequent announcement of his sexuality would just make things even better for him. He was dreaming of the exposure the station would get for this, maybe he wouldn't have been so happy if Alex was genuinely innocent.

"Jackson, the skin flakes don't mean he killed him." It wasn't a good move, his nose flared as he stared coldly into my eyes. He smacked his hand onto the desk ahead, asserting his dominance. I knew this was going to escalate.

"No it doesn't, but it's the best evidence we have. It puts him at the scene of the crime when he lied to you and claimed the attack was the last time he saw Joseph, it is enough to haul him in and question him formally," Jackson screamed back. I just sat there staring back at him with cold eyes, I knew I wouldn't win this fight but I wanted to try. "McCarthy could do it, why can't you?"

"McCarthy has arrested a kid with the mental age of twelve for a murder he confessed to but probably didn't commit. Other than the photos there is no physical evidence to tie that kid to the crime. For fuck's sake he can't even write his name, how is he going to clean up a crime scene? I want to actually investigate this case. We need a result but not like this," I screamed back, standing up in the process so that I wasn't lower than Jackson. It was hard to bring myself up to the height of a man who was almost 6 ft 7 inches, but I had to make it clear I wasn't scared of him. I wanted him to realise I could yell as much as he could and I could be just as forceful when I did.

"How dare you. McCarthy has one of the best records of any police office in this station. He actually had to investigate this, whereas you have been handed a suspect on a plate." I quickly glanced out of the room and looked at McCarthy, who was sitting there with a big grin on his face, obviously hearing our raised voices through the wall. I accepted that I had hit the point of no return and that McCarthy would soon be taking over this case. I went for it, didn't hold back, and told Jackson what I really thought of him.

"There are two suspects. Marcos is the second." The snort of derision was the last straw for me, I was going to get heard and I was going to have it happen now, I didn't care who else heard me in the process. "You're a joke of a man. How did you make it so high up the police ladder? It clearly wasn't because of your skill or ability. Maybe it's because somebody wanted you up here. Maybe Marcos paid people off to make sure you were in place so every fucking criminal act he is involved in is ignored. You are obsessed with the man, you feel I should just ignore good evidence. You feel I should ignore the history. You are as bad as he is."

"That's it, get the fuck out. You're suspended effective immediately. How dare you speak to a superior officer in such a way? You're gone!" I threw my warrant card at him and walked out of the room. As I did I noticed that Paul was rummaging through his drawers, probably looking for the forms to process Aaron. I refused to look at McCarthy, knowing that he would be wearing a particularly smug look on his face. I knew the case would go to him now he was back in Manchester, it was probably planned from the start that I would be removed. I couldn't let it go though. I knew Alex would be arrested and charged for something he was likely innocent of. Yes, the skin flakes were a problem but it was flimsy evidence at best. McCarthy wouldn't waste any time pinning this on Alex.

It wasn't loyalty, or friendship, that made me claim Alex was innocent. It was the belief that every interaction we had together was genuine, and that he didn't have it in his heart to hurt another man. Let alone the man who he clearly loved. Not in such a brutal way.

I had to find a way to prove this was the case.

•

Jackson walked out of his office with the laptop and phone in hand to see McCarthy and Paul. Whereas Paul was stunned, McCarthy was delighted at what he had seen. He had predicted that Samantha would implode during the case, and was happy to be there when it happened. She was insane, and a danger to the good name of the station. He was glad to see her gone.

"As you have both seen Samantha has been thrown off the case. It will now be spearheaded by McCarthy, with Paul helping out. I expect results, and I expect them soon," Jackson said. McCarthy nodded his head and instantly went to look over the case notes of the folder. Paul couldn't help but feel uneasy about the new arrangement. He didn't feel Samantha should be thrown off the case for not necessarily agreeing with her superior officers. He was annoyed at her comments that implied he was a homophobe, but didn't tell Jackson because he knew he had been too harsh on Alex. He wanted to provoke him though, truly understand if he was telling the truth about his relationship with Joseph, and he believed he was.

Now he couldn't help but wonder how harsh McCarthy was going to be in pursuing a potentially innocent man. It took him a moment to notice the laptop in Jackson's hands and his heart sunk. Aaron had warned against letting anybody but Samantha take that to evidence, and now it was in the hands of Jackson. Paul wanted to test his theory out.

"Sorry, may I ask a question, sir?" Paul asked. Jackson affirmed he was content with a nod of the head. "Do you want me to submit the laptop into evidence? You probably have a bit of paperwork to do for Samantha's suspension." He was unsurprised when Jackson shook his head.

"That's quite alright, Paul. I will go down and do this myself," he said, staring deeply into Paul's eyes as if challenging him to argue. Paul left it at that.

"Okay sir, I just need to go and finish off some forms," Paul stated. Jackson and McCarthy both waved him away as he walked off. He made it to a private area with nobody around and typed in a number, he had to make a phone call and appraise somebody much higher of these developments, as they could prove so costly in the end. "It's D.C. Grant. We may have gotten this all wrong, I don't think Samantha is the person we should be looking at. I think it's Jackson and McCarthy."

TWENTY-ONE

I sat on the sofa, enveloped by my silent Manchester home. In my hand a glass of Mavrodaphne, a Greek dessert wine that I favoured when I was drinking alone. As I took a sip, my thoughts once again turned to the angry scenes at the station. I knew my career was over, there was no coming back from my outburst. Much about the case had bugged me from the start. The attempts to shield Marcos from any questioning, even though Joseph had significant data on a major fraud scheme that could put him behind bars, was a worry. The loss of his freedom, money and criminal empire was a strong motive for murder. Yet Jackson didn't seem interested.

The pursuit of Alex seemed like a red herring. While his relationship being a secret could be seen as problematic, his love for Joseph seemed genuine. His motive, a loss of career, seemed weak in comparison to Marcos. He had far more to lose murdering Joseph then he did to gain. For that reason alone, I felt it was unlikely he was the culprit. Crimes of passion weren't uncommon, but the way Joseph was laid out suggested it was premeditated. That just didn't sync with Alex's situation.

The soft knock at the door brought me back to reality. I sighed at the idea of company, wanting to be alone in my thoughts and self-pity. Sadly, the lights around my property indicated I was in and refusing to answer the door would be rude. I took another large gulp of wine, finishing the glass, before making my way to answer the door.

On answering, I was pleasantly surprised to find my older brother, Shaun, standing there. A slight grin on his face and a bottle of alcohol in his hand. At 6 ft 4 inches he towered over me; he had inherited the trademark black hair like myself, but he had inherited our fathers eyes, a light brown instead of the greyish blue I had inherited from my mother.

"Shaun, it's so good to see you. I didn't realise you were back in the UK," I said, upon lunging forward and giving him a large hug. He reciprocated by putting his arms around my shoulders and pulling me close. Although we frequently spoke on the phone, we had not seen each other for nearly a year due to work commitments. "Shouldn't you be teaching right now?"

"Nah, I'm all done with that. It's my sabbatical year so I'm currently doing research for a new paper. I needed a break though, so I came back for a couple of weeks. Only just landed a couple of days ago. Here, for you," he said, pulling away from me and holding out a bottle of strange looking orange liquid. I took it and stared at him in puzzlement.

"It's mango flavoured gin, I distilled it myself. May I come in?" I moved so he could get past me and shut the door behind him. As he walked over to the sofa to make himself comfortable, I put down the bottle of gin and went to the kitchen to collect another couple of glasses. Shaun thanked me as I handed one to him. "Are you okay?" he asked, noticing my solemn mood.

"I guess," I responded briefly, while pouring another glass of wine, wanting to finish it before I started anything new. I offered a bit to Shaun, he declined saying he was happy to wait for a drink. I sat down on the chair opposite, curling my legs up underneath me. I wanted to be looking at my brother as we spoke.

"Are you okay?" Shaun asked again, emphasising the words more a second time. He knew my original answer was false. I sighed and put the wine glass on the small table next to me. I tried to keep my emotions in check.

"No I'm not. I've been suspended for refusing to arrest Alex because I still believe he is innocent. My career is probably ruined because I stood up to Jackson and accused him of taking backhanders. So no, I'm not okay," I said. Shaun nodded his head and picked up the mango gin, pouring the liquid into our glasses.

"I know, Samantha. Alex has been talking to me about the case." I wasn't surprised, they had been best friends throughout school and college, and I knew they were still close. "He knows you believe he is innocent and wants to find who murdered Joseph," Shaun stated, I sighed, it was nice that Alex had faith in me but I was no longer there to help him. Soon he would be arrested and interrogated by people who seemed to have an agenda.

"I know, I can't protect him now though. The CCTV footage, the DNA evidence and the fact he was the last to see Joseph alive will be enough to get a warrant and access to Alex and Joseph's personal records. Jackson will pursue him now until he has concrete evidence for the CPS to approve charges," I said, quietly. I felt bad. During my outburst I didn't consider the implications of my actions. My anger and frustration at being held back in my job just came out. I couldn't stop it.

"I know you aren't the investigating officer, but I also know you won't abandon him. The truth has always been important to you, that's what made you such a good detective," Shaun responded, as he sat ahead on the sofa, staring at me intensely. Although at my lowest I knew he was right. I couldn't let it lie. I felt Alex was innocent, and knew the pressure he would be put under by Jackson and McCarthy. I had to protect him, somehow.

"This is quite nice," I said, after picking up the glass of mango gin, wanting to change the subject from my failing career. Our relationship could be fractured at times, but one thing my brother and I bonded over was alcohol. Many called us alcoholics, something I would agree with, but with our past it was no wonder we both used alcohol as an escape from reality. Shaun nodded his head and sipped his drink, while I gulped mine down and poured another glass.

Only as I reached for the bottle did I realise it was empty, I tried to swig the final dregs and was disappointed when nothing came out. I was unsure how many glasses I'd had, but knew Shaun had more than I did and was drunk. Evident from his current position, sitting on the sofa opposite, head back slightly and eyes lazily drifting open and shut. He was a tired drunk. I smiled at him, but it didn't bring about a reaction I expected. He was solemn, I hoped it was the alcohol bringing him down.

"Sammi, I am so bloody sorry." I had no idea what he was apologising for. It was not for him intruding on my evening as we'd had fun. I didn't say anything. Wanting him to continue. "I should never have abandoned you as a teenager," he said, leaning forward and putting his head in his hands. It clicked immediately; he was apologising for his past sins.

"Where has this come from?" I was taken aback. When we reconnected a few years ago, we vowed never to discuss the past; the death of our parents and his leaving me and my sister. The memories of those events were still too painful and I had no desire to revisit them.

"I abandoned you. I left you to raise an eleven-year-old on your own. I am the eldest, I should have stepped up. I should have given up my university place and raised you both. You should not have sacrificed your childhood. I was selfish." Tears were beginning to form in his eyes, in that moment I saw him again as the scared twenty-year-old who had just been orphaned, not the man he had become.

"You were a kid too. You were only twenty for crying out loud. You didn't know how to raise two kid sisters. I don't blame you for your choice." I didn't quite believe my own words. At the time I was angry with him. We had just lost both my parents, and less than six months later we lost Shaun. He went back to university and we seldom heard from him, only on birthdays and Christmases did he come back to see how we were doing. The anger subsided with time, and therapy. As I matured, I began to understand his reasons for leaving. He was heartbroken at the loss of our parents and seeing us was a reminder of the pain he endured so young.

"I should have done more. I should have been there for you; I should have done more for Dad. When Mum died, I could see Dad was struggling with us all. And I just left. I felt so ashamed, I couldn't look you or Stacey in the eye. I'm just so sorry." He wiped away a tear from his eye. Everything started to become clear.

"I don't blame you. I can't. If I could have run away I would have done. But my responsibility lay with Stacey, that's just how the cards were dealt when we became orphans," I said, trying to sooth him. He smiled sadly, it was clear this was something he had wanted to discuss for a long time and needed to get off his chest. I only wished Stacey was here to hear his words also. Even though I knew she wouldn't accept them. She still believed both Shaun and I abandoned her with our choices. I sacrificed everything I wanted to ensure we could survive, and she hated me. Whereas Shaun was as dead as our parents in her eyes.

"You gave up so much, Sammi. Your entire life has been about giving Stacey the best, and hell you have given her that. Top of her class at university, and an internship at a law firm. It's everything you wanted. You gave up your dreams for your sister, and for me. I selfishly kept going at university, and I let you give up your life." He was alert now, the adrenaline was kicking in. He stood and started to pace for the room. "I mean for God's sakes, you can't even get close to another person because everybody you've ever loved has abandoned you. If I had just stayed, and taken on my responsibilities, maybe things would be different." This had been a conversation he had wanted for ten years, it was now, when I was at my lowest, he decided to finally have it.

"I don't know what to say." I was trying to process what he meant. Shaun stopped and stared at me intensely.

"I don't want you to say anything, Samantha. I want you to listen." He sat back down again, sitting forward with his hands clasped together. "I know about Michael; Alex has told me how he has fallen for you. Just listen to me when I say, don't make the same mistake I did with the love of my life, don't let him go." With that Shaun got up, I sat shell-shocked looking at where he was sitting just a moment ago. Trying to process what he said about Michael, and the person he loved. As he made his way to the door, I suddenly found my voice.

"Wait…" He stopped briefly with his hand on the door, looking over to me, waiting for my next words. "Did you know Alex was gay?" From his body language I could see he was pondering whether to answer the question. He shrugged his shoulders and nodded his head.

"Ever since college. I'll try come and see you before I leave for Harvard again, Little Sis." With that he opened the door and walked out, leaving me with more questions than answers. There was only one person I wanted to speak to, the next thing I knew I was ringing Michael's mobile.

TWENTY-TWO

INTERLUDE: THIRTEEN YEARS AGO

"Why are you insisting on going on this trip when your mum is so unwell?" Peter asked his son. With Shaun getting a place at Oxford University, and Alex signing his first professional contract, they knew this would be the last time they were together in a while. He didn't want to miss out on these college memories.

"Dad, come on. Mum is fine with me going, why can't you be cool like her?" Shaun said, as he folded up his top and put it into his rucksack. Peter sighed, he felt like the bad guy. Throughout his wife's illness their children had sacrificed much in their childhood. The holidays they couldn't take while she was undergoing chemotherapy; the days where they had to care for her as she was too weak to move from her bed, and the times they spent in hospital, believing it would be the last time they would see her. As she grew weaker, he kept them all closer and tried to limit their time away. Wanting to ensure they were all together when she met her end.

"You know what your mum is like though. She doesn't want to worry you all." Even when she was first diagnosed with terminal cancer, she was adamant she would live life to the full. Secretly, she was in tremendous pain and wanted to slip away peacefully. She had considered taking her life, but the love for her family stopped her.

"Dad, look..." Peter had now sat down on his son's bed, Shaun joined him. "We're only going to the Lake District, it's a couple of hours drive at most. I'll drive up with Alex and if anything happens to mum I will come straight back. Deal?"

"Okay, you're right. It isn't far. Just go have fun with your mates." Peter said as he got up from the bed and patted Shaun on the shoulder. It was as much affection as he could muster. Shaun went about finishing his packing, knowing that Alex would arrive any minute. He wanted them to be out quickly to beat the rush-hour traffic.

•

"I'll get it," Stasia shouted huskily, as she slowly got up from her chair, not wanting Peter and Shaun to finish their conversation yet. She wanted them to resolve their discussion before her son left for his break away. She knew she had limited time remaining, and wanted to spend it living in a harmonious and loving household.

Slowly she shuffled the few feet to the front door, trying not to show her obvious discomfort. She looked older than her thirty-six years. She was still an impressively beautiful woman; her eyes were a stunning grey, a trait that she had passed on to both of her young daughters, her son, Shaun, had inherited her husband's brown eyes. Her body was suffering from years of chemo and radiotherapy; she was small, almost skeletal at around six or seven stone; her head was wrapped in a bandana after her beautiful locks of hair had fallen out. She was a shell of her former self and just wished her pain would end.

"Hi Alex, come on in," she said with a small smile as she opened the door. Alex loved Stasia as if she were his own mum. She welcomed him into their home and treated him as a second son the first moment he came to play video games with Shaun as a teenager. His heart broke when Shaun told him her cancer was terminal. Having just come into money, he made it clear he would pay for Stasia's care at a private hospital. He wanted to pursue all avenues, but she declined. Her body was fragile, the doctors had warned her more radiotherapy could end her life sooner. It was a risk she didn't want to take. Whenever he visited, afterwards he felt hopeless seeing the bright woman wasting away in front of him.

"Hi Mrs Rodan, how are you today?" he asked, trying to sound cheerful and stifle the break in his voice. She turned slowly and walked back to her chair, seeing her struggle, Alex held her arm and gently walked back with her to the living room.

"Oh you know me, can't complain," she said, with a little chuckle as she gingerly sat back on her padded recliner; bought when she was given her final diagnoses so she could sit downstairs with her children and sooth her aching muscles. A small table next to her was full of different pills, likely pain relievers to help her through the day. The new addition though, was a supply of oxygen. It was recently discovered her lungs were failing due to the cancer spreading even further through her body. The oxygen allowed her to breathe comfortably. When they received that news, though, they were all aware the end was drawing near. They were preparing for a life without her.

"That's good. I'm glad to hear it." Alex didn't know what to say. They sat in silence for a moment. It was Stasia who broke the ice.

"Are you looking forward to your trip?"

"Yes, it'll be nice. We have felt a little… distant since I started playing semi-professional football." Although he and Shaun were close, when he moved out on loan to a club in the North West he had not had the opportunity to see him much. He was looking forward to them reconnecting, if only for a couple of days.

"I know how much Shaun has missed you. It's good that you will have a bit of time to be close again," Stasia responded, with a little smile and a wink. Alex pondered if she knew his true feelings. He had never knowingly shown any love other than that of a friend. Stasia was a very perceptive woman though.

"Hi Mummy," Shaun said, walking into the living room. Alex stood from the sofa and hugged him tight. He was jealous his friend had been blessed with good looks and he wasn't afraid to flaunt it. He wore a skin-tight shirt, showing his pecs and six-pack. Both of which he worked on with daily gym sessions. He had fantasised about touching them frequently. He brought himself back from his trance quickly when Shaun started to speak again. "Me and Alex are going to head out now. Give me a ring if you need me," he said, kissing his mum softly on the cheek. She waved off his concerns.

"It's fine, go have fun, and I'll see you when you're back," she responded, her breathing becoming laboured. Still, she didn't reach for the oxygen bottle, not wanting to show weakness.

"I love you, Mum," Shaun said, as he went to leave. If he were to never see her again, he never wanted to regret his final words to her, that was why Shaun always made a point to tell his mum he loved her. She smiled softly.

"I love you both. Now go and have fun." With that they left the house. Shaun wiped away a tear as he opened the car, loaded his luggage and got in the driver's seat. Alex followed, not knowing what to say.

•

They drove most of the trip to the Lake District in silence. It was common they would struggle to strike up a conversation. Although still close, their respective relationships had driven a wedge that neither knew how to remove. Shaun had made it clear he didn't trust Katie, begging Alex to reconsider his marriage proposal when drunk on the stag do, stating Katie only wanted his money and never loved him. Not wanting to come out with the truth, Alex defended Katie, saying he loved her and that nothing Shaun said would change that. It broke his heart to lie to him, especially when he was right. Their relationship was transactional, Alex would keep Katie in the finest things while she protected his career, there was no love between them.

Shaun was able to put that difference aside and still attend the wedding, but the pain from the drunken conversation was scarred in Alex's heart and he became distant, not wanting Shaun to find out the truth. Things only became more strained when Shaun started dating Jasmine, a beautiful, intelligent and articulate young woman. Although he knew Shaun wasn't gay, Alex couldn't hide his jealousy. He was cold towards Jasmine and it almost destroyed their friendship.

"You okay, Alex, you're quiet?" Shaun asked, as they sat in yet another traffic jam on their way to Coniston Water. He had one hand resting on the steering wheel and his head resting on the other. Normally Alex would worry if his driver didn't have two hands on the wheel, but his friend was a competent driver. He knew he was safe with him.

"Yeah, sorry, mate. Just… thinking about stuff," he said, dwelling on whether this would be the last time they spent together. He didn't want to lose Shaun, but part of him felt it was going to be the inevitable conclusion of this weekend.

"How's Katie and Marshall doing?" Shaun asked, as he clicked the indicator up and slid over into the next lane. He was paying more attention to the road than Alex's answer.

"They're good. I think she's worried about my professional contract. How she will be left alone with Marshall. But she knows it will be best for us." Even Alex didn't sound convinced of his response. Shaun could tell it was a lie, he didn't want to push any further in case his friend clammed up. He just took his hand off the wheel of the car and patted his best mate on the knee.

"It'll be fine, mate, you know it will," he responded, before putting his car in gear and crawling a little forward.

"How's Jasmine?" Alex said. He noticed the slight darkening of Shaun's features, signifying things were not going well. Although Jasmine seemed a perfect match for Shaun, Alex didn't trust her and believed she may have been cheating on him.

"She's fine. She is talking about taking a year out from college and travelling the world. She wants me to go with but… with my mum and everything… I'm not sure I can. We had a pretty big fight about it." Alex nodded his head.

"How is your mum?" Alex asked gently, knowing it was a sore subject for his best friend. For so long they had been given false hope from the specialists that she may recover, but the cancer kept returning. She spent the last three years dealing with surgery, radio and chemotherapy; her body was extremely fragile now. In the last appointment they were given the heartbreaking news the cancer had spread to her vital organs. She didn't have long left.

"She's doing what she always does. Not complaining when she is clearly in pain and staying strong for all of us. Mum is the rock in our family, I don't know what we will do when she is gone. I just wish we had more time with her." Alex wanted to comfort his best friend but couldn't. All words were meaningless, and a hug couldn't happen while driving. Shaun wiped a tear from his eye as they fell into silence again until they reached the Lake District.

•

"Hey Shaun, Alex, it's good to see you both," Justin said, as he hugged them both after they got out of the car. Altogether there would be six of them on their weekend away. A couple wanted to stay in the city and just spend their time clubbing, but the rest thought it would be more memorable if they spent time bonding and having fun in the countryside. Alex wasn't happy with any arrangement. Although he would hang out with the group, he wasn't close to them, and got tired of their ribbing about his marital status and having a child at a young age.

If only they knew the truth.

Alex and Shaun grabbed their bags and followed Justin into the cabin. It was large, with six bedrooms, a bathroom and a joint kitchen/living room. The living room was cosy with an open fire; the sofas were pretty old with floral prints and the kitchen only big enough to have one person in at a time. The counters of the kitchen were full of beer, whisky, vodka, gin, any alcohol you could think of. They were determined the weekend would get messy.

"Look who has arrived, guys," Justin said to the three friends who were engrossed in the TV, they turned around and all said their hellos. Shaun hugged everybody, followed by Alex who felt uncomfortable.

"I guess you got rid of your ball and chain for a bit then." John laughed, as he commented on his wife. Rather than make a fuss, Alex laughed along, knowing another reaction would cause tension. He wanted to get through the weekend without starting any arguments.

"Let me show you both your bedrooms so you can unpack before joining us," Justin said, ushering them out of the living room. They walked upstairs and a little way down the corridor to two rooms away from the others. "I thought you two would want to be together so we left you these two," Justin said with a knowing smile. Alex started a little, did Justin know about his feelings for Shaun or was he being over sensitive? He did everything possible to keep it quiet.

"Cool, thanks, Justin," Shaun replied, not paying attention to the comment. Justin nodded his head and walked away. Alex went into his room to scope out what he could. It was a little small, only big enough for a bed and a bit of cupboard space. Not that he minded because the intention was to be out of the room as much as possible.

"Hey Alex, everything okay?" Shaun had deposited his bag and popped his head back into his room.

"Yeah, sorry Shaun. It's just you know I feel uncomfortable when people make jokes about my marital status." It was a sore point for Alex. The lads thought that he had got married and had a family too young. He was soon to be a professional footballer and it was crazy to be tied down. But it was what Alex wanted so Shaun never pushed the point too much.

"I get that. If ever you don't feel comfortable, just let me know and we can go for a walk. Deal?" Alex brightened up and nodded his head. It allowed him to escape if he needed to, and he knew he would need to. "Come on, let's go see the guys then."

•

They sat by Coniston Water, Alex staring out at the full moon glittering against the calm water; feeling the warm breeze against his cheek and the sensation of it moving through his hair; he wrapped his arms around his knees, holding them close to his chest and resting his chin on them. Shaun lay beside him, propped up on one arm, taking swigs of vodka from the bottle he had swiped from the cabin. They had decided to go for a walk when Alex said he wanted to get a bit of fresh air, leaving the other lads to play poker.

"It's beautiful isn't it?" Shaun said. Alex shifted to look at the stars, appreciating the sight. It hadn't slipped his mind that the setting was romantic. He sighed and rested his cheek on his knees, staring over at Shaun who handed him the bottle of vodka. Alex gratefully received it, taking a swig but instantly regretted it. He wasn't used to drinking it neat, he needed to get courage for what he wanted to do next.

"Shaun, can I ask you something?" Shaun turned over and rested his head on his hand, as he did so the top button of his shirt popped open like it frequently did. For a moment Alex was distracted by the pecs of his friend, imagining running his hands over them.

"Can you promise that, no matter what, we will always be best mates?" Alex said, taking another swig of vodka and trying not to be sick.

"Of course, we'll always be mates. No matter what happens, I care a lot about you," Shaun responded, taking the bottle again and taking another sip of vodka, clearly able to handle his drink a bit better, once he stopped drinking it was at that moment Alex kissed him hard on the lips. He felt Shaun tense as they touched lips. "What the fuck?" he stammered, as Alex moved away. He lightly touched Shaun on his face and looked deep into his haunting eyes.

He didn't want the moment to end, but feared Shaun would get up and leave. Alex was pleasantly surprised when he didn't.

"I've just wanted to do it for so long, Shaun. I'm sorry," Alex said, looking away, out to Coniston Water. For a moment he thought Shaun was going to walk away, but his next action surprised him.

"Alex… look at me," Shaun whispered, as he held his friends chin. He looked deep into his eyes, and wasn't sure if it was the alcohol talking or him. "Don't apologise. This might be the alcohol, but I'm willing to give it a try if you are," Shaun said, as he kissed his friend deeply on the mouth. He discarded the bottle and let it pour over the grass, no longer caring about it. Alex didn't care if it was drunk sex, he was finally getting the man that he wanted for a long time. It was all he cared about.

•

Shaun awoke the next morning in a drunken haze. As he lay in bed, enjoying the warmth of the large blanket, his mind slowly adjusted to his surroundings. The firm bed, the scratchy but comfortable blanket surrounding his body, the warmth of Jasmine lying next to him after a wonderful night. As he tried to pull the warm body closer he noticed a sudden voice almost shouting from the fog. Confusion turned to realisation.

Jasmine wasn't next to him, it was Alex.

"No, no. Oh God, no. This can't be happening." Alex jumped up sharply from the bed and found a towel on the floor to pull around his waist. Shaun stayed there watching Alex pace around the room, looking for his clothing. It was at that moment everything came back to him. Their walk to Coniston Water, the alcohol, their first kiss, Alex's touch and muscled body. He sighed and rubbed his eyes, wondering how he would tell Jasmine. Alex's voice snapped him back to reality. "Oh my God, what have we done?" The distress was evident in Alex's voice as he found a T-Shirt and pulled it over his head. Shaun sat up, struggling under his hangover.

"Alex... stop." Was all he could say. Alex wouldn't listen though, he continued to search through the room for the remainder of his clothes.

"Why should I stop? I've made a terrible mistake, I'm not gay," he said as he picked up his trousers and begun to turn them the right way.

"We both know that is absolute bullshit," Shaun responded with a malice he didn't intend. It stopped Alex in his tracks. He almost dropped the trousers and finally faced his friend, fear and anguish in his eyes.

"What are you talking about?" He didn't remember much of their conversation the previous night, too busy savouring their actions over words. Shaun rolled his eyes and shifted to the side of the bed, the blanket covering his legs.

"You told me you were gay. You told me you'd had feelings for me since we were teenagers." He stopped when Alex sat down next to him, head in hands as he realised how much of his secret he had spilt. "What hurt the most was when you told me your marriage to Katie is a sham, a way to show the world you are straight. Do you know how much guilt I carried with me after I said Katie didn't love you? Why didn't you tell me the truth?" It was hard not to feel anger, he believed Alex would cut him out of his life and did so much to win his friends approval back. He vowed never to hurt him in such a way again.

"I wanted to tell you. Jesus, Shaun, you don't understand how hard it is to hide this." Seeing his friend in distress Shaun shuffled over and put his arms around him, pulling him in to an awkward side hug. "The only people who know are my stepsisters, my agent and Katie. Hell, my mum and Mal don't even know. I don't know how to tell them." Slowly Shaun stroked his friend's shoulder to sooth him, he leant down and kissed him tenderly on the head. "I wanted to tell you, Shaun. I don't want to be hiding who I am."

"Don't hide then."

"How can I go into my first contract as the only openly gay professional male footballer in England? Spending the entire time fending off abusive comments from 'fans' on social media and listening to their homophobic chants? It would be tough if I was an established player, let alone one at the start of his career." Shaun noticed the distress in Alex's voice. He held him tighter, wanting to comfort him. "I'm sorry, I was drunk last night and stopped caring. I wanted to be with you, and now I'm terrified I've messed up our friendship." He could feel the tears forming in his eyes, Shaun pulled away, grabbed his chin and tilted his head up.

"Alex, nothing will ever mess up our friendship. You're my best friend and I love you for that. I just wish you didn't have to hide who you truly are," Shaun said, before he kissed Alex again. He knew he wasn't gay. But the feeling of being with Alex was like nothing he had experienced before. It felt right being so close, and he wanted to cherish the moment before they had to go their separate ways.

•

They were so consumed with each other that they didn't hear their friend John get out of bed. Being a light sleeper, he rarely made it through the night and would awaken at the slightest noise. When Alex and Shaun came back he found it strange they went into the same bedroom, but wasn't shocked, assuming they just wanted to hang out and drink more. That was until he heard their moans, and it became obvious what they were doing. When he heard them talking in the morning, he decided to find out what was happening.

Silently he crept to Alex's door, hoping to hear their conversation. Instead, he was greeted by their moaning again. He stood close to the door with his ear lightly touching, listening to the squeak of the bed and Alex's soft groans. There was something about Alex that bothered him. Until Katie, he'd showed no interest in women, in fact he refused to even date. Then, suddenly, he was with Katie and less than a year later married with a child. Hearing Shaun and Alex together, it was clear his lack of interest in women was due to his sexuality. He must be gay.

John smirked to himself. With Alex signing a professional contract he wouldn't want his little secret getting out. John knew he had a nice little cash cow if he used the knowledge to his advantage.

TWENTY-THREE

PRESENT DAY

The emergence of smart phones gave the public the opportunity to get news at the touch of a button. We lived in an information age that fed off mass fear and the results could be terrifying. In a bid to inform people of the serious crimes that took place, the media corporations banded together to trial a daily 'serious crime tally' on their platforms. What they didn't count on was the devastating impact the trial would have on the mental health of the nation. Increasingly, I was hearing of more people refusing to leave their home due to concerns that they may be physically assaulted, raped or even murdered. The media refused to take responsibility, claiming they were raising awareness of the terrible crimes in the country, but when the risk of being a victim was approximately 2% it caused unnecessary anxiety to many.

It was no surprise to me when I woke up with 50+ notifications on my phone, at least half related to one breaking news story. Deciding it was better to wake up fully before taking in any information, I got up from my soft bed and went into my kitchen and made myself a coffee.

I sat down on the table, cradling my cup it in one of my hands as I flicked through the notifications. Some were just scaremongering tactics, talking about a possible new virus that was supposed to be more deadly than the Covid-19 outbreak in 2020, with others being pointless gossip. It was only when Alex Smith's name popped up did my interest peak again.

> *England International gay sex romps on weekend away as a teenager – An exclusive interview with John Young, a childhood friend of Alex Smith.*

I stared at the phone in shock as I read through the article – written by Bryony. My heart sank. Not only was Alex suffering immeasurable heartbreak due to his boyfriend being murdered, he was now being outed to the world via the media. It was selfish, damaging to Alex's reputation and designed to raise sales. One that could cost a life as it had done in the past.

As I read through, one sentence made me pause, it was about how the man he was with was 'believed to be a prominent academic'. There was only one person it could be referring to, Shaun, the only man who went to university and decided to pursue a career as a professor. The awkwardness of their return that weekend made sense now. Upon arriving back from their bonding session, the air between them was different. Gone was the loving and expressive friendship they shared, their hugs were awkward, their goodbyes fraught. It was as if something had transpired between them during the trip, they didn't want others to know about. Not long after Shaun's relationship with Jasmine collapsed, he claimed they just drifted apart but none of their family were convinced. This article was the final piece of that puzzle.

So engrossed in the article I didn't notice Michael get up, only realising he was with me when he circled his warm arms around my waist. I had spent so long pushing people away I forgot how much I enjoyed human touch. Having somebody to wake up to each morning, and to hold me tightly when I was at my most vulnerable, was a blessing. I wished it wouldn't end.

"What are you reading?" Michael asked, noticing I was

focused on the article. I didn't respond and handed him my phone once I had finished reading. The article portrayed Alex as a violent man who attacked a school friend when he confronted him about cheating on Katie when away. I remembered the man who had gone to the press, John Young, he was a habitual liar who was known to stretch the truth as a teenager. Although I believed his story to an extent, I didn't believe Alex physically attacked him to keep his silence.

The phone was ringing, and Michael's increasing grip on my waist, brought me back to reality and out of my thoughts. Michael handed my phone back, I answered without checking the caller ID.

"Sammi, it's Paul." The voice on the other end of the phone said hurriedly, I was shocked at hearing his voice as I knew Jackson would have made it clear I was persona non-grata. "I don't have much time. McCarthy is on the warpath. But if you haven't done so already turn on your TV, Alex is going to give a press conference," Paul stated and rang off. I was puzzled at why he decided to ring me, but was too exhausted to worry about it. Instead, I put my phone on the table lightly, walked to the TV and turned it on.

"What the hell is going on?" Michael asked as he followed me. The slight anger in his voice startled me a little, I looked at him briefly, seeing his hands curling into a fist. I didn't believe it was deliberate, just an unconscious reaction of a man who was worried about his friend and teammate.

"Alex is giving a press conference to respond to the article. He's confirming the story, and that he is gay." Michael looked shocked. Although it explicitly mentioned Alex had sex with another man in the article it seemed that Michael had come to the conclusion that that was a one-off. "What was written in the paper, it wasn't a one-night stand. Alex had been hiding his sexuality since his teens. He was in a relationship with the murder victim, the man he pushed, from the CCTV. The article you have just read has forced his hand; he's deciding to come out." I could see Michael attempting to process the information.

173

I was glad I could be open with him about it, but angry at the way he had found out. I hoped this came back to haunt Bryony.

"Poor Alex," he said, before we descended into silence. Waiting for the press conference with bated breath.

•

"Don't do this Alex," the agent said as he sucked on his cigar. Alex ignored him; he was done with his advice. He had hidden for too long and wanted to be free. Now that Joseph was gone, nothing else mattered. He had lost the man he loved. He wanted the world to know the truth, and that he was no longer scared of the reaction to his sexuality. He wanted to be liberated. "We can control the narrative. Say what John heard was a one-night stand? You guys were both just drunk and fooling around. It's no different to you having cheated on Katie with a woman."

"Yeah Alex, come on. It happened thirteen years ago, we can still pass this off as a one-off. It's crazy to throw your career away over this. Think of how this is going to hurt your kids, how it's going to hurt me!" Katie chimed in as she stood beside the agent. It was all she cared about, his career and the money that came with it. Nothing else mattered to her, not even their two children. All she wanted was the money and the fame of being a WAG.

"And what happens if they decide to dig a little further after we lie, and find out I have been using the services of Marcos Vincenzo to hire male escorts? What happens when they find out I was in a relationship with Joseph, it won't be long before they connect the dots and call me a murderer.

"No, I'm done with this. I can't continue to live this lie. It was fine when I was the only one getting hurt, but now Joseph is dead and I have been outed to the world by a man who heard me having sex and has accused me of reacting violently when he threatened to tell the press. It was my truth to tell when I felt ready, but he denied me that opportunity. The world needs to know my side of the story." Alex didn't cry, even though he wanted to. He felt his world collapse around him and the only way to get out was to regain some control of the situation. Having this press release was a way to do this.

"Alex…" The agent was going to reason with him again, but this time Alex cut him off with a look. He had made his decision, there was no more debating it. He had no interest in pleasing Katie and his agent anymore. It was over.

He walked out to face the scrum of the media, who had been let into his driveway for the press conference, his agent and wife silently by his side to support him. They weren't the support network he wanted though. There was another person he wished was with him, his half-sister, and solicitor, Kerrilyn. They had spoken in length on the phone about his press conference, carving out a statement that wouldn't harm any future court case against Bryony and the *Daily Scoop*. Sadly she was speaking at a conference and was unable to drop her commitment at such late notice.

An eerie silence descended over the crowd when Alex stood on the steps. For a moment he scanned the people ahead, stunned at the number of journalists who had turned up. When he started to speak he had never had such a captivated audience.

"Welcome all. This morning an article was released about me in the *Daily Scoop*, written by somebody here today. It portrays me as a vicious man who attacked a childhood friend to ensure that he didn't tell about my secret of being gay. Had Ms Penn-Seaman checked out the details, she would have found the man in question has a lengthy criminal record for blackmail and assault. He has been involved in a campaign of harassment against us and has been issued with a restraining order and an injunction." Alex paused for a moment before continuing with his statement.

"However, refuting this allegation is not the purpose of this press conference. It is to finally speak a truth I have been hiding my whole career. On the night in question, John Young did in fact hear me with another man. I am gay.

"My partner and I have been in a marriage of convenience since we were teenagers. Katie is able to continue her sexual relations outside of our marriage, as am I. Our marriage has never been consummated and our children were conceived using IVF, documentation of which can be provided." The crowd were in a stunned silence. He stared down at Bryony who was shifting uncomfortably. She had been so excited about the story of a lifetime, about Alex's alleged pattern of abuse, that she forgot to do the due diligence on her sources. She knew she no longer had credibility. She felt tears in her eyes when she heard Alex take another breath to speak again, he wasn't done.

"This is a gross invasion of my right to a personal life and I will not be taking this lightly. I am announcing, after liaising with my solicitor, Ms. Kerrilyn Marshall, that I intend to sue the *Daily Scoop* and the author of the article, Bryony Penn-Seaman, for damages to my reputation and invading my personal life. Any money received will not be kept by me, but will go to a charity to support the LGBTQIA+ community.

"It's now time for me to turn my focus to the game this afternoon. I will not be taking any questions."

With that Alex walked back into his home, ignoring the cries of the needy press wanting to hear more information. He had said his piece, and it was all he would say on the matter. Further action was now up to those around him – his legal team to take official action against the paper, and his friends and family to show their support for him. If this happened, he knew he would get through this. He was relieved to finally come out.

•

"How long have you known?" Michael asked me when the conference finished.

"Not long, only after I interviewed him for the attack on Joseph. He broke down, when we spoke to him a second time, he told us the truth. He had been in a relationship with the murder victim, he was heartbroken." The camera had gone to a reporter outside of the media scrum, she was placed at the end of the road, close enough to see Alex's property but not close enough to be interfering with their colleagues. The byline was leading on his sexuality. I zoned the soft tones of the female reporter out, too engrossed in the car in the background. Just before she wrapped up the report I paused the TV.

"What's wrong?" Michael asked, as I stared at the car. I tried to see the number plate but to no avail, it was too far from the camera.

"The car in the background. I have seen it before," I said, frustration in my voice. I attempted to rewind the footage but to no avail, the car must have arrived before I turned the channel on. I decided to phone Paul to see if he could help. I wasn't sure why but I felt I could trust him, and that he wouldn't inform Jackson of my meddling. Unless he was trying to gain my trust to trick me and take my job. I had to believe this wasn't the case though.

"Hey Paul, I have a favour to ask," I said, as he answered. Michael quietly mouthed he was leaving for training and gave him a thumbs up, he kissed me lightly on the cheek before going to my bedroom and getting changed, allowing me to focus on my call.

"Shoot, honestly I want to help you out. I have some concerns about McCarthy," he responded quietly. If he was in the office, it would be dangerous speaking about him in such a way. I hoped he would be intelligent enough to ensure neither Jackson nor McCarthy were in earshot.

"The press release, did you see the car in the background? I know I have seen it before but I can't place who owns it. Could you run the number plate?" He didn't speak, not even to confirm he was willing to do what I asked. I took his silence as confirmation, though, and that he was focused on finding a good shot of the number plate.

"Marcos Vincenzo, the car belongs to Marcos." For a moment I remained confused. Marcos had a large underground car park in his home, one I had not entered. In all my visits I had not seen the car in his possession. "Maybe you saw it at his home?" Paul said, almost as if reading my mind. I was silent for what seemed like minutes, but could have only been a few seconds. It was at that moment it hit me.

"The CCTV," I muttered quietly. Walking to my desk and powering up my laptop. I searched for the article on Alex's 'attack' on Joseph, hoping that it hadn't been taken down yet. My luck was in, I quickly hit play. "In the background, there's a car, you can't see the number plate but it is the same car."

"You're right, I believe it's the same car to," Paul agreed, clearly searching through the CCTV on his side also. I felt vindicated. If we could prove the car in the CCTV was the same as the one outside Alex's home, we could prove Marcos lied to us. He did know Joseph's whereabouts that evening. I still had questions about why he was outside of Alex's home during the press conference, but that wasn't important now.

"Leave it with me and I'll see what I can find out, Samantha. I may not get back to you today, but I promise I will look into it," Paul assured me. I wanted to argue back, tell him that, as I found the link, I should continue to dig. I stopped myself though, knowing that it was a selfish way to think. My involvement could do more harm to the investigation. I had to trust Paul and his intentions.

"Okay Paul, let me know if there is anything I can do to help," I replied. We said our goodbyes and I ended the call. A moment later Michael came back, dressed in his football training gear.

"I have to go, Sammi," he said regretfully. I jumped up and kissed him hard.

"I will see you later. Come back later," I whispered softly against his lips. He kissed me lightly and then nodded his head. Things were moving fast. We had only known each other a few days and I knew I wanted him in my life. I had concerns that I was being too clingy, we hadn't even discussed our relationship dynamic yet. I kissed him once more and let him go. Once he shut the door I went and made myself another drink.

•

After their conversation, Paul sat staring at his computer for a few more minutes. The quality of the camera wouldn't be enough to prove it was Marcos' car in both locations, nor to pursue a different angle other than Alex. Sighing, he put that thought to one side for a moment. While important, it wasn't his priority for the moment. He looked around the office, confident he was alone he got up from his desk, ensuring everything was shut down, and made his way to the evidence room.

•

The evidence room was located in the basement of the police building behind two large security doors. It was the job of the officer on duty behind the desk to enable access for all staff. On receipt of a pin code on the main door, the computer by the desk officer would send out an alert. They would then check the camera, making sure the person submitting the code matched the picture on file. The second door would be a similar prompt, but this time with a voice command and separate password. It was implemented after a series of robberies whereby key pieces of evidence went missing, resulting in some powerful criminals going free. The security protocols were designed to do two things. The first, to prevent another robbery by an unknown person and the second, if evidence did go missing, there would be a log of the last officer who was in possession of it.

Paul went through the various steps to gain access, impatient at the slow work of the officer on duty. When he was finally cleared, he entered a small room, no larger than the width of a large car. Ahead of him stood an elderly officer behind bullet proof glass. Close to retirement age, it was likely he was assigned to desk duty to tide him over until it was time to leave. Behind him was a reinforced steel, locked door that led to a small warehouse, where evidence for current crimes being investigated was held. The evidence for closed cases going back at least ten years was held in a large facility north of Burnley.

"Good morning, Detective Grant, how may I assist you?" he asked with a thick Mancunian accent.

"I need to log out some evidence from the Joseph Marsden

case," Paul responded, he could see a flicker of doubt in the officers eyes as he did. Opening his folder, he handed over the relevant request form in a bid to show he followed procedure. "I am one of the investigating officers." He also held out his badge. "You will be able to see from my ID and computer. I also have an evidence sign-out request form filled out."

"Sorry sir, but I can't sign out anything regarding this case without verbal confirmation from DCI Jackson," he responded without glancing at the form. This was an unusual practice. Any evidence relating to a criminal investigation could be signed out by any investigating officer, as long as they had filled out the relevant paperwork. Jackson overruling this suggested he had suspicious motives.

"Of course, I understand. May I borrow your phone for a second?" The officer obliged, handing him the phone. He would have used his mobile but due to the fortified nature of the basement it was impossible to get signal. He dialled the number he wanted and waited for a few moments. It was only a few seconds before the person answered.

"Good morning, Chief. I have hit an unexpected roadblock regarding the Marsden case. I need your verbal consent to log out some evidence." Paul listened for a moment as the man on the other end of the phone spoke. Less than a minute later he handed the phone to the desk officer, who gratefully received it, expecting to hear the voice of DCI Jackson. The shock on his face when he realised it wasn't him delighted Paul.

He stood in stunned silence as the man on the other side of the phone continued to speak. Paul could hear his measured, but angry, voice as he stood on the other side of the desk. He tried not to smile, he had been on the end of the chief's anger before and had delighted in seeing others suffer it. After a couple of minutes, the officer responded.

"I'm sorry, sir. I was unaware of the importance. I will help Detective Grant in anyway I can. Thank you, sir." He put the phone down and turned his attention to Paul again, looking a little sheepish as he did so. "What were you after, sir?" he asked.

"Yesterday a laptop and phone were brought in. These were initially received by myself and DS Rodan but, after her suspension, DCI Jackson agreed to bring them down." The desk officer shook his head, Paul didn't have a good feeling about it.

"Sorry sir, I haven't logged any evidence relating to the Marsden case since the day of the murder. Even then the only personnel who logged evidence in was forensics. DCI Jackson hasn't been in the evidence room for several months." It was not the news Paul wanted to hear. He asked Jackson about taking ownership of the laptop and he declined. Saying that he was happy to bring it down himself. Clearly that was never his intention, and why he made the decision that all evidence sign-outs required his approval.

"Thank you. Can I ask a favour?" The officer nodded his head. "Could you not inform Jackson of my visit? It's important this remains between us." The officer acknowledged he wouldn't. Paul turned on his heels and made his way to the door, knowing what he now had to do.

TWENTY-FOUR

Michael left for before match training as I kept searching through my laptop, cup of coffee in hand to enable my brain to stay focused on my screen. Wanting to grasp the reaction to Alex's announcement, I logged into my social media accounts and searched for his name, unsurprisingly it was the number one trend in the UK. Due to the rise in discriminatory language at football matches, and the increase in banning orders, I was cynical. I was happy to see reaction was mixed, with plenty in favour of Alex, but also sad to see some truly homophobic statements.

'Can't believe Alex came out as gay. I thought he was a bit of a mincer cunt.'

'Fucking faggot. How dare he destroys our proud club? I hope they sack him.'

'Well done Alex for coming out, but is it really our business if he likes men or women? As long as he can put on the shirt and perform for the club, that's all that matters.'

'WTF? How is that hot-arse gay? Man, I was hoping he'd leave his wife and fall in love with me.'

'Who the hell is Alex Smith and why the hell should I care if he is gay? He's just some overpaid footballer. Why is he top story when there are real issues in the world, like the fact we are all suffocating due to carbon emissions.'

'If Alex Smith had been fucking women for the past 12 years while married we would be slaughtering him, so why are people proud of his announcement that he is gay? He's still an adulterous scumbag in my mind.'

'What a proud day for football. Finally a professional at the highest level who had the courage to come out and be himself. I hope others are brave enough to follow this man's lead.'

'I hope the fans absolutely rip Alex Smith a new one in the game. Fucking HIV riddled cunt.'

'Hahaha, gay boy loves taking cock up his arse. Should be playin' 4 Brighton, fit right in.'

'Who cares if Alex is gay or not? He is still a phenomenal player who always gives his all for club and country. We should be celebrating the man, not making jokes.'

'I can't wait for the day when somebodies sexuality isn't news. It's sad that people's worth is still based on who they want to be with. I hope Alex can find some peace with his decision to come out.'

Professor Shaun Rodan – 'Alex, M8, I am so proud of you for finally being yourself. You deserve all the health and happiness in the world. I love you man.'

Katie Smith – 'As you will be aware, my husband Alex Smith made an announcement regarding his sexuality today. Coming on to here I have noticed many people express sympathies at my husband being a cheater.'

Please be aware, I am not a victim. I was aware of my place in our relationship when we first got married. I am happy that Alex has found the courage to come out and look forward to continuing our friendship for the sake of our children.'

Kerrilyn Marshall – 'All, as you are aware Alex Smith made an announcement today. If you are interested in reading the transcript please look at the below link. We are currently in the process of how we go about taking legal action against both the Daily Scoop and Bryony Penn-Seaman.'

Secondly – 'Alex, my brother, what you did today is incredible. You are a brave and wonderful man. I hope the rest of your life is filled with so much happiness. Your family are so proud of you for finally being true to who you are. We will get through this together. We all love you.'

Daily Scoop – 'As a result of this morning's press conference we have removed the Alex Smith story from our website. We will be launching an internal investigation into its publication.'

I was horrified at the abuse Shaun was receiving for supporting Alex in his time of need. Questions about his own sexuality and whether he was the man they were referring to in the article. He put his account on private and refused to interact anymore on the subject. I was, however, heartened to see others supporting him.

I considered logging in to my account to make my thoughts known, but decided to hold back as the case was still ongoing. Anything from me could put a future trial in jeopardy. Officer social media accounts were routinely scrutinised, and occasional censored. Saying anything now could push me out of my job for good, I didn't want to lose it on a technicality.

I was surprised to see Paul ringing me again. After out earlier conversation I didn't feel we had much more to discuss. Perplexed I answered to hear a slightly panicked Paul on the other end with news I didn't want to hear.

"You need to know this," he said, without saying hello.

"Where are you?" I asked, cutting him off before he was able to continue his sentence.

"I'm in my car, look… Samantha, you need to hear this," he repeated, frustrated that I had cut him off the first time. I let him continue without further interruptions. "McCarthy and Jackson are seeking a warrant to look into the financial details of Alex, they want to see if he was being blackmailed by Joseph. After that their intention is to arrest him for murder. They are confident the evidence points to his guilt." It was news I didn't want to hear.

While it didn't look good for Alex, it was all too neat for me. There was too much circumstantial evidence for me, and I hoped it would be for the CPS to.

It depended on how Jackson and McCarthy framed it.

"We need to move quickly, Sammi," Paul finished, bringing me out of a trance-like state.

"Why are you telling me this?" Confused at what was happening and how I could move in the situation. I was suspended with limited resources; I couldn't help anybody in this scenario.

"I can't tell you the full story, not yet. What I can say is that I don't believe Alex is being treated fairly and it may be due to outside influences." That stopped me for a moment. Outside influences? The terminology was vague but made me only think of one thing. Corruption. Did Paul believe that Jackson was being paid to strengthen the case against Alex. If so, only one person would gain from such a scenario.

Marcos Vincenzo.

"How can I help though? I have no access to resources and if I become involved in the case it could harm any future court case," I asked, pushing all thoughts of possible corruption out of my head for the moment. It was important to focus on one aspect at a time, and right now Alex and this case was a priority.

"I've asked Charlotte to request CCTV footage from all the clubs and buildings around where Joseph was pushed. If he was indeed there, as you claimed to have seen, then we need to see if it was Marcos who was there and not one of his chauffeurs. She will bring it around to you this afternoon. I will speak to my superiors about your involvement in the case." After my suspension the previous evening, I had been close to giving up. Believing I had failed Alex and those around me. Paul's conversation renewed my energy and gave me hope that we could still find the true culprit of this crime.

Whether it was Alex or not.

•

Michael left the stadium gym a little early to soak up the atmosphere in the stadium. He stood on the turf, cool breeze running through his hair as he imagined the sound of the crowd behind the team. Cheering as Alex scored yet another goal to push them closer to another title. He was a legend in these parts and hoped the announcement this morning wouldn't change that fact. As the chill increased, he pulled his jumper around his neck and headed back inside.

The dressing room was silent, the rest of the team would just be completing their workout. Pulling off his training jacket he started his cool down stretches, reflecting on everything that had happened this past week. Meeting Samantha, believing he would never see her again after their night together, then finding out she was investigating Alex for the push on Joseph, it was as if fate had forced them together. He knew he couldn't ignore a sign like that, and hoped Samantha felt the same.

Not long after he started stretching, Tanja and Fernandes walked in, nodding in his direction before continuing their conversation. They tried to keep their voices low but Michael could hear them mention Alex and his 'situation.' He stopped himself from saying something in anger. It was a sad way to refer to what had happened, a situation, it sounded like a problem that needed to be controlled so the club could come out with their reputation intact. They seemed uninterested that it was a man's life, and he would be struggling with his decision. He needed his team more than ever, because the fans could be unforgiving.

"I've always known there was something wrong with Alex, never seen him take an interest in other women. I mean, he married so young it was never going to last." As they left Wesley and Justin walked in. Wesley ignored Michael and walked to his locker, putting the combination in as he continued his conversation with Justin. "When that faggot came up to us a few days ago, I thought Alex recognise him. Now he tells the world he was screwing him, amazing how these queers can hide in plain sight." Wesley looked over to Michael as he said it, knowing it would set him off. Moments later he had Wesley up against a locker off the ground.

"How can you say that about your teammate? The man who has won us multiple championships and a champions league? We would be complete unknowns if it wasn't for him," Michael snarled, as the man tried to squirm away from his grip. Wesley's eyes were fear mixed with anger.

"I don't care who the fuck he is. He's a fucking queer. He's shared our dressing room for years and didn't bother to tell us. I hope he rots in hell," Wesley stated. Michael had never seen this side of him. He knew Wesley was a devout Christian, but his religious beliefs didn't excuse the homophobia.

"Guys, that's enough. Michael put him down," Tanja shouted, as she walked into the room. Michael took a while to comply.

"You crazy mother…" Wesley started.

"Enough!" Tanja shouted. Silence descended on the room, teammates fighting would harm moral and she didn't want this incident getting out in the media. Especially as their fight related to Alex.

"Look, I know the announcement was a shock. But we have to put on a united front. Some of you may not accept his sexuality, but he is still your teammate. This isn't about supporting his sexuality, but supporting him through this tough time," Tanja continued. Wesley stared at the ground, angry that he had been admonished.

"Sorry Tanja," they both responded meekly. Michael put his hand out to Wesley, but his teammate ignored him and walked off. Not wanting to show he was willing to forgive so easily.

"Michael, look I get he was slagging off Alex, but you can't do that to a teammate. We will take action against Wesley for his comments, but you know our policy on fighting. I will be speaking to Fernandes about the both of you, so expect a fine in your wages." Michael nodded his head and walked away; he had no interest in talking to Tanja about it any longer. He needed to get away and clear his head.

•

"Paul, where have you been?" McCarthy asked as Paul walked back into the room. He wasn't about to tell McCarthy the truth, that he was actively persuading Samantha to pursue the case.

"Just needed some fresh air. Know we have a long day ahead," he answered, staring down his colleague. It was clear that McCarthy didn't believe him, however, he decided to let it pass. Officers were allowed personal moments and he wasn't going to stop Paul from being secretive about his whereabouts, as long as his mind was still on the job.

"Yes, fine. I need you to do something," McCarthy began. He stood next to Paul, who had been moved to Samantha's vacant desk for the remainder of the case. "We should be able to get a warrant to look into Alex's financials soon. We need you to lead on this with the bank to see if any large sums of money have been paid out." It was all he said before walking away, he knew the evidence would be manipulated to suit their narrative regardless of the reason for large payments.

If he didn't do something soon, Alex would be in danger.

•

The smallest of suitcases had been placed by the front door, with a second luggage bag resting on top. Bryony took a peek in the top bag to find her essential toiletries and make-up. She knew what it signified and wasn't in the frame of mind to cope with it right now. The shock of the press conference was tough, and she just wanted to come home to a supportive family.

Putting her bag and keys down she walked into the living room to find Lewis in silence. He didn't turn to acknowledge his wife had come in, and just continued to stare at the opposite wall. Bryony was the one to finally break the silence.

"Where are the children?" she asked, quieter than intended. In all their years of marriage she had never seen her other half like this. They had rows, some of which became screaming matches, but the silence concerned her the most. She was terrified of how he was going to react to her presence.

"My parents. I've packed your bags for you," he stated, still refusing to look at her. She wasn't sure how to continue the conversation. She had mixed emotions. Angry that her husband could be so insensitive to her plight, and afraid at how this could be the end for her career and marriage. The second emotion won though, and she burst into tears. "What?" he asked, his voice uncaring.

"You're going to kick your pregnant wife out of the house. What kind of man are you?" she asked, not meaning for it to sound as harsh as it did. Her chest heaved from the sobs, she sat to try and calm her breathing down. Lewis finally looked her in the eye, angry at her reaction.

"Firstly, Bryony, I am not chucking you out of the house. I have rung your mum and explained you will be visiting for a while. I don't think I am in the right frame of mind to support you right now," he replied, a fury in his eyes that she had never seen before. "Secondly, I don't want your poison around our children." She went to speak but he cut her off. "When have you thought about anybody but yourself? Hmm? Answer me that? Your whole life it has been around the story, and nobody has wound your neck in.

"Now you are being sued and, sweetie, it was only a matter of time. You've lost your family, and it's possible you could lose your career. That's why I want you gone, so you can realise the severity of your actions." Lewis finished his piece and went back to ignoring his wife. Bryony tried to form a response but couldn't find the words. She was frustrated, losing everything was not an option, but she knew it was her own fault if it happened.

As she stood, she turned to say something, but decided against it. There was no point in arguing now. She was feeling too weak. Instead, she walked out, picked up her bags and left the family home. She sat in the car for a few moments to compose herself, and then drove away, wanting to get as far away as possible.

•

When Alex arrived at the stadium, he was called into the office to chat with Tanja and Fernandes. He knew that the conversation wouldn't be good and he was unlikely to keep his emotions in check. He sat opposite Tanja, who looked sympathetic to his plight, and had some idea of what he was going through. As a bisexual woman, she was no stranger to hiding her identity for her career. It was only once she retired that she come out as having been in a long-term relationship with a woman. Fernandes also tried to elicit sympathy, but he knew it was just for show. All he cared about was whether the team would come from this situation with as little embarrassment as possible.

"Please understand, Alex, we are behind you all the way," Fernandes begun. Alex stared back at his boss, not wanting to say anything. Of course, this was all for show. If he was charged with murder, he knew they would be the first to throw him under the bus. "We just wanted to check on how you are doing right now?" He wanted to be left alone to focus on the game, and try to forget about the negative energy around him.

"It's not everyday I have to stand in front of the press and tell them intimate details about my private life. I guess I will live." It was a cold response. Tanja nodded her head and bowed it a little. Fernandes remained quiet, wondering how to broach the next part without making matters worse.

"I understand." Fernandes remained calm and impassive. He knew what was going to be said next would hurt Alex and he needed to tread carefully. "When we last spoke, we discussed you taking a step back. Tanja and I believe that this may be the right time for this to happen. We are concerned there would be negative press if you played and are concerned about the abuse you may receive." The final part of the sentence seemed tagged on, to make it seem like he wasn't being homophobic or discriminatory. Ultimately though, all he cared about was the reputation of the team, not Alex's well-being.

"Surely the team will receive far more positive press if you were to stand by me throughout? Especially when you have no reason to drop me." He went to continue but Fernandes cut him off.

"There is the question of the assault, and the murder." Fernandes was confrontational. For a moment Alex remained stunned, he cleared his throat to continue his point.

"An assault I haven't been questioned for under caution, let alone charged for. No, Fernandes, you can't use that excuse. This is about my sexuality, and the fact I was outed. You wouldn't drop a player for their skin colour, so why should my sexuality be an issue? Any negative press about it frankly isn't worth our time. If you play me, it will look good for the club, standing behind the only openly gay male footballer and supporting him. No matter the difficult circumstances." Although his words were calm, Alex didn't feel it. Tanja nodded her head in agreement; she knew what it was like to suffer discrimination as a female footballer in the men's game and he doubted it was her view Alex take a step back. Maybe for his own well-being, but playing would give him the chance to put everything behind him and he'd have the solidarity of his team.

"Okay Alex, but this is your decision. If things go wrong, you will take full responsibility." With Fernandes words, Alex stood and walked out of the door. He had little interest in discussing this further, just wanting to get on with the job and forget everything that had happened.

He knew he had little change of this happening.

TWENTY-FIVE

The ringing of my doorbell brought me out of a trance. Since the announcement I'd been searching through social media and newspaper articles, wanting to get an idea of the reaction to Alex's announcement, it was mixed as expected. I quickly turned my attention to the security app on my laptop, opening the communal doorbell. A young woman stood outside, large glasses and a hat covering her face. For a few seconds I stared as she pensively kept an eye on her surroundings. After a moment I realised who it was.

"I'm buzzing you up, Charlotte," I said, holding the talk and then open function. She nodded her head and made her way into the block.

I went to the door and waited, a few moments later she arrived. The glasses were now looped around her black shirt, but the hat remained. Her long, blonde hair pulled through the strap in the back. She smiled sweetly as I pulled her in for a warm embrace. After the last couple of days it was nice to see a friendly face. She didn't say much, instead just handed me a small make-up bag, I assumed full of USB drives.

"Paul asked me to come and give you these. There is about sixty hours of footage. Please be careful." I nodded my head, she gave me a second quick hug and then left swiftly, putting her sunglasses back on as she did. It was clear the case was putting everybody on edge.

I poured myself a glass of water, inserted the first USB and fast forwarded through. Occasionally pausing when something interesting popped on screen. There were some weird yet depressing moments, including a young woman giving a man a blow job around the back of a club; an evidently high man on the street dancing with no clothing on, bouncers just watching and laughing. There was nothing of interest to the case though.

It wasn't until into the fifth hour of the tapes, and my first hour of watching, I had a breakthrough. Alex and Joseph popped up on the screen, the way Joseph cracked his face as he fell onto the kerb was more distressing from this angle. He was lucky he didn't smash his temple against the kerb, death would likely have been instantaneous. My heart broke, the last memory of his boyfriend was one of fear. At least he was in peace now.

When Joseph ran off screen, my interest peaked. Moments later a figure emerged from the bottom, back to the camera, a trail of wispy smoke following above his head from a cigarette he then discarded next to the group of men who were going in the opposite direction to Joseph. A couple of seconds later, he was out of range of the camera. His physical form matched Marcos', however, with no facial verification it could have been anybody. I fast forwarded to see if they came back towards the screen, but with no luck I abandoned the USB and inserted another.

It didn't take long for me to find another angle of both Joseph and the mystery man. Joseph came into view, running from the right of the screen. He stopped suddenly, a couple of seconds later the second man appeared. I was able to confirm it was Marcos, he lied to me about his whereabouts on the night of Joseph's murder. We now had reason to pursue somebody other than Alex.

Joseph spoke animatedly for a couple of minutes, he winced in pain when doing so. After a while Marcos led Joseph off to the left. I retrieved another USB and put it in, in the hope it would piece together more of the evening. I had success when the next CCTV picked them up entering Marcos' car, the same one parked outside Alex's home during the press conference. I thought Marcos would drive off, however, they remained in that position for forty minutes. I was curious to understand why and hoped I would get the chance to ask.

I was about to relay my findings to Paul when his number popped up on my phone. As I answered I went to speak, but he cut me off.

"I can't talk long. McCarthy is on my case," he started. I decided to remain silent, it was clear his news was important. "They're arresting Alex this afternoon, at the game. They want it to be as public as possible." I was angry. Alex was no longer being treated in an ethical manner. Both McCarthy and Jackson knew a public arrest would boost their standing and give them airtime. But it would only look good for them if Alex was guilty, they didn't consider what would happen if Alex was innocent.

"Can't you stall? I have managed to find evidence that Marcos lied to us about his alibi and I will need your support on it," I pled for help. I didn't want Alex to be forced into any more traumatic incidents when he was already close to the edge.

"I'm sorry, Sammi I can't. They want him in custody by this afternoon. I will do what I can to protect him," Paul assured me. I had to be open minded and trust in him, he seemed genuine in his resolve.

"Okay, Paul. Just keep me updated," I said, before saying my goodbyes and putting the phone down.

TWENTY-SIX

The stadium was full, it was a Saturday 3pm kick-off. Historically all games at that time were part of a media blackout, meaning none could be shown on live TV in the UK. However, with the changes in TV rights, this was removed and became a lucrative spot for Premier League teams. This match would be streamed across the world, there would likely be millions viewing the events that would follow. The new stadium only held 40,000 fans. After the pandemic, some teams opted for smaller stadium capacities with up-to-date facilities, such as comfortable and roomier seating, preferring to focus on higher ticket prices than numbers.

Against his better judgement, Fernandes agreed to start Alex. He knew he had no reason to drop him and, if he did, he could be investigated under the Equality Act. He hoped the experience would be positive, and it would give him an outlet to forget his personal circumstances. He also hoped he wouldn't receive a negative reaction from the fans, but with discriminatory behaviour on the rise in the 2020s, he knew Alex was in for a rough ride.

They lined in the tunnel waiting for the announcement to enter the pitch. Alex was standing at the back after giving his duties over to Hakeem Lewis, their vice-captain. It was a decision Fernandes welcomed. The opposition players walked past him, some stopping to ask about his well-being; others stopping to give him a hug and say they respected him for being true to himself. He choked back tears, feeling overwhelmed by the support.

The words of one particular youngster, Jason Barclay, brought him comfort. At only twenty he was considered a veteran in the Premier League, having played for the opposition first team since the age of sixteen. He was the last in the tunnel to speak with Alex.

"Thank you, Alex, I hope this is a turning point for gay footballers. Maybe one day you will inspire me to come out," Jason whispered, hugging Alex hard. At that moment he was close to tears, knowing that another youngster was hiding his sexuality made him realise he needed to be there to support more youngsters in the game. It had to be his main goal going forward.

Alex had walked out to play for the club on over five hundred occasions, today he was wracked with nerves. As the referees led the players out, Alex could feel his heart beating fast. It felt like an age until they were on the pitch, when he walked out the mood changed quickly. The boos and jeers of the minority overpowered the cheers of the fans. He lined up against his teammates, staring at the grass in a bid to ignore it. He knew it would be a long match. The players started their customary handshakes, however, when the opposition walked past, they hugged him. This time it was all of them, wanting to show their support publicly.

Throughout his career Alex had been substituted only twice for injury, never for tactical reasons. It was a statistic he was proud of and wanted to continue until retirement. As the whistle blew the abusive insults were thrown with more vigour. Although the majority crowd attempted to drown them out, the minority had organised themselves in a way that carried their abuse further. Less than five minutes into the game a flare was thrown, missing him by inches, the danger was real. During the stoppage in play, Tanja and Fernandes discussed options, and he was swiftly substituted.

As his number was called, and he walked off, Alex looked over to where the flare was thrown from. A group of supporters clashed with stewards; anger etched on their faces as their eyes followed Alex. He ignored all on the touchline and made his way down the tunnel, as he did, the announcement that discriminatory language would not be tolerated rang though the stadium, number one on the protocol to deal with abusive language. It was a hopeless endeavour. In his career he had never experienced such a toxic atmosphere in football, even when he played poorly in the World Cup he always felt the fans were on his side. Today, however, he feared for his safety.

He wanted to be alone with his thoughts. After entering the dressing room he turned to find Michael had followed. For a moment neither spoke, the only sound being Alex's heavy breathing as he considered what to do next. Barely able to curtail his emotions, he walked over to the wall of the dressing room and punched it. An audible crack could be heard in the silence, the pain seared up his knuckles and arm.

"Are you okay?" Michael asked, as Alex slumped onto the bench, looking up to the TV as the cheers rung out when they were on the attack. The jeers had stopped, it was just normal chanting for the team they loved. He felt his heart break. Not only had he lost the love of his life, but also his beloved career. He knew it would be tough to come back from this.

"I don't know. I haven't experienced anything like that before. The hatred and anger towards me, all because I dared to be my true self," Alex responded. He felt hot tears pricking against his eyes, he wiped them away quickly.

"It may not be because of that," Michael said weakly, knowing he didn't believe his own words. Fans could be unforgiving and abuse was a part of the job they all wrongly accepted. It was something he dealt with his whole career, being a black man from Southern America. He hated that his minority status was used to make him feel small, and it broke his heart to see Alex suffer in the same way.

"Mate, you're one of my closest friends, but you can't understand. No more than I can understand what it's like to be racially abused. They hate me for being gay. My career is for nothing, all those homophobes see is a man who likes other men. I feel like I've lost everything." His voice was eerily calm. Michael didn't know how to respond, instead he just slung his arm over his friend and they drifted back into silence as they watched the game continue.

As they sat contemplating what transpired, with Alex nursing his swollen hand, two unwelcome visitors walked into the dressing room followed by a frustrated security officer who had done his best to stop them. Alex nodded his head and smiled, signifying he was okay with the intrusion. The security officer left them to it.

"Alex Smith. We would like to come to the station." They both looked at Sammi's replacement in annoyance. With his small glasses; long face and slightly crooked nose, he didn't give the impression of being a hardened detective. Alex looked over to Paul briefly who had a sheepish look on his face, he then cleared his throat and turned to the replacement.

"May I ask who you are and for some ID?" The reply from Alex sounded defensive, but he wanted to cover his back before agreeing to leave. The detective took out his badge and showed it to the men.

"Please accept my apologies. I forgot I am new to this case. My name is Detective Inspector Dennis McCarthy, and you know acting Detective Constable Grant," he said, pointing to his younger colleague, who adopted a look of distaste at his new commanding officer. "I am arresting you for the murder of Joseph Marsden. You do not have to say anything, but it may harm your defence if you do not mention when questioned something which you later rely on in court. Anything you do say may be given in evidence." He had a smug look on his face as he read Alex's rights to him. Michael stood in direct eyeline of McCarthy, staring him down and making him feel uncomfortable. After only moments the older detective spoke.

"Let's not make this any more difficult than it should be," McCarthy said in Alex's direction. Michael continued to stare the man down, not flinching.

"Michael, don't." With those words Michael relented and sat back on the bench. Alex signed in relief and continued. "Okay, I'll come with you. However, I would like to have some medical treatment for my hand." The pain was starting to throb, with purple bruises developing around his knuckles. McCarthy considered the request for a moment.

"We have a first aider at the station who can take a look for you." Although not what Alex had in mind, he knew he was in no position to bargain. He nodded his head and followed both detectives out of the stadium. As they walked away, Michael remained silent, when he was in the clear he picked up his mobile phone.

"Sammi, it's me. They've arrested Alex," he said as soon as Samantha answered the phone, shocked to find she already knew this was the plan. She assured him a plan was in place, and he felt relieved. Knowing he could trust her.

TWENTY-SEVEN

"Mr Smith, you understand the reason for you arrest?" Less than an hour later Alex was sitting opposite the two detectives in the interrogation room, his hand and wrist strapped up. The officer who checked him over implored McCarthy to allow Alex to get a X-ray on his wrist, concerned that it was broken. McCarthy overruled his junior colleague, believing questioning Alex was of the utmost importance. Now he sat, his hand poorly bandaged and the pain getting increasingly worse.

"May I ask what happened to the other detective?" Alex questioned, wanting to stall. He was alone, his solicitor hadn't arrived yet as she was navigating her way through Manchester by tram. Thankfully she was in the city on a week-long conference, otherwise he would be in the cells while they tracked her down. Although Katie claimed having a solicitor over 250 miles away in Brighton was an inconvenience, she was the only person he could trust. Her status as one of the best in the country also helped.

"That's none of your concern. I am now leading this investigation, that is all you need to know." It was a short, frustrated response. Alex took pleasure on the idea he had gotten under the man's skin. "Now back to my original question. Do you know the reason for your arrest?"

"I am aware it is in connection with the murder of Joseph, and the fact I was in a sexual relationship with him," Alex responded calmly. He noticed the new detective shift uncomfortably in his seat, it couldn't be that he was a homophobe? Maybe it explained the distaste he felt when he looked at Alex. It was sad that even now homophobia was rife in the UK. It was why he had hidden his truth for a long time, the past fifteen years have been full of regret. If he could do it all again, he would have been honest from the start.

"You're correct. We would like to ask you a few questions. How was your relationship with Joseph? Were there any problems between you?" Alex stared hard at the two men in front of him, he wondered the legality of the questioning as he had asked for legal representation.

"Shouldn't you be waiting for my solicitor before you ask me any questions? I can't imagine your bosses and the CPS would be happy knowing you are questioning a suspect who has asked for legal representation. Couldn't it put the case in jeopardy?" Alex questioned. It was the one thing his solicitor had told him to say if he was being pressured without her present. He saw a wry smile fall over Detective Grant's lips, he seemed happy that the point had been made.

"Mr Smith, if you do not answer the question, I will treat you as a hostile witness." The anger in McCarthy's voice was clear, he wasn't used to people questioning his authority.

"Witness? I thought I was a suspect here. You did previously say I had been arrested. I think you may need to get your story straight, Detective." It was remarkable how calm he was sounding, but it was a façade. Internally Alex was falling apart, he didn't want to face the reality of what had happened. When he thought about it all again, he wished he hadn't pushed Joseph away, or had told him he loved him one last time. It destroyed him inside.

"Look, Mr Smith…" As he shouted the door slammed open behind them. A woman in her mid-thirties stepped in, her face etched with anger. Her light-brown hair was cut into a bob, cupping her face; her lips accentuated with soft red lipstick that gave them a plump look, and she wore a smart two-piece suit with knee length skirt. Alex felt relief when he saw her.

"Detective McCarthy, I hope you aren't speaking to my client without me," she asked, the colour drained from the senior detective's face. He and this woman had had several run-ins. She didn't agree with his interrogation style and he didn't like the fact she had a 100% success rate defending clients. McCarthy wondered how many were truly innocent. He believed she had let many murderers back onto the streets.

"Ms Marshall, I was unaware you would be representing Mr Smith in this case."

"Alex has been a client for many years. My firm has helped him on a number of occasions with contract-related matters. Now, if you could clear off, I would like to speak to Mr Smith in confidence. Thank you," Ms Marshall said, as she sat down and flipped open her briefcase. McCarthy stood in a huff; Paul followed soon after. He slammed the door on the way out of the room. The lack of confirmation the interview had been terminated suggested they weren't following protocol.

"Kerrilyn, it's good to see you, sis." Alex gave the woman a hug. He was grateful they hadn't place him in handcuffs so he could. She smiled for the first time since entering the room.

"It's good to see you too, little brother. I was worried about you," Kerrilyn replied. Although only step-siblings they had a close bond. Alex was only five when his mum remarried Mal, Kerrilyn's dad. He never knew his own father, killed in 9/11, he was one of the souls that perished when his flight hit World Trade Centre 1 as he was travelling on business. Mal treated Alex as his own, and was the main driving force behind his footballing career. It was why he was apprehensive about coming out as gay, he didn't want to disappoint the man who'd raised him. Kerrilyn was his confidant; she knew from a young age and gave him the support he needed.

"How is Joce?" he asked. Jocelyn Smith, Kerrilyn's twin sister. Their relationship was strained as teenagers and for years they didn't talk. Only recently did they reconnect and were now in the process of repairing their relationship.

"Jocelyn is worried about you; she knew getting involved

with Joseph would lead to heartbreak." She regretted the tone, but sadly it was true. They knew getting close to a member of Marcos' staff would lead to heartbreak, and felt only anger when proven right. "I'm going to be blunt here. Things look bad for you. You lied twice to the investigating officer, I understand your reasoning, but you've impeded a murder investigation and it makes you suspicious." Alex looked to the table; she was right. If he had been honest from the start maybe he wouldn't be in this situation. Maybe they'd have given him the benefit of the doubt and he wouldn't have been pursued so aggressively when a new investigator took over.

"I have a way to get you out of here today. But you have to trust me." He looked back at his solicitor as she smiled softly, he nodded his head, indicating that he trusted her judgement. With that Kerrilyn stood and opened the door as a silent sign they were ready to continue. McCarthy leant against the wall opposite with a look of contempt in his eyes, angry that the young woman had walked in making demands. He walked back into the room with a sullen Paul not far behind, they took their places opposite Alex and Kerrilyn again.

"Gentlemen, thank you for giving me the time with my client. If I may, I just want to check my understanding of the events that have led to my clients arrest." Kerrilyn stopped briefly, but didn't allow enough time for an answer. She continued almost immediately. "On the morning of the 7th March, the body of Joseph Marsden was found in his home. He had been strangled. On the same morning, at approximately midnight, he was seen on a CCTV camera being pushed to the ground by my client. Where he received injuries to his cheekbone and teeth." She stopped and turned the page. Both McCarthy and Paul wondered how she already had such detailed notes. "Since the murder you have interviewed my client several times as a witness, where he had no legal representation, however, on at least two occasions his wife was present. During these interviews you are of the opinion that my client lied to you twice. The first time about his relationship with the victim, and the second, about his whereabouts on the morning of the murder. There is no physical evidence that links my client to the murder of Joseph Marsden. Does that sum up your position?" Kerrilyn said, staring McCarthy down. She refused to be intimidated by him.

"That is correct, Ms Marshall. Now, if we could get back to the interview," McCarthy responded. Kerrilyn held her hand up to silence him again.

"I am not finished, Detective," she interjected, the anger growing in his eyes. "I have been informed that my client is not the only person to have lied to you during this investigation." She paused for effect, enjoying the angry eyes flicker to those of concern. She had him hooked. "As I understand it a file is going to be submitted to your boss regarding a second person who lied about their whereabouts that evening."

"May I ask who?" Kerrilyn detected a hint of nervousness as McCarthy spoke. She smiled a little and continued.

"Sadly, I am unable to divulge who it is, or who gave me the information, whilst the file is being put together," she said coolly, leaning back on her chair. She had the upper hand now. "However, you have to understand this makes the arrest of my client look suspicious. Based on our conversation, my client has been arrested based on circumstantial evidence and a lie; yet he is not the only person who has lied to you during the investigation. Is that correct?" McCarthy could only nod his head in agreement.

"Now, I don't want to tell you how to do your job but it's important to look at this from a trial perspective. If you pursue this interview, and charges against my client, I will be able to prove reasonable doubt to the jury within the first five minutes. If you cease this interview now, and investigate the other avenue, you will make my job harder if you do indeed feel my client should be charged with the murder of Joseph." For a moment McCarthy looked to Paul for guidance, the younger detective just shrugged his shoulders and deferred to his senior officer. He considered arguing his case, but the new evidence was enough to cause reasonable doubt. He couldn't, in good conscience, continue the interview.

"Your client is free to go. For now." With that he stood from the table and walked out the door. Paul went to leave also but the young solicitor shook her head; he sat back down.

"Could you just wait for me outside for a minute, Alex?" she asked her brother; he nodded his head and left the room. When the door clicked behind him, she turned her attention to Paul.

"Detective Grant I assume?" He nodded his head when he was addressed, not wanting to speak and suffer a grilling similar to McCarthy's. "What happened? I got a phone call from Detective Rodan this morning informing me she had been suspended and Alex would be arrested even though new evidence had come to light." Paul paused for a moment. Processing the words. He did not understand how Samantha would know to speak with Kerrilyn. Before he could ask, the young woman must have understood his confusion and continued.

"We all grew up together, well in a way. Alex is my step-brother. Samantha has an older brother called Shaun, who happens to be Alex's best friend and the man they were referring to in the article printed this morning." He couldn't hide the shock in his eyes at the admission. All this time he was concerned that Jackson and McCarthy had an ulterior motive, but it seemed Samantha also had one. He feared that this connection could cast doubt on the entire investigation and make it impossible to secure a conviction no matter who the culprit was. Too many people had a stake in his case.

"Does Samantha know about her brother and Alex?" he asked, wanting to understand if she may have outside influences for wanting to protect Alex.

"Oh no, at the time the only people who knew were me and my twin sister." She stopped for a moment and thought about it. "She probably knows now though, the article wasn't subtle about the second man. But please, tell me what happened?"

"Samantha was suspended," he started, surprised at the lack of reaction from Kerrilyn. "She was being pressured into arresting Alex, but believed the evidence didn't merit an arrest yet. She has been suspended with full pay." He stopped briefly, again collecting his thoughts before sharing them with the woman. "I am concerned, though. Jackson and McCarthy are determined to see Alex go down for this murder. If they find out what you have told me, and they do charge Alex, Samantha is also in danger of being charged with assisting an offender and perverting the course of justice."

"We need to find a way to stop that then," she said, looking at her watch. "I need to go, Detective, I will speak with you soon." With that Kerrilyn stood and left the room, leaving Paul to wonder how they would all survive this case with their careers in check.

TWENTY-EIGHT

Although an avid football fan I didn't turn on to see the 3pm kick-off, wanting to avoid anything that may trigger my thoughts on the case. Instead, I choose to spend time doing something I loved, baking. It was a skill I picked up from my mum when she was alive, we would spend hours in the kitchen together making Romanian cakes and breads. On days when she was a little tired, or in too much pain, I would take the lead with her reading the recipe to me. I decided on Cozonac, a Romanian sweet bread that would commonly be eaten at Christmas or Easter. Although neither holiday was close, I liked to cook it when I had some free time.

It wasn't until my phone rang that I realised the game had started, it shocked me to see Michael's number on my caller ID. On answering he informed me Alex had been arrested, less than twenty minutes after he had started the match. I thanked him and then set my plan in motion, making sure that there was enough reasonable doubt to get Alex released for now. I thought it had worked, however, nearly three hours later there was still no information.

The doorbell rung as I pulled out the latest batch of bread. I pulled out my phone and checked the blink system, after verifying the person's identity I informed them to come up to my flat and I would be with them shortly. After quickly washing my hands and taking off my apron I went and answered the door to Kerrilyn Marshall and embraced her warmly.

"It's good to see you, Sammi," she said as I hugged her tightly. Although we had recently spoken on the phone we hadn't seen each other for a long time. She was the woman I aspired to be when I grew up. Intelligent, beautiful and funny, a combination I envied. Her reputation as a defence lawyer was fierce thanks to one famous case. A man had been charged with murdering his former lover and, although evidence pointed to his guilt, Kerrilyn argued the woman had been abusive and he acted in self-defence. He was cleared of murder, but guilty of manslaughter on the grounds of diminished responsibility and served five years in jail. I didn't agree with the verdict, but I respected her for getting the result for her client.

Many others didn't though.

"Come on in," I said, uncoupling from her. She followed me and sat on the chair next to the kitchen countertop. "Drink?" I offered, filling the kettle up by the tap. She held up her hand and shook her head.

"No thanks, this will only be a short visit." I put the kettle down and flicked it on, wanting to make myself a coffee. The lack of sleep since the start of the case was starting to catch up with me, and I wanted to be more alert for my conversation with Kerrilyn. "Paul knows," I sighed, knowing the meaning of the two words immediately. It was only a matter of time before he found I had a connection to Alex, and now it could harm my chances of getting back on the case.

"What did he say?" I asked, pouring the hot water over a couple of teaspoons of coffee. I went to the fridge and topped it up with milk, before walking over and sitting beside Kerrilyn.

"He is concerned Jackson and McCarthy may use it against you, claim that you have been assisting an offender. He wants to help." If it wasn't for the past day I would have questioned if that was true, however, he had given me the support I needed to pursue alternative avenues that didn't include Alex. That being said I still wondered if he had an ulterior motive and was concerned it could come back to me in an uncomfortable way.

"That's good to know," I said, sipping my coffee for a brief moment, letting the warm liquid run down my throat and feeling revitalised. "How is Alex?" I was keen to change the conversation, not wanting to dwell on the potential end of my career.

"He's broken. I can see it in his eyes. Losing the man he loved was hard enough, but to be the main suspect in the murder of his death has destroyed him. I just wish there was more I could do to help." She briefly looked down at her phone, checking the time. She either had a prior engagement or a train to catch.

"You stopped the interrogation today, that is more than enough."

"That was you though. Until your phone call I had no idea how I was going to get him out of that situation. You really came through for us." It was the first time I had seen a vulnerability with Kerrilyn. She had defended numerous clients who had stronger evidence against them, and never wavered in her resolve. The fact she and Alex have a strong bond was dampening her ability to work. I understood, but we all needed to remain impartial.

"I get that. It's hard to think logically when it's somebody you care about." She nodded her head. "There is something I wanted to ask you about. It's about Katie and Alex."

"Of course, anything."

"I know their marriage is just a way to protect Alex's career, but when I spoke to them things seemed odd. It's hard to explain, but I got the feeling they hated each other."

"They do," she responded bluntly, but then decided to elaborate further. "It hasn't always been like this though. When they first met, they really did enjoy spending time together. They did everything a normal couple would do, minus the obvious. So, when Alex asked Katie to marry him, she was over the moon. We all told them it was a mistake, but they were young and impressionable. They thought the good times would continue."

"What happened?" I had gotten up to take my coffee cup to the sink and check on my bread, it was still warm after coming out of the oven but had a nice bouncy feel as I touched the top. It had worked. I sat back down to listen to Kerrilyn recount the story.

"Katie started to resent Alex, and even started to hate him. We don't know exactly when this happened, Jocelyn believes it was when he started playing football as a professional and the reality of her life set in. But I think it was before. I believe it was after the Lake District."

"You mean where Alex and my brother slept together?" I interjected, making the woman feel uncomfortable. She paused for a moment, considering her response, before continuing.

"That's something you will have to discuss with your brother. I have enough family drama of my own at the moment." The comeback was the confirmation I needed. Had it not been true she would have denied it but, by telling me to talk to Shaun, she was confirming something happened. I allowed her to continue. "After that they started fighting more. Just words to begin with. Katie complaining Alex didn't support her with Marshall, and Alex saying it was what she signed up for. But more recently, over the past year or so, things have become… violent."

"Violent, how?"

"Recently I've noticed marks on his body, bruises, scratches and once even a scald mark on his chest. When I confronted him, he told me it happened during a game, or training, but it was obvious there was more." She opened up her phone and flicked through it, showing it to me when she found what she was looking for. "I took this photo without him noticing. It's blurred but you can see a sizeable bruise on his arm, as if somebody forcibly grabbed him." I nodded my head and she put her phone away. "We begged him to leave her, but he wouldn't."

"Why not?" I asked, interjecting again. She sighed a little and ran her hands through her soft brown hair.

"Because she was blackmailing him. She told him that if he divorced her, she would go to the media and come clean about his sexuality. She would leak the text messages between him and Joseph, and the bank records to show he had been paying for male escorts. She had him by the balls." Her eyes flitted with anger. She was protective of her family, especially Alex. "Something changed in him recently though. He originally wanted to come out at the end of his career but in the past few weeks he had been talking to a divorce lawyer at my firm. When I spoke to him about it, he said he didn't care anymore. He just wanted to be free from the lie and from Katie. I told him to be careful, I didn't know how Katie would react to the news."

"Do you know if he told her?" I was learning a lot from Kerrilyn at this moment, I was grateful she was willing to be honest with me.

"I don't think he did. Alex has been careful. She may have found something out while snooping but nobody would have told her"

"Do you think she could have killed Joseph had she found out?" Up until this moment, I hadn't considered her as a viable suspect. Too consumed in my pursuit of Marcos, and my protection of Alex, but if it was true she had violent tendencies and was starting to harm Alex, it was a question I needed to ask.

"I don't know. With her anger issues, I'd say it's possible." It was enough for me to consider another angle to this murder. If she had found out about Alex's plans to divorce her, she would stand to lose the most. She was quick to verify Alex's alibi, but maybe it was to protect herself, and not her husband.

"Sammi, I am going to have to go soon, Terrance is meeting me up here for dinner, but there was something I needed to discuss with you quickly," Kerrilyn said, as she started to respond to a message, likely making plans with her husband Terrance Marshall, the Prime Minister. When he was originally voted in, it had a detrimental effect on their relationship. With Terrance based in London, and Kerrilyn having a practice in Brighton, they could go days without seeing each other. Rumours of an impending separation began, tanking Terrance's poll numbers briefly. They undertook relationship counselling in a bid to make it work, and now set aside at least two days of alone time together per week. Today was one of them.

"Sure, whatever you need."

"It's about Stacey." My heart sank at the words. As her legal guardian I had many phone calls that started with that sentence, and the talk was seldom good. Although she matured with age, and her attitude softened, I was aware of the cruel streak that continued to lace her thinking. When she moved to Sussex, her parting gift was the announcement it was to get away from me. Although hurt, I asked Kerrilyn to keep an eye out. Due to their age differences, Stacey didn't know Kerrilyn, so wasn't too suspicious when one of the guest lecturers offered her an internship at her law firm.

"She hasn't gotten into trouble at work has she?" I felt my heart pounding in my chest.

"Absolutely not. Her grades are impeccable and she is extremely popular in my office. It's about her personal life." She stopped briefly to compose herself, my mind was starting to think of numerous possibilities. "A couple of weeks ago, Marcos visit me. He tried to recruit me as his defence lawyer. Knowing his history, though, I refused to get involved. I work in a moral grey area, but it does not fall into that. Anyway, I am going off on a tangent.

"I don't know how, but Marcos struck up a conversation with your sister. They took a liking to each other and he has been sending her gifts to the office. I can't give much more detail on the nature of their relationship though, if they are dating or this is just flirtation." I could feel the anger rising. Marcos' interest in my sister wasn't a coincidence. He was a well-connected crime boss who was known to research those he came up against. I was certain he knew every detail of my life; who my parents were; my sibling's location and even about my blossoming relationship. It was terrifying, but I didn't want to consider it now. If he did have an interest in Stacey, then it was likely to hurt me.

"Thanks for keeping me in the loop. There isn't anything I can do though. If I try and broach the subject with her, she will just pull further away." My sister had made efforts to go no contact with me in the past. Only through intervention from Shaun did she eventually relent and keep limited contact, which normally led to a couple of phone calls a year. I wasn't looking to push her even further away.

"No worries, Samantha. I'll keep an eye on her and let you know if there are any developments," Kerrilyn responded. The phone on the table started to vibrate vigorously, a smile developed on her face as she looked down at the identity of the person ringing. I could tell from her facial expressions it was her husband. "Sorry, I really need to go now. It was fun chatting to you. Next time I'm in Manchester we will go out for a few drinks." She stood up from the chair – I gave her a quick hug and walked her to the door.

•

As we said our goodbyes on the doorstep, I became distracted when a familiar face walked up to us. Kerrilyn heard the footsteps also and turned around, when she looked back to me she was as confused as I felt.

"What are you doing here, Paul? How did you know where I live?" He looked embarrassed as I asked the question, and looked over briefly to Kerrilyn.

"I needed to see you and I took a shot that Kerrilyn would be coming over after our little chat at the station. I followed her," he replied. I suppressed a chuckle as he recounted the details, especially as it was likely he could gain access to my personal address through our computer systems. In case of emergency, staff phone numbers and addresses were readily available, so that if they were reported a no show somebody from the office could attend their property immediately. It seemed a better way than stalking.

"I'll see you soon, Sammi," Kerrilyn said, as she hugged me again and gave me a quick peck on the cheek, she gave a little wave and walked off, turning her attention to her phone and ringing her husband. I moved to let Paul enter my property.

"You know it's creepy to admit you followed a woman around

the streets of Manchester, right?" I said, shutting the door behind us. He shrugged his shoulders and walked to the seats in the kitchen, perching himself on the chair that Kerrilyn had just left.

"What have you found?" he asked, getting straight to business. I pulled my laptop case from the draw and brought it over, sitting back at the table. I pulled out printed pictures of Marcos' car and slid them to Paul, he picked them up to examine them. "We've already established this is Marcos' car," he stated matter-of-factly. I then handed over the second photo of Marcos and Joseph talking in the street, followed immediately by a photo of them getting in Marcos' car. "He lied about his whereabouts that night."

"There's more. They stayed parked there for at least forty minutes. On at least two occasions Joseph got out and went to walk away, but Marcos persuaded him back into the car. They both then drove off in the direction of Joseph's flat." I put down further photos from the CCTV, of Joseph getting out of the car in an agitated state; Marcos following him out and putting him back in; and then finally them driving away forty minutes later. We finally knew what happened in between Joseph getting attacked and his murder. As Paul examined them, I continued. "We need to find out what they were discussing and what happened after they drove off."

"We can't take this information to Jackson and McCarthy because they will find a way to bury it," he said, putting the photos down and looking at me intensely. "I think we need to go to the assistant chief constable." I was sceptical about his idea, unsure how we would get a conversation with him as one of the busiest men in the country.

"And how do we do that?" I vocalised my scepticism, causing Paul to smile.

"I have contacts in his office. If I frame it right, he will be happy to see us." I needed to trust Paul's judgement, we had been backed into a corner and this was the best way forward. He examined the photos again and then turned his attention to me. "I want to be honest with you about something though, Sammi.

I may have to do this alone. If Jackson and McCarthy find out you know Alex, it could put the case in jeopardy," I sighed, a little annoyed that this was happening. I didn't feel comfortable leaving Alex's fate in somebody else's hands, but if it was the only way to exonerate Alex, I had to accept it.

"I understand, but if there is a way for me to continue on this case, I want to do it." He nodded his head, understanding my position.

"We will get whoever did this. Even if it was Marcos, he won't get away with another crime." With that Paul stood and said his goodbyes, before I was able to get up and show him our he was out the door. For a moment I pondered whether to text Michael and ask him to come over, instead deciding an evening of solitude wasn't a bad thing.

•

"What are you doing here?" Alex asked, as he turned the light on in his living room. Katie sat on the sofa, her perfectly manicured hands cupped around a tumbler of whisky. Her hair was a mess, and lipstick was smeared across her cheek. It was easy to guess where she had been, but less clear the age of who she was doing it with.

"I thought I'd come and see how you were feeling after that car crash of a football match. I nearly left; you've kept me waiting so long." Her words were slurred and full of spite, the alcohol had exacerbated her anger and Alex feared she would react violently. He stood on the other side of the room, out of striking distance.

"Well Katie, if I had known you were in my house, I would have rushed home sooner to throw you out." On leaving the station he'd hailed a taxi to the hospital, wanting to see if the assessment from the officer was correct. It took a couple of hours, but he was relieved when receiving the news that there was no break in his wrist or hand, just a bruise. After being bandaged up again he was sent on his way. "You know what, I've had a shit day. My personal life is now out in the open; I have been subjected to abuse; I was arrested for murdering the man I loved and now I come home to find you here. Even though I told you this morning to get out and not come back." He was not a confrontational person, but the pain and frustration of the past few days had gotten to much. He regretted his actions when he managed to duck the whisky glass flying at his head at the last second.

"Now you listen here, Mister," Katie began, standing up from the sofa. He instinctively flinched and moved backwards to increase the distance more. "You need to be careful how you speak to me. I have protected you for your all adult life, and deserve more respect. You got it?"

"Just clean up this mess and fuck off out of my house," Alex responded before walking upstairs, he had no interest in continuing to stroke her ego. He'd had enough, unsure of how much he could handle having this abusive woman in his life while grieving for his career and boyfriend. He just wanted it all to end, even if that meant taking matters into his own hands.

TWENTY-NINE

The melodic ringtone from my phone rang on the other side of the room, my eyes adjusted to the dark as I raised my head to investigate the noise. I stared at the softly lit phone, wondering whether it was worth getting out of the warm duvet wrapped around my naked body. Now I was no longer on the case, I didn't see why I should have my sleep disturbed. Yet I felt something deep in the pit of my stomach, an intuition that something was wrong. I relaxed a little when the phone rang off, but it was short lived when it quickly started to ring for a second time.

Realising it was important, I jumped out of bed, hissing a little as the cold hit my skin. I scrambled to the phone and checked the name before answering, surprised to find it was Michael.

"Yes darling, what is it?" I asked, realising it sounded sarcastic, an unintended consequence of being woken up early again. He responded in a stressed manner, talking fast. I wasn't able to pick up on much of what he was saying. Wanting to slow him down I interjected. "Michael, calm. Tell me what's wrong, slowly."

"It's Alex," he paused for a moment, trying to regain his breath. I listened to his heavy breathing for a moment, wanting to give him the time to process the thoughts in his mind. "I found him, he was… his wrists had been…" He stopped again, trying to suppress the sobs. I didn't need him to continue, I had worked out what happened. My heart sunk; I couldn't stand the idea of losing another person.

"Is he alive?" I asked, my fingers mentally crossed. It seemed like an age before he responded. I didn't want it to end like this. Selfishly my thoughts turned to the case, if Alex died, we were unlikely to find the truth about Joseph. McCarthy and Jackson would spin it to suggest he couldn't handle the guilt anymore. If he was innocent, however, it would backfire on them both.

"Yes, he's alive, for now." He stopped briefly, there was mumbling as he spoke to somebody on the other side of the phone. "They're taking him to North Manchester General Hospital. They're concerned the wounds are deep and he may not make it." The stress in his voice was starting to get worse. I knew I had to remain strong.

"Okay, you need to go with him to hospital. He will need a friend if he wakes up. I'm going to find a way to end this." I sounded vaguely threatening, as if I would circumvent the rule of law to get the culprit. I needed to do it legally and by the book though, to ensure that justice was truly served. Even if that meant stepping back and enabling Paul to lead the case.

"Please help him. He's hurting badly, he needs the cloud removed from his head to give him the space to heal." It was a passionate plea. I knew he was right. Alex was struggling and needed all the support he could get. I was one of the few people who could provide it.

"I'll let you know what happens." It was all I could respond with before putting the phone down. I hoped that he could trust my intentions and that I would support him. After sending a brief text to Shaun, explaining Alex had been taken to hospital, I rung up Paul. Time was now of the essence and I wanted to move forward quickly.

"Please tell me you have had some luck with the assistant chief?" I asked, not bothering to say hello. The urgency in my voice was evident and I wanted to get straight down to business.

"I have a meeting this afternoon, is everything okay?" He was calm, I came to the realisation that, unless the media had caught wind of the story, he wouldn't know that Alex had been taken to hospital. My heart ached when I thought about it, he had been backed into a corner and felt the only way out was to take his own life. It was devastating for those who loved him.

"We can't wait a morning. Alex tried to commit suicide. Michael has gone to the hospital with him." I relayed the information that Michael had told me this morning, about how he was found and where he was being taken. It was only once I finished speaking, he pitched in.

"Leave it with me, I will see what I can do." He put the phone down without me thanking him. As the adrenaline left my body I realised I was still naked. I shivered as I walked over to the wardrobe to find my dressing gown to sling over my shoulders, pulling it close in a bid to warm faster. Only a few minutes later I received another phone call from Paul. "Get to his office by 8am, he will see us as a priority." I was surprised that I was being summoned also, but didn't pay too much mind as I got myself ready.

•

Within the hour I was sitting in the assistant chief's office. It was decorated to a higher standard than the station offices we had. Like many seniors he wasn't fully based in the area of the country he oversaw. Now, with collaborative working, which became top priority after a terrorist attack in 2025 that claimed the lives of 156 people, his main office was down in London with all deputies and chief constables around the country. The office in Manchester was used once or twice every couple of weeks, to give him a base for his meetings with subordinates who held the fort during his absence. Him having time to hear us out was an honour.

The secretary beckoned me into the office. He was a tall striking man who looked like a recent university graduate. His hair was blond and he had deep-blue, piercing eyes that sent shivers down my spine. Had I not been seeing Michael I would have handed him my number; it was best not to complicate my personal life any further though.

Paul was already in the office, staring out of the large glass window. The assistant was speaking in hushed tones and stopped when I entered. One of the most inspired men on the force, he was a beacon of light to those who struggled through life. As a young uniformed officer, he was shot and blinded in one eye by a suspect who had a concealed weapon. After a period of sick leave, he came back, determined to clear up street crime. He had one of the highest arrest records, and continued even after his health faltered. At the age of forty he was promoted to assistant chief constable, and five years later looked to be on the fast track to becoming chief constable.

"Detective Rodan, please have a seat," he said, gesticulating to the empty chair. I did so and balanced the file I had compiled on my legs. "As you know I am Assistant Chief Constable David Turnball, I have been informed by Detective Inspector Grant that this meeting is urgent." At that moment I was thrown. Detective Inspector? I turned to look at my colleague, wondering if I had heard correctly. His face gave nothing away though.

"Detective Inspector?" I mumbled softly, not intending to say the words aloud. I intended to confirm that the meeting was indeed urgent, but my mind had faltered at this new revelation.

"Yes, we have a bit of explaining to do and then we can go through the case specifics," he said, standing up from his chair. "A while ago we received a tip-off about corruption in your office. However, we had no concrete evidence. As such I sent in an expert, Paul Grant." He stopped briefly before sitting down, looking me intensely in the eyes. "Initially we believed you could be the corrupt one. You had been the lead for many cases involving Marcos, yet seemingly, failed to get a conviction. It wasn't until this case we realised our mistake and started to look elsewhere, at Jackson and McCarthy."

"Forgive me for being blunt, sir, you believed I was corrupt and aided Marcos in avoiding prosecution? What mental gymnastics did you have to do to jump to that conclusion?" I managed to compose myself and avoid swearing at one of the most powerful men in the city. It was Paul who interjected with a response to my protests.

"Yes. When you underwent vetting, we discovered that your father was a close contact of Marcos, and was known to use his services. He was found in a sting operation at one of his properties. During recruitment there was no evidence that you were aware of this, so we passed you. However, recently Jackson claimed that you knew more than you were letting on." He paused briefly, the chief nodded his head, an indication he should continue. "We didn't approach you about it because we didn't want to tarnish the image of your father. Let me be clear, this was after the death of your mother that he was found in the arms of an escort, not when your mother was battling cancer." He stopped again, allowing me to process the information. It saddened me to know his life was so unfulfilled when my mum died, and the only way he could handle the grief was by using Marcos' services. I felt a stab of pain in my heart as I realised the arrest was what likely pushed him towards suicide.

"When working on the case with you, though, I came to realise you wanted to put Marcos behind bars. I saw the anger in your eyes when you spoke about him. I decided to look elsewhere, while continuing to keep you out of the loop. The two events that made me focus on Jackson and McCarthy were when they suspended you, and the laptop and phone went missing from evidence." My heart sank. The laptop, the item that Joseph had worked so hard to keep out of the clutches of Marcos, looked to be heading back to him. I felt I had failed him. Pushing it aside, I turned my attention back to the matter at hand.

"I may not have the greatest reputation. I know people are aware of my partying lifestyle, and how I like to play the field a bit. But I am a good police officer. I have served the badge well since I was eighteen, and I would never sell out my own kind. Remember that in future." I thought it would be the end of my career, but the ACC nodded his head.

"Please, tell me about your case," he replied, signalling an end to the corruption matter. I looked down at my file, composing myself before telling the story. I hoped he was willing to help.

"Joseph Marsden, thirty-seven years old, escort for Marcos Vincenzo, and previous suspect in a robbery case. Murdered on the morning of 7th March 2028. He was found in his flat, a silk scarf around his neck a second scarf in his mouth, and suggestions of sexual activity." I pushed over the picture of Joseph at the murder scene, David looked at it with interest and beckoned me to continue. "Our first break in the case was an article in the *Daily Scoop*, that Joseph had been assaulted by Alex Smith, a high-profile footballer. On questioning him we found that he was in a sexual relationship with Joseph and had been for almost six months.

"After this we hit a wall. Jackson wanted me to pursue Alex as the most credible suspect, whereas I felt we hadn't leant on Marcos enough. After my suspension, Paul procured CCTV images from the night of the assault for me to examine. It was here I discovered vital evidence had been overlooked." I placed the photo of Marcos and Joseph on the desk and David picked them up. I continued as he examined them intensely. "As you can see, Marcos lied when we initially spoke with him, he claimed he hadn't seen Joseph that evening when in fact he was the last person to see him alive. I would like to pursue this avenue of investigation and find out whether Marcos has more knowledge of the murder than he claims to."

"Thank you. I am happy for this investigation to continue. Paul has briefed me on your history with Alex Smith, but I feel you are still the right person to lead. Paul will assist you," the assistant responded. I was relieved. "It goes without saying, but both McCarthy and Jackson need to be kept out of the loop. I will inform them they will be taken off the Joseph Marsden case as it is no longer seen as a top priority, especially with the main suspect in hospital." I reeled a little at the comment, but before speaking realised it was how he would frame it to Jackson. I breathed a little sigh of relief. "I am also aware of comments that Ms Marshall made when getting Alex released, about how a file was being put together. I will make them aware the evidence was insufficient, and the matter was closed." He stopped again, staring at me with his piercing brown eyes. "You have forty-eight hours. If we fail to secure a suspect in that time the crime will be designated a cold case. Understood?"

"Loud and clear, sir." Although the time frame was short, I understood why a quick resolution was necessary. The situation had reflected badly on the police force, especially now the news would trickle out that Alex has been hospitalised after trying to take his own life. Questions would be raised about the police involvement in it, and in all likelihood the department would be investigated by the IOPC. However, if we were to find a new suspect, we could sweep that bad news under the carpet.

"You may go," David Turnball said. I got up and left almost immediately, Paul remained seated for a moment, they clearly had another matter that they needed to discuss without me. I left the office and jumped in my car, using the privacy as an opportunity to check on Alex.

"Oh, thank God you rang, Samantha." I felt my heart stop briefly as Michael started with those words. As I went to speak my throat dried up, my mind had gone blank and was focused on the worst-case scenario. Thankfully Michael didn't leave me in suspense, and continued. "Alex is stable. He's going to be okay, the wounds were deep and he required stitches but... he'll be okay." I let out an audible sigh of relief, I hadn't been aware I was holding my breath until that moment.

"Thank you for being there this morning. I know it was a traumatic experience for you." I could feel the tears prick my eyes. Although it was Shaun who found my father's body, I knew the trauma he endured trying to process it. The guilt he felt for not getting there soon enough to save him; the nightmares he had of the lifeless corpse hanging from the banister; him withdrawing himself from the family and falling into a booze trap, and finally, the endless bouts of therapy to deal with all of the above. The idea of Michael going through the same broke my heart. "I'm back on the investigation, I will do all I can to help Alex."

"Be careful," he whispered softly. I knew he meant for the sake of my reputation but I feared for my safety also. If Marcos was really involved in the murder, then he could find a way to remove me permanently. I couldn't think in such a way though.

We said our goodbyes. I ended the call and, as I did so, there was a knock on my window. I stopped a yelp of surprise that had formed on my lips. I gestured for him to get in the car, and he walked around and joined me in the passenger seat. As he did so he got straight to business.

"Is Alex okay?" he asked, sounding concerned. I eyed him wearily, still not trusting his true intentions. It was possible the concern was for the police and not for Alex, I batted that thought away though and answered his question.

"Stable. Wounds are pretty deep; he's had stitches but he will survive with no permanent damage." For me something didn't feel right with the situation, although Alex was hurting, the method of how he attempted suicide seemed out of character. I knew I had to share my concerns with Paul.

"Okay, hear me out. No matter how tenuous this sounds, stick with me." Paul looked perplexed but nodded his head. "I don't believe Alex tried to kill himself. Alex is terrified of blood; I've seen him faint at the smallest drop. It just seems illogical for him to take that way out when he wouldn't be able to follow through. And there's something else, when I spoke with Kerrilyn she informed me that Katie is becoming increasingly violent towards Alex. She's been physically assaulting him. Isn't it possible she may have played a part in his attempted suicide?" I knew his interest was peaked when he nodded his head. He silently contemplated my point, I allowed him to do so. Wanting us to be on the same page for the rest of the investigation.

"There's something else," he suddenly said, I gave him my full attention. "When we arrested Alex yesterday, he had sustained an injury to his hand. After his substitution he punched a wall. One of the officers at the station checked his hand and recommended he be taken to hospital before interrogation due to concerns it was broken. McCarthy wanted the interview to take place immediately.

I don't know what the outcome was, however, I question if he would have had the strength to inflict those kinds of wounds to himself. I think you're right. There is more to this story." I was glad of the information. It was enough to convince me there was more to this attempted suicide than we first thought.

"It's possible we are now looking at an attempted murder as well as a murder," I said, frustrated that it had now gone this far. In my mind, one person had now raced to the top of my suspect list. A woman who, up until last night, I hadn't even considered a suspect, Katie Smith. She had the most to gain from both deaths.

"So how do you want to play it?"

"I think we need to follow the avenues we already have. First speak with Marcos again and question him about the lie. Then we head to the hospital to speak with Alex, if he's conscious, and a doctor to understand if he could have inflicted the wounds himself."

"Lead the way," Paul said, as I had finished. I turned on the ignition and stuck my car into drive. We had limited time remaining, and I felt we had lost too much already by sitting in the car park. It was time to track down a murderer.

•

Michael sat beside Alex's bed, his head in his hands, fighting back tears as thoughts turned to the last couple of days. Even with all that occurred, he never dreamed Alex would take such drastic action. His never-say-die attitude is what made him a popular footballer, to see him crumble in such a way was traumatic. He lay in bed, sleeping, the heart monitor beeping softly, indicating he was alive, comforted Michael.

"How is he doing?" A soft, but distressed voice, said behind him. Michael turned around, ready for a fight with a member of the media. Instead, a young man stood, eyes brimming with tears, as he looked to Alex. Michael considered the idea he was a crazed superfan, but he looked vaguely familiar. He decided to indulge him.

"He's going to be okay. Sorry, but who are you?" he asked a little abruptly. The young man walked in and put his hand out.

"Shaun Rodan, you must be Michael. I've heard a lot about you." Michael took his hand and shook it. It made sense now. Facially, he had similar features to his younger sister; they shared similar thick, dark hair also. The only noticeable difference was his eye colour, brown rather than grey, and significantly taller at 6 ft 5 inches. Michael couldn't help but wonder if this was the man the article was talking about yesterday.

"It's nice to meet you. I just wish it was under better circumstances," Michael responded. Shaun nodded his head solemnly, and looked down to Alex, watching his small soft breaths as he slept peacefully. He was happy to see he could breathe on his own, it was a positive sign.

"Do you mind if I have a bit of time alone with him?" Michael didn't say anything, just left the room. He was aware of their close relationship and didn't want to get in the way. Once the door shut, Shaun felt a weakness in his legs, he dropped to the vacant chair. The trauma from his father's suicide came flooding back to him when Sammi messaged him with the news. He prayed there had been a mistake, that he hadn't tried to find a way out. But seeing him in the bed, it made it all real.

"Why did you do this, Alex?" he whispered, fighting back the sobs forming in his chest. He felt responsible. On returning to his hotel room last night, he'd noticed a missed call from Alex. Due to the late hour, he ignored him. Had he answered, maybe it would have been enough to disrupt his plans. "I'm sorry I didn't ring you back last night, I wish I had and then maybe this wouldn't have happened.

"When Samantha texted me, I froze. All I could think about was my dad and how he was successful in ending his life. I was convinced you would be to, and it was at that moment I realised I can't live without you." The tears were falling freely now, he tried to wipe them away, embarrassed and angry at his selfishness. His needs weren't important and, if Alex felt he couldn't continue living, it wasn't up to Shaun to persuade him otherwise. But it was difficult. He had never cared so deeply for another person, let alone one who didn't reciprocate and was a man. He knew he wasn't gay, but it was different with Alex. He loved him and wanted to be with him, the prospect of him dying broke his heart.

"I know this is a terrible time, but I have to tell you this. I love you, Alex, ever since that night together in the Lake District, I have been in love with you. You're the man I want to be with, and I'm sorry it's taken me this long to say anything." He bent down and kissed him softly on the forehead before leaving. He didn't want to face an awkward interaction, or take Alex away from Michael any longer. A tear formed in the corner of Alex's eye, he felt the pain in his heart at the words. After fifteen years, he finally had the words he wanted for so long. He just hoped he could reciprocate once this was all over.

•

"All okay?" Michael enquired as Shaun left the room and shut the door. He stood outside sipping a cup of coffee, regretting the cost he paid for the overly watery concoction. If he wasn't in desperate need of a caffeine fix he would have binned it.

"He's still asleep. I'm glad he's okay though." His eyes were red from the tears, he wiped his face to prevent more falling. "I don't normally give unsolicited advice but I'm going to give you some. My sister is a wonderful young woman, but our history damaged us all. If she tries to push you away, or struggles to trust you, just be patient."

"I will be." Michael was confused about the warning. Other than their first meeting, she trusted him with a lot of her history. He loved that about her.

"Take care, man." Shaun shook Michael's free hand and walked away, leaving the younger man to go keep Alex company.

THIRTY

We were greeted at the door by Marcos' wife, looking trashy and unkempt. Although only 10am she held a large glass of wine in one hand, and a cigarette in the other. Her hair was a falling apart beehive, and her eyes were caked in thick make-up that had run over her face. Her dress was short, just below her hips. Either they had been up all night or she had gone to sleep in her evening clothes. The look of disgust on her face aged her five years at that moment.

"It's the coppers for you M," she said, moving to let us in. Her voice was hoarse, due to smoking from a young age. Marcos joined us in the hallway, his eyes fierce with anger that he had intruders again.

"What the hell are you doing here?" Marcos aggressively asked. I stared in contempt and walked into the living room without invitation, knowing it was the only way I'd gain access. I sat on his sofa, staring at him and daring him to throw me out. His rage intensified; his hand curled in a ball, a subtle threat of a physical altercation. He didn't move towards me though.

"We won't take up too much of your time. We just need to ask a couple of questions, about this," I stated, putting the photo down on the table ahead. He walked over and looked in horror, he knew we had found his alibi to be a lie. Whether he killed Joseph… that was another story.

"Fuck," he said, looking down at image. He picked it up to examine it closer. As he did, I thought there was a brief flicker of emotion in his eyes. It couldn't be though, Marcos cared for nobody but himself. It didn't seem credible he would be hurting over Joseph's death.

"Care to explain?" He sat down on the chair opposite me, looking bemused. He sighed, realising he needed to be honest. Only because he had been caught, though.

"I believed Joseph was involved in the theft of my jewellery. Even now, I thought he knew more than he was letting on at the time. So, I've been following him in the hope I would catch him doing something illegal," he responded, putting the phone down. I knew it was a lie, he wasn't interested in finding out Joseph's illegal activities. He wanted to understand if he was meeting the authorities to see if they were building a case. Not wanting to share my scepticism, I let him continue. "When Joseph got hurt, I wanted to help him. But he was hysterical. I took him back to the car to try and calm him down. We were parked a while because I was trying to persuade him to go to hospital, but he was refusing to go." I was shocked on hearing those words, my face betrayed my thoughts, Marcos picked up before continuing.

"Don't be surprised, Detective, I may be an arsehole but Joseph was in pain and I wanted to make sure he was okay. But he wouldn't go for fear of getting Alex in trouble, as he knew the police would have to get involved. I took him back to his flat, and that was it. He went in and I left." He finished his story. It couldn't have been long after that Joseph was murdered. Either Marcos was one of the last to see him alive, or he saw something pertinent to the case.

"Before you left, did you see anybody you recognised at his property?" He thought for a moment and nodded his head briefly. He realised it was time to be truthful, any further lies could result in a charge for perverting the course of justice. While I would relish that thought, he was too smart to be jailed for such a minor crime in his eyes.

"I saw two people that night, Detective. Alex Smith, who was there less than five minutes, and a woman." He stopped for a moment, leaving us both in suspense. "It was Katie Smith."

THIRTY-ONE

"Marcos may have seen Katie at the scene, but it isn't enough to bring her in." I looked out at the cars speeding past us as we sat in the layby less than ten minutes from Marcos' home. I wanted to take a moment to process the information he had given us. Confirmation Katie was at Joseph's home the night of his murder was circumstantial, there was no physical evidence to link her to the murder. Paul's silence concerned me, I wondered if he was plotting to take over the investigation. "We need to speak with Alex first, find out what happened last night." I looked over at Paul who was making notes, he stopped when he noticed I was paying him attention.

"For what it's worth, I don't believe Alex is guilty, which is why I went above Jackson and McCarthy and got you reinstated. We can't drag Katie in on Marcos' word though; we need to find evidence that ties her to the murder scene. We have an advantage though. With Alex also being a suspect, we should be able to obtain a search warrant for their home, we can find something that links her there," I agreed, with the circumstantial evidence against both it meant that we could push for a warrant and find more evidence that could implicate either. I hoped it would be Katie rather than Alex.

"Okay, let's go to Alex first. I'm keen to see what we can find from there."

As we walked into North Manchester General Hospital, I started to get a sick feeling in the pit of my stomach. Growing up with a sick mum, I made frequent trips to the hospital, never knowing if she would be coming home with us. Since her death, I had not set foot in a hospital, this was the first time. And I hoped, for a while, it would be the last. I entered the reception, leaving Paul outside for a moment as he was trying to arrange a warrant to search the Smith's home. I was surprised it hadn't been arranged by Jackson during their pursuit of Alex. Once he had finished, he followed me in.

"Good Morning, I am looking for Alex Smith's room." I greeted the receptionist behind the main helpdesk.

"Sorry, visiting hours are over, you'll have to come back tomorrow," she responded bluntly, without looking up from the computer. I glanced at Paul who shrugged his shoulders. Not willing to be pushed around I slammed my hand on her desk, prompting her to give her consideration.

"Oh good, I got your attention. Now, if we were visitors we would be turning up during visiting hours. My name is Detective Sergeant Rodan, and this is Detective Inspector Grant, we are currently investigating a murder and need to speak to Alex." I held up my warrant card, to allow her to verify my identity. "Now, either you can tell me where he is, or I can make your life very uncomfortable for hindering an active investigation." She stared at me coldly, I responded in kind until she spoke. I would not be intimidated by her.

"He's on floor 5. Trauma centre, in a private room. The nurse on the front desk will be able to help." I smiled sweetly and thanked her for her help, prompting a grunt in annoyance. It wasn't that I intended to annoy people, I just believed in playing hardball when I needed to get my way. I didn't care if people hated me for it.

We made our way up in the lift to the trauma centre, in silence all the time. I opened my phone and messaged Michael, wanting to check on his mental state after this morning. In the couple of minutes between floors he hadn't responded. On leaving the lift, I put my phone on silent, not wanting to be disrupted during this interview.

A young nurse sat at the trauma centre reception, a bright smile on her face as we walked over. I showed her my warrant card, wanting to avoid a repeat of the main reception and make more enemies.

"Good Morning, we are here to speak with Alex Smith. Would that be possible?" She quickly typed something into her computer, and then gave us her full attention only moments later.

"The doctor is currently doing his rounds and will be seeing Alex soon. Are you able to wait a few moments?"

"We would actually like to get the doctor's opinion on something. If that's possible?" Paul stepped forward and replied. I gave him the space to do so, as my superior in the Greater Manchester Police, he was entitled to take over at points.

"Oh absolutely. Please follow me." She got up from her desk and moved a little sign to the front, stating she would be gone a few moments. Paul allowed me to follow directly behind her, and he took the back again. Her bright and cheerful chatter filled the halls as we walked down past the various private rooms. It reminded me of the older nurse who cared for my mum towards the end of her life, somebody who loved her job and was committed to helping people. It was a shame that so many with her demeanour had left the NHS due to poor wages, deciding to work in private healthcare. The disparity for health between the rich and the poor was troubling.

"Here you go," she said cheerfully, stopping outside a private room at the end of the hall. I looked through the glass, seeing a sombre looking Alex talking to a grey-haired doctor. I knocked softly on the door to announce myself. The doctor beckoned me to come in.

"Excuse me, sorry to interrupt. My name is Detective Sergeant Rodan, I need to speak with Alex about what happened this morning. If possible, Doctor, we would also like to ask you something?" He looked a little perplexed at being asked for his input. Turning back to Alex he thanked him for his time and joined us outside of the room, I shut the door, signalling to a distressed Alex we would be back in a moment.

"I can spare a couple of minutes, Detective. What would you like my help with?" I gestured to Paul to take over, he had more of an understanding of the previous day and would be able to phrase the questions a little better. I intended on taking over when we spoke with Alex.

"I guess first is about how Alex is doing at the moment?" It was best to ask about his mental state for when we spoke with him. He was a man already on the edge and neither of us wanted our actions to push him further.

"Without going into too much detail, physically he's fine. His wounds are not as deep as we first feared and we are happy he isn't in any immediate danger." He hesitated slightly before continuing. "But mentally, he is in a bad place. I have referred him to our in-house psychologists for further support." I wasn't shocked. It was common in cases of suicide for all to be referred, even those who were close to the victim. We all received counselling after our father killed himself, not that it dispelled any of the trauma we felt.

"Thank you for that update. Now to the matter at hand. Yesterday afternoon, before Alex was arrested, he sustained an injury to his right hand after punching a wall. With that in mind, could it have impeded his ability to inflict these wounds himself?" As Paul asked, the doctor was pensive.

"That is a difficult question to answer as there are multiple different factors at play. To start with, I would need to understand whether Alex has a high tolerance for pain, if so the aching in his hand wouldn't have been an issue. If he didn't, my next question would be whether he had any pain relief beforehand, as many of my patients who have attempted suicide in this way before did in the past. If neither of those factors are applicable though, I would say yes, it would have impeded his ability to inflict the wounds." It was a non-committal response, but it did enable an element of doubt in what really happened last night. Hopefully Alex could fill in the spaces.

"Thank you, Doctor, may we go speak with Alex now?" The doctor gestured for us to leave, I thanked him and we entered Alex's room.

The room was eerily silent, the only sound being Alex's gentle breaths as he sat staring impassively at the wall. I sat on the chair next to the bed, Paul leant against on the wall, Alex didn't react to our presence. Not wanting to engage with us.

"Alex, how are you feeling?" I asked sympathetically, still he didn't stir. I noted the change in his breathing, the heaviness of it, indicating he was becoming stressed. Realising he wouldn't answer I moved on to the matter at hand. "I need you to tell us what happened last night," I said softly. For a few moments there was still nothing, Then, sighing, he looked down to the fresh bandages that encashed his wrists and hand.

"I don't know," he whispered, curling his one good hand up into a ball. He winced at the pain emanating from his wrist. "I can remember coming home and finding Katie in the house. We had an argument and I told her to leave. After that I remember having a few beers, and that's where my memory fails."

"What do you mean?"

"The doctor said it could be me blocking out the trauma, but I don't remember anything beyond the drinking. I'm just completely drawing a blank." I could hear the stress in his voice as he was trying to remember. Wanting to alleviate it, I tried a different tactic.

"Going back to before, you said you argued with Katie and told her to leave. Did she leave?" If we could get confirmation she didn't, and place her at the scene, it would link her to two possible crimes.

"My house is large, it's possible she stayed after I told her to leave. I can say with certainty I didn't see her leave, though." It was enough for me. Although still circumstantial, Katie potentially being at Alex's home on the day of his suicide could have meant two things. Either she was involved or, even if she wasn't, she didn't seek medical help for him. Either way I had some uncomfortable questions for her.

"Alex, I'm considering the possibility somebody else was involved in your suicide attempt. As you can't remember what happened, would you agree to a drugs test?" Testing him for illegal, or legal, substances could help us understand whether he was conscious at the time of the alleged attempt. If he had been drugged, it would all but confirm it was attempted murder.

"Absolutely, I want to understand what happened." He looked down to his wrists, when he faced me again there were tears brimming in his eyes. "I had thought about killing myself, I even had plans of how I would do it. But I couldn't leave my kids, not with that woman. Please find out what happened, Samantha." He was unravelling. I patted him gently on the shoulder. I turned to speak to Paul, surprised to find he had silently left the room.

"I'll find out what happened, Alex, I promise. Now get some rest," I replied, squeezing his arm before joining my colleague. I felt we were getting closer to the truth.

THIRTY-TWO

"Okay, thank you, sir. That's wonderful news," Paul said as I slid into the driver's seat. He ended the call and I looked over to him in anticipation. "We have a warrant to search Alex and Katie Smith's home, on top of that a lab tech will visit Alex to take a blood and urine sample for a drugs test." It was positive news. Although Alex couldn't be ruled out as a suspect, it was looking like the attack on Joseph was being used to make Alex look guilty of murder.

"I think Katie did it," I said with conviction. "I believe Katie was outside Joseph's home that evening and, after Alex left, she forced her way into the property. After murdering him she hoped we would look to Alex as our prime suspect. The evidence was there to secure a charge through the CPS…" I stopped for a moment, resting my chin on the steering wheel and stared at the wall ahead. "When Alex came out, she panicked. She truly believed he would rather go to jail than be truthful about himself. It made her realise maybe we would investigate other avenues.

"Last night, when he was released, she couldn't take the chance that he was still the only suspect. She drugged him, slit his wrists and left him to fucking die." It was only a theory but felt the most plausible one under the circumstances. Katie was the number-one suspect in my eyes now and played a part in Alex's downfall.

"It's just finding that proof now and exonerating Alex," Paul responded. I nodded my head. It wouldn't be easy, but the warrant to search their property was the first step to solving this. I turned the engine on and pulled away from the parking space, intending to get to Katie's as quickly as possible. In normal circumstances I would call for uniformed backup to support us, but to keep Jackson and McCarthy out of the loop we would need to go it alone.

I only hoped they weren't there.

•

A uniformed officer greeted us on arrival at Horribon Lane, he extended his hand as I put my foot on the brake and slowed to a crawl, stopping only feet in front of him. He walked over to Paul's side of the car; my colleague obligingly wound the window down to facilitate a conversation. I looked to the journalists in the mirror behind, most too focused on presenting their live reports. I turned my attention back to the officer.

"Good morning. What can I do for you?" the young officer asked. As he looked at us both I took the time to examine him. He was young, likely only just out of training. I had no doubt this was one of his first assignments. Paul looked to me and smiled softly, indicating he would take it from here.

"Good morning. I don't believe we have met. I am Detective Grant, and this is Detective Rodan." I waved with my arm still resting on the wheel. "We are here to visit the Smith household."

"Sorry, sir, I can't let you through. Detective Chief Inspector Jackson's orders, he is now running the case with Detective McCarthy. He also gave me strict instructions to contact him if you were to show up." I wasn't shocked. Jackson taking the reigns was inevitable once Alex had been released from custody.

"Look PC…" Paul stopped, giving the young man an opening to provide his name.

"Robertson, sir," he replied swiftly.

"PC Robertson. I understand your position, but you also

need to understand mine." Paul produced a letter from his jacket pocket, I was curious as to the nature of it. He opened it and held it out to the young PC who examined its contents. "As you can see, Jackson and McCarthy no longer have authority on this investigation. I am now acting investigating officer with Detective Rodan here as my backup. If you contact Jackson, I will make our boss aware you violated his orders. If you allow us though, I will ensure you are looked on favourably when this is all over. Do you understand?" He looked at Paul and then me, nodding his head in affirmation. I couldn't help but glance into the mirror again. We had made enough noise to alert the media, who were now filming our interaction. I hoped it was not live, but had no doubt it would make the news later if it wasn't.

PC Robertson moved out of our way, grabbed the barrier and moved it for us. I put the car into gear and started to roll forward, waving thanks as we went past him. After we were clear he set the barrier into its original position and stood back.

"I have to say, boss, I enjoyed seeing you so assertive." I had a large grin on my face. Paul looked over to me and smiled as I weaved my way around the cars parked precariously on each side of the road.

"Why thank you, Detective," he responded, before laughing to himself a little, resting his hand on his arm. "And don't worry about that letter naming me acting investigating officer. It's just for insurance, it means if things go wrong I will be taking the fall."

"But why?" I asked, slowly manoeuvring so my car window was in line with Alex's intercom. I decided to keep the window shut so we could talk in private for a moment.

"Our assistant chief likes you. He thinks you have potential, but he also knows your background. So he wants to protect you from any potential misconduct hearings. I'll be fine, he can sweep mine away, but with you it will be more difficult. You lead the case, but if something goes wrong, I take the fall." I was shocked. The assistant and Paul willingly putting their careers on the line made me feel emotional.

"Thank you," I said softly, trying not to choke up. Paul smiled and I decided to focus on the matter at hand.

I opened my window and pressed the intercom, informing Katie we were here to speak with her about Alex's attempted suicide. Rather than respond the gates opened and I slowly rolled my car through, parking up by Alex's Ferrari and turning off the engine.

"We need a plan," I said, changing the subject. Paul waited for me to elaborate. "Although we have a warrant, I think it's best to see if she agrees to a voluntary search. You should lead the search as I have concerns she will accuse me of planting evidence. Do you have a body camera?" With the rise in attacks on police officers, and allegations of police brutality, it was mandated all uniformed personnel would require body cameras from 2023. This didn't extend to non-uniform, but I, as well as others, would use them for property searches so that there were no allegations of improper conduct. Especially during a solo search.

"Of course," he said, pulling it from the glove compartment. I hadn't noticed him put it there, and realised he must have stored it when I was out of the car. I was grateful, it would make any evidence difficult to argue.

"Let's go." I got out of the car, hoping that we would find something else on Katie. It was a frustrating investigation, due to how we were finding information it was difficult to put a coherent strategy in place. I was confident we were heading in the right direction now.

"Detectives, how good to see you. Please come in." She had a relaxed attitude, one that didn't sync with the situation. We followed closely behind as she walked away. "Would you like a drink?" I looked around the room, memories of Alex were already being removed. Pictures of him had been taken off the wall and thrown into a large box, along with the medals from various titles he'd won. It was sad she cared so little for him she was willing to throw his stuff away while he recuperated in hospital.

"No thank you, Katie. We have received new information regarding the murder of Joseph Marsden. Are you happy for us to look around?" She seemed hesitant, considering whether she could deny our request. This changed quickly though.

"Whatever you need. I'm happy to help." Paul took that as his cue to leave, and walked away. I heard the click of the camera on his chest as he did so. He spoke softly into it on the start of his search. I choose to stay with Katie for the moment.

"How are you holding up?" I asked softly with a smile, wanting her to believe I was on her side. She didn't need to know we were searching for evidence to implicate her as well as Alex at the moment.

"I'm shocked. I never though Alex would try to take his own life. I guess it can't be a good look for him though?" she responded coldly, taking a sip of her drink as she stared, daring me to deny it. I tried to hold back my emotions.

"Alex has experienced some life-altering trauma. His partner died; his career is on the verge of ruin and he was outed to the world via the media. It's likely anybody in his position would consider that avenue if they were backed into a corner." I tried to be diplomatic in my response, making her believe we still were under the assumption Alex had tried to take his own life. I didn't want to tip her off that we were looking at another avenue.

"Well, he was selfish. He has two kids and does this. He's only ever cared about himself." Knowing I was in danger of arguing with Katie, I stood up.

"Are you happy for me to go and assist my colleague?" I asked, not really concerned about her response. She nodded and took another swig of wine. I left her with her thoughts and walked upstairs, clicking on my camera as I did. I found Paul in the master bedroom, rifling through a drawer. "Anything?" He looked up and solemnly shook his head. I sighed, I had a feeling in the pit of my stomach that this would be more difficult than we first thought.

"There must be something." I pulled out a pair of unused latex gloves that I stored in my pocket and put them on. After ensuring they tightly wrapped my hands, I moved into the en-suite bathroom, unprepared at the sight that would greet me.

"Jesus," I said, looking at the crimson bath water that hadn't been emptied. I wondered how much blood he lost before Michael found him. Although I knew the water gave an incorrect picture, I still wondered how he survived. I walked over, briefly running my fingers across the dried blood that had stained the perfect white bathtub. On the side lay the razor blade. Reaching into my pocket I pulled out an evidence bag, placed it in, and sealed it. If we were lucky, it could have fingerprints on.

"Did you find a suicide note?" I said, a lack of a suicide note wouldn't prove anything either way, but I was still interested in finding one. As I walked back into the bedroom, Paul was standing over a desk reading through something on the table.

"It's typed, not signed. Anybody could have written it." He picked up the note and sealed it in an evidence bag, again ensuring that everything had been touched using gloves in case of fingerprints or DNA trace.

"What does it say?" I asked, as I cast my eyes around the bedroom, wanting to see if there was anything Paul could have missed.

"My dearest family,

You may be wondering why I have taken this action. The truth is I can no longer live with the guilt.

Due to my own actions, I have lost my family; my career, my fans and the man I loved. A man, who I brutally killed a few mornings ago. He wanted a deeper commitment, me to leave my life behind. But I couldn't do it, and he couldn't understand. We fought..."

"Okay stop, I've heard enough." Paul put the note back on the table. "None of this makes sense. If this is his note, and he wanted to confess to murder, why didn't he just tell us at the hospital?"

"Maybe he thought Katie would get rid of it?" Paul queried. It's possible, but that would be misplaced faith in a woman who would gain more from him being jailed.

"Why would he put his faith in a woman who, by his own admission, hates him? If anything, she'd have handed us the note." Paul concurred by nodding his head. The note was concerning, although it wasn't signed it would still be viewed as a confession of murder. I needed to find a way to shift the focus back to Katie. "Did you find a laptop when you were looking?" He picked up the item from the bed and handed it to me, I started to remove it from the evidence bag he had put it in.

"We shouldn't do that," he said, knowing my plan before I enacted it. Under the Communications Act 2024, looking through a suspect's communications device without permission could result in a dismissal. It didn't concern me though as I didn't see Alex as a suspect, and I knew he wouldn't make a complaint.

After booting up the laptop I found it was not password protected, and took me straight to the front page. Conveniently the author of the note had left it in a prominent place, so we didn't have to search too hard.

"Well, the note is here." Paul looked over my shoulder as I searched through the file properties. I noted the date and time it was composed. I breathed a sigh of relief; it was finally positive news. "Alex couldn't have written it."

"Why do you say that?" I pulled out my phone and moved out the way so he could get the file on camera also.

"The time of file creation. It was after Michael found Alex in the bathtub. I have a call log on my phone and can be certain of this." I showed him the time of Michael's call, and put it next to the screen ahead for a side-by-side comparison. There was an hour's difference between them. Somebody was trying to cover their tracks.

"It's still not enough to arrest anybody." Paul walked out of the bedroom, and into Alex's office next door. I shut down the laptop, put it back in the evidence bag and followed him in. The office was small, a desk in the middle with a second computer on it, and book shelves full with coaching, sports science and fitness books. I knew Alex was keen to gain some qualifications so he could move into coaching once his playing career was over, this must have been the office to dedicate time to his studies.

As I shuffled through some papers on the desk, Paul searched the rest of the room, looking for any possible hiding places. He slowly walked up past the shelves, occasionally moving books, rifling through them. He moved one of the smaller shelves to look behind, but to no avail. It wasn't until a few moments later his eyes were drawn to the skirting board near the back of the room.

"Detective Rodan, look at this." I stopped what I was doing, approached him and bent down to examine it, seeing it had recently been cut open. "Do you think somebody was trying to hide something?" I didn't answer, instead I prised the board away from the wall, breaking a couple of fingernails in the process.

Somebody had been using it as a hiding place. Once opened a large supply of pain relief and sleeping tablets fell out, behind a couple of bottles of 96% proof vodka, alcohol that wasn't sold the UK and could only be imported from abroad with a licence. Due to the darkness in the space, I used my phone as a light, examining behind the pills in the hope I would find clarity on why this had been stashed behind a skirting board. I noticed the envelope propped at the side behind a bottle of vodka. After grabbing it, I opened it up and quickly scanned through the contents.

"It's a second suicide note." My heart lifted as I examined a little more deeply. It was hand written and signed by Alex. This was the break we had been hoping for. For the purposes of the camera and Paul, I started to read its contents.

> "To my children, my fans, my team and my love,
>
> I'm sorry for the pain I have caused. I'm sorry for not being truthful about myself and deceiving millions of fans. I'm sorry, to all the young footballers who have been scared to be who they are because of their sexuality. Had I stepped up earlier, maybe it would have been different for them.
>
> I'm sorry to Joseph, the man I loved, because I couldn't protect him from his fate. I hurt him and left him, thinking

I would get one more chance to make it up to him. I regret my actions.

But most of all I'm sorry to Marshall and Katriona, I never wanted you to be in the public eye but my selfishness has made this the case. You are my world, and Daddy loves you very much.

It is time to confess what I know.

On the night of the attack I went to Joseph's flat, in a bid to reconcile with him. He was hurt and angry. I didn't blame him, and left not long afterwards.

As I was leaving, there was another person around Joseph's home. It was dark, and I couldn't make them out. But I do know it was a woman. Although I could not be certain, I believe it was my wife, Katie Smith.

I wanted to inform the police sooner. But I feared repercussions. For months, Katie has been physically assaulting me and I feared this anger would go further. I needed to protect my family.

I am sorry for the prolonged suffering I have caused.

Tears brimmed in my eyes as I read through the note a second time. He was a broken man, somebody who had been pushed to the edge after losing everything and blaming himself for it. It broke my heart to read how he put up with the attacks and lied to protect those he loved. It reminded me of my dad. Taking his own life to protect his family from the truth of what he had done. I wiped away a stray tear as it fell down my cheek.

"This is definitely Alex's suicide note. He was going to end his own life and throw Katie to the wolves. But she got there first." Now we had found the note we had confirmation that Katie was at the murder scene; and suffers from violent tendencies. Although Alex didn't see her clearly, two witnesses confirming they saw a woman of similar build to Katie was enough to bring her in, especially as it meant she'd lied about her alibi. "Bag this and the pills, I'm going to speak with Katie." I handed the note to Paul as he was pulling out a new evidence bag from his jacket pocket. He nodded his head as I walked past and made my way downstairs.

Katie was sitting where I had left her, a newly refilled glass of wine in her hand. On her lap a glossy homes' magazine, provided by one of the most exclusive estate agents within the county, she was flicking through it using her empty hand. It was clear her intention was to move elsewhere once Alex had been charged with murder. As I walked into the room, she looked back to me, a wry smile on her lips.

"Everything okay?" Her tone was calm, she was still under the impression she was not a viable suspect.

"Katie Smith, I am arresting you for the murder of Joseph Marsden and the attempted murder of Alex Smith. You do not have to say anything, but it may harm your defence if you do not mention when questioned something which you later rely on in court. Anything you do say may be given in evidence. Do you understand?" She downed the wine in her glass, not wanting to waste a drop. I watched as she walked to the coats by the front door and slowly put on a sleek, black leather jacket, buttoning it up as she stared in my direction.

"Let's go then." I was surprised at how receptive she was to the arrest, I opened the door and led her to the car. I didn't feel the need for handcuffs, concerned how it would impact her children, especially Marshall. No doubt he was still reeling from his dad's press conference and hospitalisation, seeing his mum arrested would be the icing on the cake. I wanted to give the perception she was just helping us with our enquiries, or we were taking her to visit Alex in hospital.

I hoped we would soon have a conclusion to this whole sordid affair, for Alex's sake.

THIRTY-THREE

Before leaving the Smith's property I instructed Paul to pull in Agent Danvers for questioning. His involvement in the murder was unknown for the moment, however, he had perverted the course of justice by providing a false alibi for Katie, a crime that could carry a sentence of ten years in jail. If it were found he was an accessory to murder, this could push any possible sentence even higher.

As I drove Katie through the main roads down to Manchester, I dialled the Greater Manchester Police and requested to be put through to Jackson as a matter of urgency. He was the only person who could grant access to the interview rooms during my suspension, it was time to key him into the situation.

"What the hell do you want, Samantha? You are suspended." It was the blunt response I expected when I got patched through to him. In the distance I could hear the sound of breathing, indicating that I was likely on speaker phone. I had no doubt the other person in the room was Dennis, no doubt discussing the investigation and how they could approach Alex once he was released from hospital.

"I need access to two interview rooms. Paul and I are bringing in two possible suspects for the murder of Joseph Marsden." The unidentified person choked in the background at the words, I smiled to myself, relishing being on their bad side. Before Jackson could interject, I continued. "I have been reinstated by Assistant Chief Constable David Turnball due to concerns about corruption surrounding the case. If you are in any doubt he will be happy to discuss this with you further. In the meantime, I would be grateful if those rooms are ready for when I get back." I hung up before he was able to respond, imagining the angry and terrified glances they were giving one another at my final comment.

They knew their careers were, in effect, over.

•

I stared at the woman on the monitor, taking her in. Her ever-changing hair colour highlighted in the bright interview room; flecks of red and copper danced as she played with it. With her other hand she tapped her fake nails on the table in front of her, she twisted her wrist to check the time on her jewel-encrusted watch, keeping a note of how long she had been left to wait. Although some colleagues enjoyed making their suspect stew, we had little time to question a person and any delay could be critical. The twenty-four hours initially available was vital. I decided to use this break to observe her reaction for now, but once Paul arrived it was down to business.

"Ready?" Paul said, walking into the room. It was confirmation that he had brought in the agent. He went to walk back out, but I held my hand up indicating we needed to wait a little longer. He leant against the wall momentarily, blocking the door a little. He was surprised when it opened and bumped into his elbow. Moving sharply, he let the person enter the room. "Sergeant Dawkins?" She shut the door and look at both confused.

"What is going on? I thought you had been suspended, Samantha?" She squeezed past Paul and sat in the vacant chair, moving her shoulders uncomfortably at the weight of her stab proof vest. I started to feel claustrophobic, the room was small and only built for two. Having so many in a confined space frightened me, I focused on my breathing to try and ignore the thoughts of wanting to get out.

"I had, but this investigation has taken a weird turn and I was reinstated. I've been informed McCarthy and Jackson are being investigated for corruption." Paul looked at me in annoyance as I told Charlotte, she was the only person I trusted other than Paul. Working in the team as long as she had, she was bound to realise there was something off about both of her superiors. It was why she dropped to uniform, she had concerns in the past they would try and turn her also. "We have brought in two suspects for the murder of Joseph, I want you to observe the interviews from in here."

"Why? I'm just a uniformed officer. I have no place observing this case." Arms folded, she stared at me with hard eyes. A silent indication she knew there was more than I was saying. I sighed and ran my hand through my hair.

"I'm too close to this case, Charlotte. I'm desperate to find closure and it could make me sloppy in questioning. You were one of the best in your time out of uniform, you might be able to pick up on something we miss." She still looked a little hesitant, possibly considering what may happen if her superiors were to find out. Paul clearly understood this and took over.

"If you are concerned about Jackson and McCarthy, don't be. I've handed in my report to the assistant chief, and he is going to sign off on their suspension imminently." It was news to me; I was impressed at how seriously they were taking the situation. "With them gone, maybe we could look into you being reinstated as a detective." Her eyes lit up at the news, it was what Charlotte had wanted for a while. Although she enjoyed being a beat cop, she preferred the investigation side. She nodded her head.

"Okay, I'll help." She turned to the monitors ahead, taking off her jacket and stab proof vest. Out of her pocket she pulled out a small notebook and started keenly observing the two suspects, making notes of their demeanour. I turned my attentions back to Paul.

"You ready?" I asked, picking up the file as Paul nodded his head. I gestured to Charlotte that we were leaving and she waved her hand in acknowledgement. It was time to finish this case once and for all.

•

The prisoner's dilemma is a well-known example of game theory, and one I lived by in these situations. It is the idea that a person will act entirely in their own self-interest, something I prayed would be the case today. Although we had eye-witness testimony to suggest Katie had lied, it would not be enough. We needed to rely on her confession, or Agent Danvers recanting her alibi.

As I opened the door to the agent he looked up from his hands. Worry etched his face for a moment, but the mask fell almost instantly. He looked haggard, closer to his true age than when we first met. He leant back against his chair as I sat down opposite, trying to show a façade of calm in the situation. It was not working.

"Interview with Samuel Danvers, aged fifty-seven, in connection with the murder of Joseph Marsden. Begins at 12.45pm on Saturday 11th March. In attendance are Detective Sergeant Rodan and Detective Inspector Grant. Observing from the technical room is Sergeant Dawkins," I said for the purposes of the camera, before turning my attention to the agent. I placed the file ahead of me, letting him see the front page. "Mr Danvers, thank you for coming in. As you are aware we are investigating the murder of Joseph Marsden. We would like to ask you a couple of questions regarding that night in particular. Could you please confirm for the purposes of the camera that you have not requested legal counsel, is that correct?"

"Yes, that's correct." His voice was crisp and clear, with an edge of cockiness to it. I smirked softly, he was too relaxed, that could lead to mistakes.

"Thank you. Mr Danvers, could you remind us how you knew Joseph Marsden?"

"I wouldn't say I really knew Joseph. He was dating my

player, Alex Smith, I met him once or twice." He shifted a little in his chair.

"And what did you think of him?" Paul asked, we hadn't rehearsed the tag team, it just seemed to come naturally to us. This was the first time all case we had truly been in sync.

"He seemed a nice, respectable young man. He made Alex happy, that was all I cared about." The small shift in his eyes suggested a lie. It was unlikely he cared about Alex's happiness; in reality it was about the money he could make him.

"Thank you. Now I want to discuss the night of the murder." I flicked through the file until I was at his statement, transcribed by one of the freelance secretaries that we use for this type of work. Vetted of course, ensuring she was above board. "When we asked you about an alibi you claimed you were with Katie Smith. Is this correct?" A small nod of the head, I continued. "Could you confirm what time you were with her from and to?"

"We met at my place at 10pm, and she was with me until 6am."

"In those eight hours, were you with Katie at all times. Or were you apart for any length of time?"

"We were together all night. We never spent more than two or three minutes away from each other at any one time." His confidence seemed rehearsed, I looked down at the file again. Pretending to examine pages, showing a level of unpreparedness to relax him even more.

"That's interesting. Especially as there are witnesses who place Katie at the scene of the murder." There was a small hesitation in his eyes, but it disappeared in an instant. I tapped my nails on the table, waiting for his answer.

"They must be mistaken. As I said when we first met, I was with Katie all evening until 6am. Long after Joseph was murdered." He was calm, confident in his words. At that moment I felt the vibration of the phone on my leg. Reaching into my pocket I touched the screen to see a two-word message from Charlotte, 'He's lying.' I was glad she had confirmed my own suspicions. I put the phone away and considered my next move.

I could continue to press Danvers, but felt it wouldn't get me anywhere. Looking to Paul I nodded my head, an indication I was done for the moment.

"Interview terminated at 1pm. Detective's Rodan and Grant will now exit the room."

•

Without taking a break we went into the adjoining room. Paul led as I followed with my file, sitting down opposite the young woman, just thumbing through the paperwork ahead of me. When she realised I wasn't going to speak, she decided to make the first move.

"This all being filmed?" she asked, nodding to the camera on the ceiling. It was directed at Katie so we could record all of her movements. It was invaluable data for psychology experts, often people say more with their actions than with their words. Video recording was a wonderful invention.

"For the purposes of the camera. Interview with Katie Smith, aged thirty-two, in connection with the murder of Joseph Marsden. Time is… 1.02pm. In attendance is Detective Sergeant Rodan and Detective Inspector Grant. Observing in the technical room is Sergeant Dawkins."

"Large promotion there for you?" Katie sneered as she looked at Paul. We both ignored her comment and got down to business.

"Katie Smith, could you confirm for the tape that you were offered legal representation but have subsequently waived this right? Is this correct?" The woman nodded her head, looking smug. It was clear she thought she was here to help us in our enquiries and nothing more, even with us reading the Miranda rights.

"You are correct, only the guilty need a lawyer."

"Thank you. Ms Smith, how well did you know the victim Joseph Marsden?"

"I knew a little about him. He was in a committed relationship with my husband. We didn't move in the same social circles thought." She went to bite her nail, but decided against it when seeing the acrylic. Not wanting to damage her perfect manicure.

"We have it on good authority that you may have known Joseph in an intimate capacity. That you bought his services on a couple of occasions." I was treading on dangerous ground with the allegation, one she reacted to with disgust. However, I hoped pushing her on this matter would cause her to slip up.

"No, that is completely untrue. Marcos did offer Joseph to me in the past but I would never sleep with a queer." She trailed off once she realised what she said. She had confirmed that she was using Marcos services as well. This was a delightful turn of events and gave me more links. She didn't just know Joseph through Alex; she was aware of him in other circles as well.

"For the camera, could you confirm you have been using Marcos services as well?" I asked. She nodded her head sheepishly, knowing she could not backtrack now. The new information contradicted the claims she had been having an affair with Samuel Danvers. A fact we already knew to be false, but I was grateful she confirmed this under questioning. Katie was unaware she had implicated herself.

"Yes, for the past five years or so I have been buying the services of young men from him." She refused to keep eye contact, indicating her shame. I silently celebrated this new information, hoping it would take us closer to the truth and get Alex his life back.

"To clarify, can you confirm you have never had sexual intercourse with Joseph Marsden?"

"Never." The response was so quiet I wasn't sure she had spoken. Instead, I looked back to my notes and persevered.

"Ms Smith, could you remind us where you were the morning of March 7th between 1.30am and 4am?" She stared with cold eyes. Her hands dug into the table ahead, breaking off an acrylic nail, not that she was aware. She was focused on calming the rage she felt towards me.

"You know where I was, I was with Alex's agent," she responded. I was surprised she continued to peddle the lie even when, by her own admission, she was buying sex from one of the most powerful men in the region. I acknowledged her story and continued, knowing that the next part would hit her for six.

"Thank you. Now I want to move on to the morning that Alex was found half dead. Could you tell me where you were then Ms Smith?" Her breathing stopped for a short while, her hands turned white as she grabbed the table in anger. A second nail nearly broke away, but she stopped in time.

"Alex asked me to leave, so I did. I was in a hotel with one of Marcos' men." It was a weak alibi, and one that was easy to disprove. Thanks to Marcos' new found helpfulness it would only take a quick phone call to find if this was the truth. I looked to Paul who was sending a message on his phone, I hoped he was on the same wavelength as me and asking Charlotte to check the alibi. If we were in luck, we would find out quickly.

"Okay, Ms Smith. Thank you. May I ask one final question?" She nodded her head, I felt she knew her time was coming to an end. She was starting to look terrified. "We were hoping you could help with an issue that has been bugging us for a while. Why do you think your husband would try and slit his wrists when we found receipts and large quantities of legal drugs hidden in the wall cavity of your property?" Her facial features dropped, she started to chew on her broken, non-acrylic nail. I could see the fear in her eyes as she considered how she was going to get out of this.

"You see, Ms Smith. I know for a fact that Alex is terrified of blood. To the extent he has been to therapy over it." It was clearly news to the woman ahead who just stared back with wide eyes. Paul produced both suicide notes and placed them on the table ahead of us as I moved forward with questioning. "I have no doubt Alex had spoken of his plans to end his life. What happened? Was he taking too long? Did you snap?"

"I... I..." As she stammered my phone vibrated against my pocket again, as did Pauls. We both looked simultaneously. I was surprised as the swiftness of the reply from Marcos. Not only did he confirm Katie had lied in her most recent alibi, but he also provided us with the client list for that evening. I was impressed he was willing to support us, but knew it was only to take the heat of himself.

"You see, Katie, we have already verified your alibi is fake. A colleague of mine spoke with Marcos, and he has informed us you were not using his services on the morning Alex was found. He provided the client list to us." I put my phone on the table ahead, she peaked over and scanned through the names, then looked back to me. I took the phone away and continued. "We are also conducting drug tests on Alex. When we spoke to him in hospital, he told us he could not remember the events leading up to his alleged suicide attempt. Which led us to believe, somebody else was involved. We are checking his body for drugs that may have contributed to this loss of memory." I stopped again for dramatic effect; the nail Katie was biting was now down to the skin. I had her where I wanted her. "If there's something you want to tell us, now would be the moment to come clean."

"Where should I begin?" She had a coldness in her voice as she stared deep into my eyes, regaining her composure. It was a remarkable turnaround for a woman who looked on edge a few seconds ago.

"Let's start with the murder of Joseph."

"Ah Joseph, the bane of my existence. He was fun, friendly and most of all a bloke. Qualities that Alex loved. Knowing he couldn't meet a guy under normal circumstances, Alex decided to use Marcos' male escort service. When he met Joseph, they instantly clicked, he specifically requested him each night." She stopped a moment, twirling her hair around her finger. "Then… their love blossomed into something more. Marcos granted Joseph permission to start a romantic relationship." She saw the confused look on my face, eliciting a laugh. "Oh no, he continued to pay Marcos. Just in a different way.

"You would be amazed to know how much Alex paid for male escorts. Marcos wasn't just going to take that financial hit, was he? So… he offered him a deal. Joseph would be able to start a relationship with him, as long as Alex paid £300,000 a year for

Marcos to keep quiet." Her laugh was akin to a witch's cackle, by all accounts Marcos has been blackmailing Alex into silence. It didn't surprise me, though I doubted we would take it further. Alex was unlikely to want to testify against him.

"Everything was going fine, until recently. Joseph had been acting sketchy, he was snapping at Alex and becoming stressed when the conversation of their relationship came up. Of course, Alex took this as a sign he wanted them to be official and out to the world. That's when I got scared." I remembered my conversation with Kerrilyn, how Alex had kicked off divorce proceedings. Before I was able to press more, Katie continued. "Before our marriage, we signed a prenup. When we first got married, I wasn't interested in having children, but Alex wanted a family. So we signed a contract. If we were to divorce, regardless of who instigated it, I would relinquish all rights to my kids.

"Recently I've realised I didn't want that. Marshall and Katriona are my life now. I couldn't imagine life without them. I spoke with the agent about it and he decided we should 'get rid of the competition'. As, not only would I end up losing everything, Alex would too by being a pariah in the footballing community. We thought that if we scared Joseph off, tried to persuade him to leave Alex alone, things would go back to normal. But things just got out of hand.

"When I turned up and saw him, a red mist descended over me. I forced my way into his house. I didn't mean to hurt him, just… scare him a little. I admit I went too far and sexually assaulted him, but I didn't have the strength to murder him," she stated defiantly. It was a major turn of events. She had now admitted to being at Joseph's residence the night he was murdered, and harming him. I wasn't sure I believed she did not murder him though, and pushed for further clarity.

"Go on then, who murdered him?" I could have phrased the question more professionally, but my patience was starting to wear thin. I didn't want to be jerked around anymore and wished to shut the case down quickly.

"Samuel Danvers. He was the one who strangled him."

"And why should I believe you when you have lied throughout this investigation?" I asked coldly, noting her lips had curled into a smirk.

"Because he has more to lose. His career has been plagued with rumours about misconduct towards his female clients, and Alex is his only client left. He has too much to lose from this scandal." I relaxed in my chair, staring her down for a moment. I didn't believe her story. It was a poorly thrown-together statement. Paul took decisive action and decided to terminate the interview. I knew the next course of action was to speak with the agent to hear his side.

I had no doubt she was lying, it was just whether her accomplice would be willing to testify to that in court.

•

"You don't believe her do you?" Charlotte asked, as I shut the door to Katie's interview room. She was standing opposite with her back leaning against the wall, picking apart an orange and sliding segments into her mouth. She offered a bit to Paul who declined, shrugging her shoulders, she continued, staring at me with inquisitive eyes.

"I don't believe a word she says. She has been lying from the start. But I can't prove she didn't strangle Joseph." Even if the agent dismissed her story, it was his word against hers. We would have to charge both with murder and hope there wasn't enough reasonable doubt to avoid conviction.

"So what now?" Paul chimed in as Charlotte continued to suck on an orange segment.

"We go and interview Samuel Danvers. If he points the finger at Katie I guess we have to consider charging them both." They both nodded their heads in agreement. Charlotte silently went back into the observation room; I opened the door to find the agent sitting with his head in hands.

"Interview with Mr Samuel Danvers will commence at 1.45pm, on Saturday 11th March. Detectives Grant and Rodan in attendance," Paul said for the tape as we sat back down. For a moment I considered my tack, then I decided to go the extreme route.

"Mr Samuel Danvers. We would like to inform you we are currently putting together a file for the CPS, recommending you be charged with the murder of Joseph…"

"Wait, what?"

"You do not have to say…"

"No, you have this all wrong. I didn't fucking murder anybody," he screamed, pounding his fists on the table. I could feel Paul's eyes boring into my skull. I ignored him and continued to stare levelly at the agent. His ragged breathing was the only noise that could be heard in the room. I allowed him to calm down before continuing.

"That's not what Katie Smith told us. She confirmed that the alibi you both provided was false. She sexually assaulted Joseph, but you ultimately strangled him." His face was a mixture of shock, disgust and anger. However, there was no hint of concern in his eyes. For me that was a sure sign Katie was stretching the truth.

"That fucking lying bitch." He slammed his fists onto the table again. From this reaction I could see he had a temper, but was it one that would compel him to murder an innocent man? I couldn't make that judgement. Most would react in a similar way when they were backed into a corner and told they would be charged with murder.

"You have a temper, Mr Danvers?" I pointed out, deliberately goading him.

"And how do you expect me to react when I am being falsely accused of murder?" His nostrils flared. I shrugged my shoulders, ignoring his question.

"Tell me what happened then." I gave him the floor, leaning back in my chair. He looked at us both coldly before going in to his story.

"You have to believe me when I say I didn't want to be involved in any of this. Katie rang me at home, in tears and freaking out. I asked what happened, but she was too stressed for me to understand. She just started screaming about how she was with a dead body and didn't know what to do. I guess I wanted to help, so I asked for her location to visit. She told me it was an accident; that it was an erotic game gone wrong. When I turned up though, I knew I had been lied to.

"Joseph was dead. I had no doubt she had forced herself on him and strangled him with a silk scarf. I walked in on her mutilating his genitalia. I told her I would call the police but she told me that I was an accessory after the fact and should keep my mouth shut if I knew what was good for us. I should never have done it, but I agreed to stay quiet. I secretly hoped it was an accident, but I knew she was a sick and perverted woman. She frequented Marcos' services and was known to have an acquired taste. She has a whole PR team dedicated to ensuring it didn't get out in the media. So, when I saw her with Joseph's body, I wasn't shocked." His head dropped, this had eaten away at him for a while and he was glad to get things off his chest.

"I just want to clarify something about Katie. What do you mean sick and perverted with an acquired taste?" Although not imperative to the murder case, it would enable me to paint a picture of her if it was to go to trial; or if they required her to undergo a psychological evaluation.

"Two things. She liked young boys, barely legal teenagers who had just turned sixteen. She relished in harming them. She was also obsessed with gay men. She fantasised on many occasions about drugging Alex and forcing herself onto him. Forcing him… to impregnate her naturally. I don't know if this happened, but I begged for her to seek therapy when she told me that." I held my hand to my mouth, trying to stifle the little yelp that was forming on my lips. Turning to Paul I could see he looked a little green in the face. This woman was sick and needed professional help.

"Why not come forward?" The uncomfortable silence spoke volumes. He didn't want to come forward because he knew the result if he did. He knew his most influential clients would be in jeopardy. Alex wouldn't survive the scandal. "Let's move on. What can you tell me about the attempted murder of Alex Smith?" He sighed and looked at the ground.

"I never expected her to go that far. After he came out to the world, Katie became angry. She was inconsolable. She knew her life would be over." He stopped briefly, trying to regain his composure. "She decided to take action. She devised a plan to make it look like Alex commit suicide. I never expected her to go through with it. I never imagined she'd kill my prized asset." His description of Alex angered me. He wasn't a person to them, just a commodity. His sexuality got in the way of their ambitions and they needed action to rectify this. He may not have wanted to be involved in the murder, but he benefit from it as much as Katie.

"Mr Danvers, why should I believe you when you refuse to recant your alibi, even though we have proof it was a lie?" I was grateful for Paul when he stepped in. My mind was struggling to process everything due to the rage at his statement.

"Because I have everything documented. Her statement regarding wanting to drug Alex. Her obsession with gay men. Her garbled voicemail. The text messaged she sent after the fact. Everything is documented on my phone. And I will willingly submit that to the police if it will clear me of murder." My heart leapt with a small semblance of joy at that moment. It was the killer blow we needed to convict Katie. I thanked the agent and terminated the interview. We finally had our woman.

•

"Katie Smith, due to new evidence being submitted, we will be processing a request to charge you with the murder and sexual assault of Joseph Marsden and the attempted murder of Alex Smith." I stood in the doorway, holding the door and waiting for a response. She just stared, trying to comprehend my words.

"You fucking bitch. You have ruined everything," she screamed at the top of her lungs, getting up from the table. Instead of responding I hastily shut the door and called for Charlotte to restrain her. Relief washed over me when I realised it was finally over. We had got our killer.

THIRTY-FOUR

Michael sat beside a softly sleeping Alex. He was no longer hooked up to the heart monitor and able to breathe on his own. As I walked in, the first sound was of Alex's gentle snoring, it soothed me to know he was sleeping peacefully. Michael looked up from his book and offered a weak smile, I could see the trauma in his eyes. Determined not to have his life damaged by this one incident, I noted to get him counselling to process what he experienced.

"Is everything okay, Sammi?" he asked, as I walked over and fell into his arms. He held me close to his hard chest, I sighed and relaxed my body into his. As I stood listening to his breathing, I looked down at Alex. Noting the small streaks of blood that had started to seep through his bandages. Knowing he was likely due for a change of them soon.

"No, but things will recover." As I spoke Alex opened his eyes a touch, staring up at me and Michael. I jumped a little, not expecting him to wake up so quickly at the sound of my voice.

"Samantha," he whispered. I uncoupled myself from Michael and sat on the edge of Alex's bed, placing my hand on his shoulder. I was conflicted, I didn't know whether I should tell him who I had arrested for Joseph's murder. The news would devastate him, but part of me knew he would rather find out through me than through the media. He had lost the man he loved and needed to be told any outcome in a sensitive and dignified manner.

"Alex, I am sorry to have to bring you this news." Pausing for a moment, I looked over to Michael, he beckoned me to continue. "We are pursuing charges in the Joseph Marsden investigation. Your wife Katie will be charged with Joseph's murder and sexual assault, she will also face a further charge of attempted murder and perverting the course of justice." He stared at me wordlessly, trying to process the information. Michael stood next to me, his hand resting on Alex's arm, comforting him.

The silence was disconcerting. Neither Michael nor I spoke for a while, waiting for Alex to react, but he just stared at his strapped-up wrists. It was difficult to understand his mood. I expected tears, or anger, instead he seemed to be in a trance-like state. It was as if his mind had just stopped, he was numb.

"Maybe you should go," Michael whispered, not harshly. I agreed, knowing my presence wasn't helping. I squeezed Alex's hand and walked off, leaving him to process what I had informed him in peace. I hoped he would be able to get through this for the sake of his two children. They needed their father now.

On leaving the hospital reception I found Paul leaning against the pool car, looking like an expectant father who couldn't keep still in the hospital. I walked over and perched next to him, putting my head in my hands. I was in desperate need of a drink and to try and process everything that had happened. It had been less than twelve hours before I had received the news of Alex's alleged attempted suicide. In that time, I was reinstated as a detective, had discovered a deeper plot and was bringing charges against the woman who had caused all the misery and pain to her husband. It was too much to process. I knew I would end up with a large bottle of wine on the way home.

"Did you tell him?" He didn't look at me, just at the hospital entrance as he spoke.

"I did," I responded quietly. Not wanting to make myself heard too loudly. I felt I had destroyed the last part of a man who was supposed to be a friend. Yes, it was the job, but it didn't make it easier. I cared about Alex, and causing the final heartbreak in his story was too much for me. I couldn't just be dispassionate in this case.

"I'm really sorry, Samantha," Paul responded, putting his hand on my shoulder. I shrugged and pushed myself off the car.

"I'm going to get the tram home. You take the car back. I'll see you in the morning I guess." Paul let me walk away without another word, he knew that forcing me to stay wouldn't be beneficial. I needed time to myself to go through everything that happened and consider whether I wanted to continue in the police force. This case had deeply scarred me. Not because of my close friendship with Alex, but because I was unsure if I could trust my colleagues in the future. Finding out my bosses were being investigated for corruption; my 'junior' colleague was actually a senior officer looking into this, and that they'd all hidden my father's secret, hurt.

I just hoped in time I would be able to forgive and forget, but that was for the future me to worry about.

THIRTY-FIVE

He sat in the visitor's room, shifting uncomfortably on the hard metal chair. The walls were grey with flecks of paint falling off; the floors grimy with an unknown substance. He stared down at his hands that rested on the hard metal table. Only two days ago he had been in hospital, his wrists taped up after an alleged suicide attempt. After the initial fears he wouldn't survive, it quickly became apparent the wounds weren't as deep as believed. He was let out after a day so that the bed would be used for somebody else more in need. The deal was he would rest at home, and not do any strenuous activities. Facing his assailant wouldn't fall into that category surely?

A guard arrived in the room, pulling Katie behind him by the handcuffs. He pushed her down onto the chair and looked to Alex.

"I will be outside. If she does anything, push the panic button under the table," he said, not waiting for Alex to respond before walking back out of the room. Alex turned his attention to his wife, who now looked a shell of her former self. The luxuries she'd enjoyed as a married woman were no more, but even he was surprised at her appearance. Her normally fluffy and kempt long hair was matted and greasy, she likely wouldn't have washed or brushed it since being held on remand. Her nails were down to the cuticle where she had been biting them. Her weight was suffering also, in a few days she had lost close to half a stone, looking almost skeletal. The grey tracksuit engulfed her tiny frame, Alex wondered how long she would last in a place like this.

"What do you want?" She stared at him with disgust

"Hello wife," Alex's response was laced with malice. She looked murderous, clearly in her mind wondering why she hadn't done the job properly and killed Alex when she had the chance. "How are you doing?" She stared at him with cold eyes.

"We both know you don't care." She was correct, he didn't. However, under the circumstances it was the best question he could begin with. He was finding being civil difficult, her vicious streak had cost him the man he loved, he didn't care if she rotted in jail.

"No you're right. I'll get down to why I'm here then. Why did you do it?" He wasn't expecting an answer, but wanted to face her and ask for his own piece of mind.

"Because I knew the truth. You were going to divorce me for that fucking whore. How do you think that made me feel? You were going to take my children away from me and take them into a corrupted household. Being raised by a gay man was one thing, but two gay men? It's immoral." Alex did his best to remain calm, he struggled to process seeing this side of her. He could understand if she attacked him for the break-up of their marriage, but not the idea that their kids being raised by two gay men was somehow immoral. The idea broke his heart.

"I shouldn't have gone behind your back about the divorce, but can you blame me? You have a vicious streak in you. I had so many bruises from where you threw things and hit me. I could not tell you about my meetings with a solicitor." He stopped momentarily; he could feel the tears pricking against his eyes as he thought back to all the times Katie physically abused him. The broken ribs he suffered when she threw a chair at him; the black eye and cut from a glass shattering in his face and the daily bruises on his arms and legs from where she punched him. The physical scars had healed, but the mental ones remained. "But you have to understand, I wasn't there to just secure our divorce. No matter what I think about you as a person, you are a good mum, and I wanted you to have a relationship with our children. I wouldn't take a child as young as Kat away from her mother. In my meetings with the solicitor, we spoke about revoking the old contract and creating a new one."

"You wouldn't have prevented me from seeing my own children?" Her voice was small as she responded, she had done much of this out of fear of losing her children. She had become adamant that Alex was going to force her out of her home, destitute, with nobody to love. All the while she was plotting her revenge on Joseph, he was working in secret to make sure her kids had a relationship with their mother. Her heart broke at the realisation of what she had done.

"I'm not a monster like you. Taking that course of action would have been harmful to everybody, especially Kat. But now, you have messed up any chance of seeing those children ever again. Do you really think I'm going to bring them to jail to visit their mother?" Alex stood up and rested his hands on the table ahead. He needed to have that feeling of power, and felt being higher than her would enable it. "Marshall is an intelligent lad; I can't lie to him about what you did. But I can lie to little Katriona. She idolises you, and loves you. Do you know what she told me recently? That she wanted to be like mummy when she was older. How can I break it to her that her mother is a murderer and attempted to murder her dad?

"I can't, and I won't. The best thing for me to do is tell her you are dead. It will break her little heart, but no more than the truth. You have destroyed this family, and want to hurt us even more by pleading not guilty." She went to speak but he cut her off swiftly. "Samantha told me. She was informed by the CPS you are pushing for a not guilty plea. How do you think that makes me feel?

"I will tell you. I feel the only person you care about is yourself. You don't understand the impact pleading not guilty would have on your children. The constant media intrusion on their lives while the trial is ongoing. It could ruin their childhood. If you truly loved them, you would do all you could to protect them by pleading guilty. I can't see it happening though. You're a lowlife piece of scum." The words were horrific, but Katie knew Alex was right. It still didn't stop the tears streaming down her cheeks. She had never considered the impact on her children. All she wanted was Joseph and Alex gone from her life by any means necessary. Now she had caused pain to those she loved the most.

"I… I…" She snivelled. But it was too late. Alex knocked on the door to alert the guard he was done. The man obliged by opening it, escorting him a little way down the corridor towards a second guard. As this happened Katie continued to weep in the locked visitor room. She had never felt so alone.

•

On arriving home, the first thing that hit Alex hardest was the silence. Although his relationship with Katie was strictly for show, he missed having companionship. It was only in the past two years they had grown to hate one another. When they first married, they had attended parties and sporting events together; travelling the world for football. On their downtime they loved nothing more than to watch a film or go on 'date' nights to the theatre. It wasn't love in a conventional sense but, they respected each other. She never tried to exploit his sexuality to her own advantage, she was supportive and it was why he wanted her to play the role of his wife. He just wished it hadn't become so toxic.

He sat in the silence for a moment, the only sound coming from the bottle of beer in his hand as he took another swig. The sound of the doorbell brought him back to his senses. He picked up his phone and opened the ring app. He was confused when he saw nobody at the gate intercom, but realised he had left it unlocked. On changing to the front door view Shaun came into focus. Alex sighed, he considered pretending he was out but knew Shaun wouldn't leave so easily. He pressed the talk button.

"I'll be there in a sec, mate." He took another sip of beer before putting the bottle on the table. Nothing could prepare him for the awkward conversation that was going to follow. He got up and made his way to the door.

"Hey Shaun," he said softly, opening the door. Shaun looked sombre and smiled encouragingly as he saw Alex.

"Hey, can I come in?" he asked. Alex moved, a silent invitation that Shaun could enter. He shut the door behind them both and walked back to his sofa, picking up his beer off the table and taking another swig before showing it to Shaun.

"Want one?" Shaun shook his head.

"No thanks, I drove." Alex nodded his head and took another drink, there was a hint of a sardonic smile on his face. Shaun decided to sit on the chair opposite his friend, so he could examine his body language as they spoke. During his criminology studies he had become an expert in reading people via their movements rather their words. He knew it would be useful for this chat. "How are you feeling?" As soon as the words left his mouth Shaun regretted them. He felt like a professional dealing with a patient rather than a best friend. Alex didn't respond, instead continuing to down his bottle of beer. Once finished he retrieved a new one from the fridge, sitting back down once it was opened and continuing his efforts to get drunk. An uncomfortable silence punctuated the room. Shaun was wishing he had taken up the offer of a beer now.

"Where's Kat and Marshall?" By changing topic, Shaun hoped he would strike up a conversation. Alex side-eyed his friend as he continued to drink. Sighing, he finally relented, put down his beer and stared at his best friend uncomfortably.

"Marshall is at a friend's house. He refuses to talk to me at the moment. He's embarrassed about his gay dad. He's a teenager, he'll get over it." Alex winced and touched his wrists lightly as he spoke, clearly still in pain. "Kat is with mum and Mal for a few days. I can't face her. I'm struggling to work out how to tell her…" He stopped briefly and looked away, trying to compose himself. "Tell her that Mummy is never coming back, and it's all Daddy's fault." He grabbed the beer by the neck and headed over to the window, looking out over the reservoir. The still water calmed his ragged breaths and stopped the tears forming in his eyes. He found water peaceful and could stare at it for hours, it was why he had bought a house here. He knew it would be beneficial for his mental health.

"You can't blame yourself for this," Shaun raised his voice a little, he knew his friend was in a fragile place but was angry at his self-pitying attitude. He became alarmed when Alex laughed dryly before taking another swig of beer. He finished the bottle and turned back around.

"But I can. I have ruined the lives of so many people because I didn't listen to you when we were teenagers. You're right, I should have come out. It would have saved so much pain." He went to the fridge, this time intercepted by Shaun who put his hand on the door, preventing him from opening it. Alex sighed and sat on the dining room chair, resting his elbow on the table and putting his head in his hands.

"If I had just told the truth, I could have met a man normally, not through Marcos. Joseph probably wouldn't have met me and wouldn't be dead. Katie could have been with somebody who loved her unconditionally. My two kids wouldn't have lost their mother. Your sister wouldn't have nearly lost her job by trying to do everything she could to protect me. She believed in my innocence from the start and she was nearly fired for that." He stopped for a moment, wincing as he gingerly touched his wrists. "But you know what else? Just staring at you! The man who declared his love for me. Shaun, you and Jasmine were perfect together, and I screwed up your relationship and your life."

"I know you're grieving. But you can't put all the blame on yourself," Shaun responded softly. He wanted nothing more than to hug his friend but decided to stay leaning up against the fridge for the moment. "You did what you had to so that you could have a career and protect yourself. It isn't your fault the world wouldn't have accepted the real you. You were right. Why put yourself through that much pain and abuse when you could hide it?" Shaun stopped again, the urge for alcohol had grown. He opened the fridge and grabbed two beers, using the bottle opener on the side of the cabinets to open them. He handed one to Alex who gratefully received it and started to drink.

"And me and Jasmine… you didn't mess anything up," Shaun continued, after taking a sip of beer, he sat opposite Alex and ran his hand through his thick dark hair. "We were pretty much over anyway. I realised she was a self-centred person after the way she reacted when I told her I wouldn't go on a gap year. She told me my mum had been ill a long time and I needed to live my life. She even said it didn't matter if I was able to say goodbye when she died because I had already done it when she was last taken to hospital. You did nothing wrong." Silence dropped between them once again, neither knowing how to continue. Alex stood and walked back to the living room, sitting on the sofa. He played with the label of the beer bottle, picking it off and discarding it on the coffee table. He then started to down it in one go. Shaun watched his friend with alarm as he polished off a third beer, wondering if he had drunk more before he'd arrived.

"You remember that night in the Lake District, under the stars? When we sat there drinking a bottle of vodka, I just found the setting so romantic. At the time I just imagined sharing that moment with the person I loved the most, but then I realised I was with that person. When you kissed me, everything clicked into place. It felt so natural being with you that evening."

"But you're not gay," Alex said softly, putting his bottle on the table. He didn't look his friend in the eye.

"If I had a pound for every time you've said that I could probably retire." Shaun laughed a little. "My sexuality is not important. I am attracted to you and it's not like what happened was a one-time thing. Hell, living together in lockdown during your 'break-up' with Katie proved that. But I don't want to argue now, Alex, not when you're grieving." They were silent again, Shaun just left Alex with his thoughts. He sighed before continuing. "Do you want me to leave?" Alex shook his head, he could feel the tears in his eyes and knew his resolve was collapsing.

"I just wanted a hug and to be told it will all be okay." Shaun obligingly moved to sit next to Alex, putting his arms around him and pulling him close to his chest.

"It will be okay, I promise." It was the last words that Alex heard. For the first time in days, he finally felt relaxed enough to fall asleep in Shaun's arms.

THIRTY-SIX

Marcos sat in his large living room; head thrown back as the woman in front of him wrapped her lips around his hard dick. He took a sip out of the glass in his left hand, a thirty-year-old Scotch Whisky, with his right he pushed his escort's head down, forcing himself deeper into her mouth. He was lost in the sensation and didn't hear the footsteps of his servant walking into the room, he only responded when she cleared her throat.

"Can't you see I'm busy?" he snapped, moaning afterwards as he felt the young woman on her knees deep throat him. It felt incredible and proved once again he'd made the right choice making her his slave girl.

"Sorry boss, there are two men here to see you, they say they're detectives," she replied. He wasn't paying too much attention; the woman had now wrapped her hands around his dick. He put his whisky glass down beside him and grabbed her head, forcing himself even deeper into her mouth. She started struggling as she was adjusting to Marcos taking over, but he didn't care. It turned him on even more, having the woman writhing around and struggling under the pressure. He got off on harming others, and this was making him harder.

"Tell them to come in. I'm nearly done with this whore," He grunted as she started to use her tongue. It wasn't until he had finally cum did he realise the servant had left and two detectives had replaced her. The young woman got up with tears in her eyes and ran out the room, holding her hand over her mouth to stop herself throwing up.

"Do you treat all your staff like that?" McCarthy spoke, his voice laced with a sneer. Rather than arrange himself for his company, Marcos picked up his glass and took a long sip. He didn't care what these people thought of his present state.

"Gentleman, you have some balls coming here like this," he said putting his penis back into his trousers. "I mean you have hardly covered yourself in glory. All you had to do was arrest Alex, it wasn't a difficult task. Yet you managed to spectacularly fail at it even when he was the only viable suspect."

"Easy? The moment we assigned Samantha to that case we failed. You said we could control her, but at every step she was determined to prove Alex innocent. And then, when all hope looked lost for Alex, you told her that Katie was at the crime scene. If you didn't want them to know she was involved why the hell did you tell her?" Jackson shouted back at the crime boss. Marcos rung a bell and waited in silence until one of his girls filled his glass.

"That's good stuff." He enjoyed the anger on Jackson's face as he ignored the question. "Have either of you played chess, gentlemen? You see, with chess you need to plan several moves in advance and juggle that with multiple strategies at one time. My preferred strategy was Alex's arrest, but once Samantha found the CCTV of me with Joseph, I needed to change tack. Had I denied seeing him, Samantha and her little corruption buddy would have continued to dig and found I was at Joseph's for longer than I claimed to be. It wouldn't have been a good look."

"How do you know Katie will stay silent?" It was a valid question from Dennis, Marcos laughed.

"Everybody has a weakness, for Katie it's her family. She may have been on board with this but she certainly doesn't want those two lovely kids of hers taken away from their dad and put into a life of care. She will remain silent for as long as I can hold that over her. Danvers was a more difficult prospect though, for a slug he is a surprisingly virtuous man with few vices. Sadly, the reports of his inappropriate behaviour against women were incorrect, so I just agreed to pay for some of the best lawyers in the country to ensure he never had to see a jail cell." He stopped momentarily, taking another sip of his drink, letting the warm smooth liquid run down his throat before continuing. "So, gentlemen, do you have anything else? Because I am starting to wonder if you are taping this interaction to save your own skin at your gross misconduct hearing."

Jackson reached into the bag that Marcos only just noticed and pulled out a phone and laptop, putting it carefully on the table in front of them. Marcos looked perplexed at the items and then back at the men.

"I believe this is what you were looking for in Joseph's home? A laptop and phone, with some compelling evidence about some of your crimes. Most notably the fraudulent claim for your jewellery being stolen." Marcos looked impressed.

"And where did you get this?"

"Some man came in, claiming he stole it from Joseph's home. But when we went to check the arrest records, it was locked under a 'need to know' file. The only person who could grant access was the ACC," Jackson revealed.

"Clever people, seems like you weren't the only two trying to cover your tracks. Well, I believe this concludes our business," Marcos said, as he leant over to pick up the laptop, only for another hand to also come down on the laptop. He looked up in anger.

"Our business will never conclude, Marcos. Our careers are gone now because we got into bed with you. We have enough to burn you and bring you down if we wanted. What price are you willing to pay for our silence?" McCarthy said, his face red with rage.

"Think it might be advisable to call off your attack dog, Jackson." Marcos refused to look at McCarthy. The detective removed his hand and stood back, still looking at the crime boss with a seething look of contempt in his eyes. "As I have already said. Everybody has a weakness. Do you really think I would have nothing on you two?" Both men shifted uncomfortably now and looked at the floor, Marcos smiled, he didn't want to stop there though, determined to make them more uncomfortable.

"I mean, Jackson, your wife is a wonderful woman. You know she was so welcoming when I visited your home the other day. Gloria isn't it? Yeah Gloria. Beautiful, highly intelligent and articulate. She was so proud of your achievements. The fact that you managed to rise to the ranks of detective chief inspector. How do you think she would feel if she found out the truth? That you sold your soul to corruption?" He stopped for a moment to punctuate his point before continuing. "And your daughter, hmm, eighteen isn't she? A wonderful specimen. Very focused on her studies and her training. Isn't she training for the Olympics? A lovely swimmer's body, she would do incredibly well in my escort service. A virgin as well, such a rarity." Jackson had a look of defeat on his face. Marcos then turned his attention to McCarthy, whose eyes were darting around the room in fear.

"And McCarthy, don't you think the police will want to know that you have been keeping the company of young women? I think Hannah's story is particularly compelling. You know the young girl who was on her knees as you walked in? The first time you started fucking her she was only fifteen years old. Oh I realise she looks much older, but you must have had a clue." McCarthy almost looked green at what he was told.

"You told me she was eighteen when I first shagged her," he shouted, the crime lord ahead of him just laughed.

"Oh but who will believe you? All I need to do is tell Hannah to go to your bosses and make a complaint about how you raped her. She's a good little actress. It'll all be backed up by the video and pictures we have on you as well." The laughter was terrifying. Both McCarthy and Jackson knew they had been beaten. "If you keep your mouth shut, you will keep the money I have already paid you. If either of you make a sound, the money will be syphoned out of your account by some of the greatest hackers in the country with a money trail so complex not even an intelligence agency will find out what has happened." He took a sip of his whisky and saw the defeatist reaction on both of their faces, they had been hung out to dry.

"If you are lucky, you may avoid corruption charges, but gross misconduct will likely be the end of your careers. I hope it was worth it." The two detectives knew what would happen, they would both have a black mark against their names and their chances of getting another job would be slim. Jackson knew the money from Marcos would keep his family in food, but not for long. He feared he would not be able to provide for them in the long term, whereas McCarthy knew if his indiscretion got out, he would go to jail. Policemen don't survive, let alone ones that harm children.

They knew Marcos had won.

EPILOGUE

A month after his murder, Joseph Marsden was finally laid to rest. Only three people attended the funeral, me, Michael, and Alex. We sat in the church, Michael and I with our arms around a devastated Alex, the tears silently falling down his cheeks as he watched his beloved get cremated. When we left, we asked what Alex would do with the ashes. He said he would keep them with him forever, by getting his beloved turned into a memorial ring. He couldn't part with the man's last mortal remains.

Many people believed he would go back to playing football after a period of grieving. It was a surprise when he'd announced his retirement within weeks of coming out. Citing that if fans couldn't accept him fully, then they didn't deserve to see him play for the country or club again. Those detractors for his decision claimed he let the abusers win and he was weak, however, I thought it was a brave decision. He had a family to raise now and wished to keep them safe from harm, there is nothing more noble than that.

Shaun went back to Harvard before the funeral; it surprised me he didn't stick around to support Alex. I never received a response to my texts asking why he didn't attend the funeral. On broaching the subject with Alex, he became evasive and moved the conversation on. I choose not to push any further and decided to speak to Shaun at a later date.

Bryony lost her job, her credibility and her unborn baby. The stress of the threat of being sued were too much for her and she suffered gravely for it. The only saving grace was it brought her and her husband closer together, he was determined not to let this situation destroy their marriage and they have decided to have another go of things.

Jackson and McCarthy were both suspended from the force after we charged Katie. It had become apparent that both had been taking bribes from a number of powerful and influential members of society. There were quiet whispers that one of those was Marcos but sadly, as of yet, no evidence has been found to prove that. We all know it is true but, sadly, Marcos is too intelligent to leave a paper trail of his misdeeds. McCarthy was also charged with child grooming, having sex with a minor and statutory rape. An anonymous 'tip' came in to say that he had seen intimate pictures of McCarthy with an underage girl named Hannah. I knew who had set him up, but I no longer cared or felt sorry for him.

Katie changed her plea from not guilty to guilty soon after her talk with Alex. When I spoke to the CPS they confirmed it was because she didn't want to put Alex through any more pain. It would have been a noble gesture had she not attempted to murder him. All charges against his agent were dropped after she claimed she'd acted alone. The media were merciless though, and he was blacklisted, his career was now over.

With the detective chief inspector slot going at Greater Manchester Police, Paul was promoted and moved out of corruption. He was initially very unfairly received, however, it did not take long for him to change opinions and he was known to be a popular leader. I wished him all the best in his future success.

As for me, you would expect an ending with accolades and promotions galore? Unfortunately, that was not the case. Although I was promoted, it was out of the city that I loved and grew up in. Sadly, the news of my nightly escapades, and relationship with a potential witness, was discovered, and it was deemed an embarrassment to the force. While the chief constable wanted me to be investigated for gross misconduct, the assistant had my back. He found a role in Sussex Police in Brighton, and I was promoted to detective inspector. It wasn't a bad move, however... it was a difficult one. I loved living in Lancashire and felt a ting of sadness having to leave. Thankfully, my sister was at the University of Sussex so I wouldn't be completely alone, and at least I would be able to keep an eye on her and monitor her developing relationship with Marcos.

Michael and me? Well... Michael opted to look for a new contract elsewhere. He bought himself out of the one in Manchester due to lack of game time, and decided to head down to Brighton as well. We never dreamed he would be snapped up so quickly by another team though. We will just have to see how everything goes on the relationship front.

This book is printed on paper from sustainable sources managed under the Forest Stewardship Council (FSC) scheme.

It has been printed in the UK to reduce transportation miles and their impact upon the environment.

For every new title that Matador publishes, we plant a tree to offset CO_2, partnering with the More Trees scheme.

For more about how Matador offsets its environmental impact, see www.troubador.co.uk/about/